THE PROMETHEUS SAGA 2

A Speculative Fiction Anthology

Front and back cover designs by Charles A. Cornell

Cover images licensed from Shutterstock.com

The Prometheus Saga 2/ A Speculative Fiction Anthology -- 2nd ed. PRINT June 2023

ISBN: 978-1-960974-04-4 (Ebook)

ISBN: 978-1-960974-05-1 (PB)

Contents

About The Alvarium Experiment

The Alvarium Experiment is a consortium of writers working "independently together" to create short stories based on a central premise. The name comes from the Latin *alvarium,* meaning beehive, a colony working towards a common goal for the benefit of all involved.

The Prometheus Saga 2 is the fourth collection published by this Hive Mind of award-winning and bestselling authors. Stories from the first, *The Prometheus Saga,* collectively won seven literary awards including five prestigious Royal Palm Literary Awards from the Florida Writers Association. The second anthology, *Return to Earth,* has multiple stories that have received recognition for awards.

To follow The Alvarium Experiment's current and future projects online, please join the conversation:

Website:
alvariumexperiment.wixsite.com/prometheussaga
Facebook Page:
www.Facebook.com/alvariumbooks
or @alvariumbooks

About The Prometheus Saga 2

The Prometheus Saga is the fourth project of the Alvarium Experiment, a consortium of accomplished and award-winning authors. Each author was given a central premise of an alien probe living on Earth from the start of humankind as a human with an analytical, computerized brain, a nearly immortal functioning human body, with the ability to experience all human pleasures except procreation, eschew food and sleep, heal itself, awaken from apparent death, sample DNA in order to pupate into different genders and ages at any time of its choosing, and an objective outlook that discourages judgement and emotional development. The probe, Prometheus, is unaware of its purpose, but discerns its differences, is aware that the directives it sometimes hears within its head are not its own, and over its thousands years of existence has developed its own mental reckoning towards human situations, emotions, and its place within the humankind.

The authors were allowed the freedom to interpret this premise within the timeframe of human history to current day. Except for time period as Prometheus cannot be two places at once, the authors were generally unaware of the contents of each others' stories before they were individually published. The stories do not need to be read in any particular order as any story can become an entry point for the reader.

The Prometheus Saga 2 stories and authors are:

"The Seventeenth Slave" by Jade Kerrion. Fu Hao, daughter of a chieftain, accepts the greatest of honors--to be one of King Wu Ding's sixty wives--propelling her to power in the Shang Dynasty and into the annals of history. No one speaks of the mysterious "amah" who attended Fu Hao from her first to last breath. More devoted than a mother and possessed of the wisdom of ages, the amah transforms a girl-child into a queen, high priestess, and warlord. This is Fu Hao's story. And this is the story of the long-forgotten seventeenth slave…

Visit Jade at www.jadekerrion.com.

"The Tower House Prisoner" by Ken Pelham. Captain Farnham, given the unhappy task of bringing to heel a renegade English lord in a backwater of 17th century Ireland, frees a most peculiar prisoner and finds himself embroiled in the hysteria of the witch hunt. Can he uncover the truth of the tower house prisoner without being led himself to the hangman's noose?

Visit Ken at www.kenpelham.com.

"**Her Midnight Ride**" by Bria Burton. Awed by an extraordinary patriot spy, sixteen-year-old Sybil Ludington longs for a chance to prove her worth to the cause of American Independence. When the British attack the city of Danbury, she volunteers for a dangerous mission, one she may not survive.

Visit Bria at www.briaburton.com.

"Remuda" by Elle Andrews Patt. It's 1886 and seventeen-year-old Ranger Jacobs finally has the chance to prove his commitment to Jacobs Cattle Company by overseeing the remuda on a high-priced cattle drive. When his favorite horse dies, Ranger's new mount tests his mettle, launching him on a journey of discovery that threatens to destroy his lifelong dreams of taking over the company his grandfather built. Not to mention shatter his heart. Will contact with Prometheus shape Ranger's destiny or leave his future in the hands of fate?

Visit Elle at www.elleandrewspatt.com.

"**Knowledge is Power**" by T.L. Woolsley. In New Orleans in the midst of the Roaring Twenties, there are plenty of places to go drinking and dancing. For one young woman, all the fun can't distract her from the bully at work who makes her life miserable. A new co-worker encourages her to stand up for herself. Soon the bully will find out . . . Knowledge is Power.

Visit T.L. Woolsley at www.tlwoolsley.com.

"**Highball**" by Kristin Durfee. A veterinarian in gangster-ridden Chicago discovers a dog in need of his help. When it turns out the animal is involved in the Bugs Moran crime syndicate, the vet gets a front row seat to the inner workings of the Chicago crime family and their impending tragedy.

Visit Kristin at www.kristindurfee.com.

"The Orchid Man" by Charles A. Cornell. Vietnam, 1968. A student of Chinese medicine is kidnapped by Vietcong guerrillas. American helicopters arrive to face a large North Vietnamese force. All hell is about to be unleashed on the jungle and its hidden orchid garden, a place in later years that holds powerful emotions for those who survived the Vietnam War.

Visit Charles at www.charlesacornell.com.

"Dragon Lure" by John Hope. In the final days of seventh grade, a simple teenage video game addiction spirals into an unthinkable myriad of computer hacks and murder for two friends who soon find themselves in the middle of a complex game of espionage.

Visit John at www.johnhopewriting.com.

Introduction

What's past is prologue . . .
—William Shakespeare, The Tempest

The individual keeps watch on other individuals. Societies keep watch on other societies. Civilizations keep watch on other civilizations. It has always been so. Keeping watch is sometimes benevolent, sometimes malevolent. It is most certainly prudent.

It is not a trait exclusive to the human species.

Out of such prudence an advanced intelligence, far across the vastness of space, delivered to Earth a probe 40,000 years ago, to observe and report the progress of the human species. This probe was "born" here fully formed, a human being, engineered from the DNA of *Homo sapiens*. It possessed our skin, our organs, our skeleton, our muscles.

And it still lives among us.

The probe keeps watch.

The probe is one of us. Almost. It possesses a nuclear quantum computer brain, emitting a low-level electromagnetic field. It manipulates DNA and stem cells, healing itself as needed. It dies but remains immortal. It enters human societies, adopting any guise, any race, any gender, any age it wishes, following a three-month metamorphosis. It witnesses the events, great and small, good and bad, that shape our destiny.

The probe keeps watch.

Everything it sees, hears, feels, experiences, and thinks, it flashes instantaneously across a thousand light-years, in real-time quantum-entangled communication with the intelligence that sent it here.

The probe keeps watch. And sometimes it acts.

—The Authors of the Prometheus Saga

THE PROMETHEUS SAGA 2

THE SEVENTEENTH SLAVE

Jade Kerrion

1192 BCE

They buried me alive.

I was one of seventeen slaves selected to serve the Lady Fu Hao in the afterlife, the only one who walked down the steps into her tomb. The others had opted for a final meal of sweet buns infused with herbal concoctions. Their slumbering bodies were arranged in the chamber beneath her lacquered casket. Sleep eased into death.

As for me, the end was easier to face. It was never final.

Death, however, was far from my thoughts as I lay at the head of her casket. It was my right. The midwife who delivered her from her mother's womb had placed her directly in my arms. I was the first to hold her.

I was the last to bid her farewell.

The rhythmic clangs of the gongs anchored the sonorous, melodic chants of the monks. The air, heavily infused with incense, made my nose run, as it always did. It would almost be a relief to exchange this life, made tedious by the Shang rituals, for another.

Yet, incense or not, I would have stayed as long as she needed me.

Fu Hao's mother had been a thin, sickly creature, so I, her nurse, her *amah*, tended to the infant from the moment of her birth. I fed her and rocked her when her white baby teeth pushed through her aching gums—her red face scrunched up, tears streaming down her chubby cheeks. She kicked; she wailed; her fists pounded the air. Even then, she railed at things she could not control.

I steadied Fu Hao's first steps. I taught her how to read. We spent long days wandering the steppes on the outskirts of the town. Far from the scrutiny of others, I showed her how to ride a horse and wield a dagger-axe. Her preferred defense was to attack; no one ever expected it of the solemn-faced young woman. She was faster than she was strong, the precision of her skill always triumphant over brute force. I told her stories of ancient battles, and together, we analyzed military strategies and tactics. When she asked me how I—a simple nurse—knew so much about the art of war, I evaded her question.

How could I reply when I did not know the answer? I had lived one life after another, in one body after another—and I never understood why.

Yet, in Fu Hao, I almost found the answer. My life revolved around raising her. I was the person she smiled at, the person she yelled at, the person who dressed her for her wedding.

She was nineteen then, well beyond marriageable age. Her mother had despaired for her. Her father might have too, if he—the tribe's leader—were not so absorbed in walking the fine line between peace and independence. Fu Hao's family lands bordered those of the Shang, and the Shang king, Wu Ding, was acquisitive.

Fortunately, Wu Ding did not believe war was the answer to everything. He made peace and extended his influence with sixty-four neighboring tribes by marrying women from those tribes.

Fu Hao was among the sixty-four.

On her wedding day, she scowled at her hazy reflection in the bronze mirror as I dressed her for the ceremony. "When will he lose interest in me?"

"Why would the king lose interest in you?" I secured a stray strand of hair with a pin and tucked it under her headdress.

She spread her arms, the gesture encompassing King Wu Ding's massive wedding entourage, which included many of his other wives. "I could not get from any of them more than two minutes of conversation that did not involve clothes or food. I'm going to be the king's mad wife, stalking the corridors, mumbling to herself, and tearing her hair out for lack of intelligent conversation."

I chuckled. Fu Hao did not tend toward melodrama, but she was not incapable of exaggeration.

Her scowl deepened. "This is not funny. Why didn't my father pick someone else to give to that man?"

"Probably because that man, the *king*—" I reminded her, "—would not have settled for anyone less than you."

"I'm too old to marry. Too old to change my ways."

At nineteen, no less. I nodded sagely. It was always safer to let her talk her way back to rationality, than to attempt to argue her into it. "I hear that the capital city is beautiful."

"I don't want to go to Yin. It's crowded and dirty. Too many people make me nervous. I want to do what I want—not what a dirty old man wants."

"The king is quite clean—his slaves were scurrying around preparing his bath just yesterday—and not too old." I pressed my hands down on Fu Hao's shoulders. The pressure steadied her, as it always did. Her breathing slowed. She sat up straight, head high, and stared at herself in the mirror.

Fu Hao was not particularly pretty, but her direct gaze was compelling. Her keen intelligence made her beautiful.

"It's a marriage, not imprisonment," I reminded her. "What you make of it is up to you."

"I will not be one of seventy."

"Sixty-four," I corrected gently. "And I don't recommend poisoning the others."

Her eyebrows arched, and I immediately regretted putting that thought in her mind. She seemed to contemplate it for a moment, then sighed. "It would take a really long time, wouldn't it? But what else do I have to do with all that time on my hands?"

I hoped she was joking, but with Fu Hao, one could never be sure. I lingered on the outer edges of the voluminous tent erected for the wedding ceremony, which dragged on for hours with rituals, divinations, and sacrifices to the high god Di, the powers of nature, and innumerable ancestors. I would have left—my nose dribbled constantly from the pungent incense—but I stayed for her. Fu Hao remained mostly stoic; she rolled her eyes only once, when a sacrifice was made to a long-deceased concubine of a past emperor.

Wu Ding and Fu Hao scarcely looked at each other. It did not bode well for them.

In the morning, another slave sought me out. Fu Hao had sent for me.

I walked into her wedding chamber. She sat on a stool, staring at herself in the mirror as she combed out her hair. I took the brush from her to finish the task. For a long moment, neither of us said anything until I broke the silence with, "Well?"

"We talked," she said simply.

In her voice, I heard wonder, not belligerency, and I waited.

The long strokes of the brush through her hair calmed her, as it always had. A faint flush crept into her cheeks. "We did…other things too, but mostly we talked." Fu Hao expelled her breath in a soft sigh. A smile touched her lips. "I think we could be friends."

My smile concealed the ache deep in my chest. "I will supervise the packing of your belongings. In a week, he will return to Yin, and you with him."

Fu Hao's gaze met mine in the reflection of her mirror. "The other slaves can pack for me. You will pack your things. You are coming with me."

Her command, casually issued, rebirthed hope in me and restored joy to my days. I followed Fu Hao to the Shang capital city of Yin, but we did not stay long. The king's aged father died, forcing Wu Ding into a three-year period of mourning. Sulking in the royal palace for three years would have driven Fu Hao insane, so she talked her husband into a tour of the country.

Naturally, I accompanied Fu Hao, preparing her tea in the morning and evening. I supervised the slaves who washed her clothes, polished her dagger-axes, groomed her warhorses, and fed her dogs. I inspected the kitchens where elaborate multi-course meals were prepared for her and her husband. I was her *amah,* and in China's semi-matriarchal slave culture—the same culture that allowed Fu Hao to rise through the ranks to become Wu Ding's most favored consort—I was honored as the manager of her household.

Those three years were among the happiest of Fu Hao's life. She rode beside her husband to inspect crops and irrigation systems. At meetings with local officials, she sat next to the king, who seemed content to let his wife ask questions on all matters of public interests, from agriculture to trade, from crime rates to foreign treaties. In the evenings, I brought her tea to her bedroom, then withdrew. Often Fu Hao and Wu Ding, engaged in private heated debate over what to do with the *hsiung nu*, the barbarians clamoring on the empire's frontiers, did not even seem to notice that I had come and gone.

The next day, though, the tea cups were always empty. That morning, as I often did, I took up the hairbrush and drew it through Fu Hao's long hair. She wore an ornate gown, one she reserved for the most solemn rituals. She toyed with her glittering jade pendant, a wedding gift from her husband. "You are thinking hard," I said quietly as I gathered her hair and pinned it away from her face.

"I leave for the north. Tonight. You will come with me."

"Of course," I answered immediately, then an awful thought occurred to me. "Does the king know?"

She glared at me from her reflection in the mirror.

The door opened and the king walked into the room. I lowered my head and my gaze, for whatever good it did. To the king, I was merely an accessory, one that was present wherever his wife was. Wu Ding looked at Fu Hao. "They are waiting for you."

I glanced at Fu Hao. For an instant, her direct gaze quavered. I pressed my hands on her shoulders, steadying her. Her shoulders straight, her head held high, she followed her husband from the room.

I trailed behind Fu Hao and the king to the large room where religious ceremonies were conducted. The air was already cloudy with heavy incense. My nose started running and my eyes stung, but I squinted as the diviner inscribed questions on the tortoise shell. He raised it above his head, invoked the high god and the ancestors, then ceremoniously cracked it upon the bronze altar.

The old priest bent low, his eyes narrowed as he divined the answers from the cracks in the tortoise shell. He straightened and stared at Fu Hao.

I held my breath.

The diviner spoke, his voice resonant with authority. "The ancestors will spread their blessings over you."

The king smiled. His gesture summoned two servants carrying a large bronze *jue* between them. The three-legged drinking vessel, used for ceremonial rituals, was presented to Fu Hao, who bowed and accepted it with gracious formality.

The formality evaporated the moment Fu Hao stepped out of the room. She waved her hand in front of her face to dismiss the fragrant fumes. Her gaze fell on me. "Have you finished packing?" Her sharp tone quivered with impatience.

I stammered. "Uh, where we are going?"

"To defend our borders from the Tu Fang."

THE BRONZE *JUE* marked Fu Hao's first military commission from her husband, the king. Political expediency and military emergency made it inevitable. The two leading Shang military commanders were spearheading campaigns in the southeast and the southwest when the Tu Fang threatened the northern boundaries. Fu Hao stepped in because—it was the sort of person she was.

She understood the geography of the land; she handled dagger-axes and warhorses better than many soldiers; and her aptitude for military strategy was keener even than the king's greatest generals. The right to lead was conferred by the *jue*, but the respect of her troops she earned by leading them into battle.

"What would you have done if the divinations did not favor

you?" I asked her one cool morning as we stood outside her tent. The stink of men and horses surrounded us, as did the smell of smoke from the extinguished camp fires. Her horse was already saddled, and she wore leather armor over her simple clothes. Her dagger-axe, mounted on a pole like a spear-head, gleamed in the rising sun.

She arched her eyebrow. "You told me to make of this marriage what I would. Why would I let a cracked tortoise shell get in my way?" She took a final sip of her tea and handed the cup back to me before mounting her black horse.

"You would have ignored the divination?"

She shrugged. "I would have turned the tortoise shell until the priest read in the cracks what I wanted him to read."

I laughed and watched as she rode to take her place at the head of her army. My heartbeat quickened as it always did for her. I believed in no god, but I prayed for Fu Hao's safe return.

She did not return that night, nor the next morning. It was past noon the next day when her army finally returned to the camp, all of her men filthy, many of them wounded.

Terror cramped my stomach.

The whinny of horses and the stamp of hooves drowned out the shouts of men. My gaze swept across the beasts. There were far too many steeds without riders—far more than Fu Hao had led into war and most of them bore the crudely hewn Tu Fang leather saddles. My fear melted into the glimmer of hope. Had we won?

The vicious, victorious grins on the faces of the Shang troops confirmed it. Even so, it was hours before I found Fu Hao in the tents of her men, tending to the wounded. Hope soared into joy. "I am not hurt," she insisted, fending me off when I tried to examine her.

I tried not to flutter around her like an anxious mother hen. "You have to sit, you have to rest."

"Just get me some tea." Fu Hao dismissed me with a flick of her wrist. "I will eat later."

Later turned out to be many hours past midnight. I was waiting in her tent when she returned, her limbs dragging with exhaustion. Her smile, however, was radiant. I had never seen her so happy, nor so filthy. Her clothes would have to be burnt. I scrubbed nearly forty hours of battle grime from her body. She was already falling asleep as I dried her hair and brushed out the knots.

To my eyes, she was still just Fu Hao—a little girl turned woman, too brilliant and willful to be ordinary.

To everyone else, she had changed. Fu Hao had left Yin as the king's favored consort. She would return to the capital city as his favorite general. She had routed the Tu Fang so decisively that they never rose again to challenge the Shang empire.

The acclaim and favor of the people made it easy for Wu Ding to exalt her as high priestess. Fu Hao conducted sacrifices to appease the high god and to honor the king's ancestors. She shattered tortoise shells and ox scapula, and scrutinized the cracks with perfect solemnity and reverence.

I watched her from the doorway of the ceremonial chambers. She always turned the cracked shells and bones until they proclaimed what she wanted them to say. The other priests exchanged nervous glances, but no one told the king.

Especially not after Fu Hao delivered to Wu Ding a son, Xiao Yi, in the fifth year of their marriage.

The delighted king granted her a fiefdom on the borders of his empire.

"So, you'll be leaving Yin?" I asked Fu Hao after she ordered me to begin packing. "But to leave the king…and his seventy other wives—"

"Sixty-three," she corrected. "It's crowded here in the royal palace."

"But aren't you afraid you'll lose your standing as the king's favored consort?"

She dismissed my concern with a wave of her hand. "I am and will always be his favored consort. He has given to me a city from which to defend his borders and wage war against other nations. The generals Zhi and Hou Gao now report to me. I command 13,000 men, and I will establish order in the frontiers of the Shang empire." Her eyes narrowed on me. "Besides, you need the fresh air. The incense is making your cough worse."

"I am—"

Fu Hao strode past me to issue orders to the slaves who maintained her armory and cared for her warhorses. Her armory was more extensive than her wardrobe, and her horses were finicky brutes who charged fearlessly into war but were picky about the quality of their hay.

"—fine," I said to her back. I did not even realize she had noticed my reaction to the incense.

I followed Fu Hao; that I would do so was never in question. I was her *amah*. She was my sole care. Over the next decade, always accompanied by her son and his entourage of household slaves, she travelled frequently between her fiefdom and the capital city of Yin, and led two more successful military campaigns; the first against the Qiang Fang in the northwest; the second against the Yi Fang in the southeast and southwest.

Fu Hao returned from the second campaign triumphant, but exhausted in victory.

She dismounted from her horse, and staggered against me, as if the weight of her leather armor were too heavy for her. "You must rest!" I insisted, holding her up as her other slaves hurried toward us. They caught her before she fell, and carried her to the royal chambers.

The most esteemed medicine men in the royal palace rushed to her bedside. "She is fatigued," they insisted at the conclusion of their examination, and sent instructions to the kitchen to brew herbal tonics, infused with ox blood, to help her recover her strength.

The oracle readers proclaimed that Fu Hao's ailment was temporary and she would live many more years. I glanced at the dark scowl on the king's face and the worried furrow between his eyes, then stared down at the cracks in the tortoise shell. It hardly even mattered what the oracle bones proclaimed. The priests valued their lives; they would only have told the king what he wanted to hear.

Wu Ding would not have tolerated any suggestion that Fu Hao —his most celebrated general, his revered high priestess, his beloved wife and consort—would die.

To even *think* it was treason.

No one was ready to lose her.

I tended to Fu Hao every hour of every day. Her son, Xiao Yi, spent most of his waking hours with her—a more faithful shadow than any of her six dogs. "He looks more like his father every day," Fu Hao observed quietly as Xiao Yi played in the private courtyard, accessible only from her chambers.

Cherished by an overly protective mother, Xiao Yi was willful and conceited, but he was not without his virtues. "The scholars say he has a quick mind and a quick tongue," I told her. "He is drunk on legends of you."

"Legends?" Fu Hao laughed, but the sound edged toward a cough. It left her straining for breath. "I am only thirty-five. Legends demand decades of greatness, but my son will someday be proud to call me his mother." She glanced at the great bronze battle axe propped against her bedroom wall. "I am not yet there."

"If you're talking about ever actually carrying that axe—"

She laughed again, and it ended in a hacking wheeze. "I almost broke my wrist the day I lifted it. That axe was made for ceremony and ritual, not for battle. My little dagger-axe is all I need in a fight."

"You cannot go back into battle."

Her chin lifted. "Cannot?"

"Your body cannot take the strain of one military campaign after another. You are hardly returned from one before you head out on another—"

"Perhaps you should let the Qiang Fang and the Yi Fang know not to attack our borders while I'm catching up on my precious sleep."

"The Shang have other generals—"

"The oracles have said—"

"You made that stuff up."

Fu Hao's eyes widened, and she pressed her finger to my lips. "Quiet." She glanced around, but no one had paid us any attention.

I glared at her. "We both know you do. The oracle bones only say what you want them to say."

Fu Hao shrugged, and for an instant, she looked like a young girl instead of a war-weary general. "The borders of my life have expanded beyond anything I imagined. Wu Ding shared his world with me. I could never have experienced any of this if I had not married him."

I caressed her hair. "You were born for greatness, Fu Hao, with or without Wu Ding. Your name will live forever."

I RAN my hand over the smooth lacquer of Fu Hao's coffin. The seemingly endless line of servants entering the tomb with burial offerings had tapered off. The underground chamber had been filled with hairpins and arrowheads made of bone; expensive pieces of jade, opal, and ivory; bronze vessels, bells, mirrors, and weapons—including four massive battle axes, none of which she had actually carried into battle. The ceremonial *jue*, including one weighing almost twenty pounds, proclaimed her military supremacy, unmatched in life and immortalized in death.

That *jue* had been given to Fu Hao after she recovered from her illness, and before her final battle with the Ba Fung. King Wu Ding himself led his troops against a neighboring tribe allied with the Ba Fung. Lured by the possibility of killing the Shang king, the Ba Fung joined in the battle—walking straight into the ambush set by Fu Hao. The Shang army, with Fu Hao and her subordinate generals leading the charge, swept in and crushed the Ba Fung.

Fu Hao returned to Yin, exhausted by her victory. She might have slowly recovered as she had after her campaign against the Yi Fang, if not for the death of her son. I sat by her bedside, my hands wrapped around hers, when Wu Ding, his voice breaking, told her of Xiao Yi's accident. He had been thrown and trampled by her favorite warhorse. Fu Hao turned her face toward the private courtyard where her son used to play. She said nothing. She did not even cry.

She merely faded away, her food and herbal draughts untouched. Her will to live, her reason for greatness, had died with Xiao Yi.

Fu Hao's funeral ceremony had lasted for days and finally culminated in the filling of her tomb with burial offerings worth a princely fortune. Her tomb was permanent and hers alone. Unlike the king's other wives, her body would not be interred with his. She had been more than a wife and consort.

She had been the Shang empire's high priestess and war general.

Her six dogs, slaughtered to accompany her into the afterlife, lay beside her sixteen drugged slaves. Seventeen, including me. One for each year of her life as Wu Ding's consort. The king stood, silent and hollow-eyed, above her tomb as the slaves gathered to fill it.

I suspected it would not be long before he followed Fu Hao into the afterlife.

Dirt splattered onto my face. They were burying me alive. I closed my eyes and allowed my fingers to trail off the lacquered casket. I was the first to hold Fu Hao; I made certain I was the last to bid her farewell.

It was finally time for me to leave.

1976 CE

I SQUINTED against the sun and used it to set my bearings. The modern Chinese city of Anyang, built over the ruins of Yin, threw off my sense of direction. The mess the archeological team had made of the dig site did not help.

Zheng Zhenxiang, squat, bespectacled, and filled with boundless energy, scurried among her team, ordering them to use their *Louyang* shovels to probe the ground for rammed earth walls. She had convinced the local government to delay their plans to level a hillock outside the village of Xiaotun, but she was running out of time.

And she was searching in the wrong spot.

She had no idea what treasure lay beneath.

Fu Hao's name had been virtually extinguished from the annals of history, her triumphs as a queen, a high priestess, and a general purged in the less-enlightened Chinese dynasties that followed.

No one remembered her.

But I did.

I had promised her that her name would live forever.

It was time to make good on that promise.

I glanced once more at the sun, then strode over to the base of the hillock. *Right about here.* I pushed the long handled *Louyang* shovel into the earth. I pulled it up, its metal tip stained with red lacquer. A jade pendant hanging from one of its hooks glittered in the sun.

I smiled. Centuries…millennia before, that pendant had graced Fu Hao's neck when she was still merely a wife and consort. Before she became a general and ascended into legend.

"Over here!" I shouted in Chinese. Zheng Zhenxiang scurried over. Her eyes widened as she pushed me aside to examine my findings.

It did not bother me. Here, in this lifetime, I was merely a day laborer, hired to dig out an ancient hillock. Let Zhenxiang claim the credit for uncovering the tomb of a Shang dynasty queen. Fu Hao's resting place had been found. The bronze vessels and oracle bones in her tomb would restore her name and her fame.

And beneath her tomb, they would find the bones of six dogs and sixteen slaves.

No one would ever know there was ever a seventeenth slave.

Except me.

AUTHOR'S NOTES – JADE KERRION

MU XIN, the brilliant NSA analyst, is a *Double Helix* fan favorite, equally loved and hated for her startling perspectives, shrewd insights, and ruthless conclusions. She is the clone of the Shang dynasty's most famous queen, general, and high priestess—Fu Hao.

The Seventeenth Slave breathes life into the story of the young woman who rose through the ranks of China's semi-matriarchal slave culture to become King Wu Ding's most favored consort. Fu Hao led 13,000 men in successful defense of the Shang borders and was the mastermind behind the earliest recorded large-scale ambush in Chinese history.

In 1976, Fu Hao's tomb was unearthed, intact with its lacquered coffin, bronze and jade treasures, and the skeletons of the sixteen slaves chosen to serve her in the afterlife. Her tomb is now open to the public.

You can enjoy Xin's story at http://books2read.com/xin. Happy reading!

—JK

THE TOWER HOUSE PRISONER

Ken Pelham

Ireland, North of Cashel, 1605

Captain William Farnham studied the tower house from the edge of the renegade's dead fields. The dawn's fog had dissolved and light came thin and pale, a jaundice afflicting the sun's beams. Farnham took a bite of apple, tossed the core aside, and wiped his mouth on his sleeve. He thanked God and cursed Him in the same breath. Just enough good light for killing.

The long, bleak siege, three months in, would soon be over, its end assured this day. His vehement request had been at last granted by plump administrators in Dublin Castle, scratching at carved oak desks, imbibing French wine, and playing at love with whores in featherbeds.

Lord, how he hated Ireland. Step outside Dublin's walls and you entered a backward, barbaric country. Why King James insisted upon English ownership of such a land was beyond him, yet royals throughout Europe scrabbled and clawed for any dirt they happened upon in their mad zeal for colonies. Ireland abounded in no riches, unless rocks be riches. The Irish scurried about as savages, or nearly so, speaking their gibberish tongue and wallowing in fleas and filth.

The only thing worse than an Irishman was an Englishman that had gone Irish. Like Lord John Merriwether, the little fool that dwelt in this tower house, this pitiful excuse for a real castle. The towers dotted the Irish countryside, looming over all. They rendered English lords godlike in the eyes of Irish bumpkins who themselves dwelt in rude huts and hovels. And though pretend castles fed arrogance and a sense of invincibility, they impressed veteran English soldiers not at all.

Still, Merriwether's two dozen defenders had accounted themselves well, repulsing the two frontal assaults that had been ordered at the beginning of the campaign by quill-pushers in Dublin before the fight had settled more sensibly into siege. Safe within their sturdy walls, they had lost perhaps three of their number, while Farnham had lost sixteen men dead, another eighteen wounded beyond use. Men he counted true and brave and worthy.

Farnham turned from the tower house, confident it would remain quiet. It lay outside the ranges of the King's archers, and his siege lines outside those of the tower's.

He signaled his men to bring forward the engine of destruction that would put an end to this campaign. From the wood forty yards behind, his men emerged, a quintuplet leading, and two great horses following and hauling the cannon.

Merriwether had been seduced by the barbaric ways and redhaired charms of his Irish wife. The hearty nobleman of England began sliding into this depravity a good decade ago, slow to collect taxes at first, slower still to install proper English ways, and—most unpardonably of all—siphoning off more than his fair share of revenues.

Marrying local did that to you.

Laxness among the governing lords festered, leading many to lapse into local custom and morals. Impatient, the King commanded Dublin to bring the scattered errant lords back into line, and sent hand-picked emissaries afield to discuss the matter, gently or firmly according to need, with the wayward lords. Some capitulated without so much as a harsh word. Others resisted. Merriwether, a particularly quarrelsome sort, took another, more foolish step.

He imprisoned Catherine Stokes, the King's own emissary.

Dublin did not need guidance from King James in this matter. They knew that if the situation were not rectified they would soon be dealt with themselves. So they mustered a force barely large enough for the task, positioned the unlucky Farnham in its lead, and sent them to take Merriwether Castle and fetch both rebel and emissary back to Dublin, posthaste.

Captain Farnham knew what to expect. He had brokered similar situations, peacefully and without loss of life as luck would have it, twice before. Succeed or not, it was unlikely the emissary still lived. Once the Crown refused to pay ransom, food and water to the prisoner became whims of the captor. And when under siege, a lord parcels and conserves his foodstuffs wisely.

Farnham had entreated Merriwether in straightforward fashion. Release His Majesty's agent, he'd told the man. Beg for leniency and perhaps be spared, albeit most likely forced into hard labor, or exiled to some hard, foreign shore. At least earn a measure of mercy for your family and servants.

Merriwether had grown nervous and claimed that Catherine Stokes and her lone guard had come and issued outrageous demands and then left, heading west. That was the last he'd heard of the woman. The traitor then ended negotiations abruptly. He would not surrender.

Merriwether had lied, of course; the Crown's spies in the province assured Dublin that the lady had entered the tower house and never left. That spoke the worst for the poor emissary. She had likely been cut from rations and left for dead, a common practice among ransoming lords. Or simply murdered and buried.

The sky brightened and Farnham squinted into the distance. Defenders were assembling atop the tower to watch the cannon being wheeled into place. Merriwether, Farnham gathered, had never witnessed artillery in action. Most small-minded local lords hadn't, safe in their provincial ignorance. New, fearsome weapons terrorized peasants and royals alike across Europe, rendering useless the old ways of warfare to which even many English clung. Farnham knew better. He'd used the new weapons. Stonework, so reliable a defense for centuries, now afforded merely a heavy tomb in which defenders might be buried.

Merriwether was to receive his first lesson in modern warfare.

The men stuffed the cannon with gunpowder and wadding, rodded it in, and rolled the forty-pound ball into the barrel.

"Light it, Captain?" asked Carter. The gunnery lads drew near, one holding the glowing igniter, eagerness in his eyes.

Farnham shook his head and turned again to the tower house. Merriwether could not mistake what came next. Surely he knew of cannon and what terrible destructions could be wrought by it. But knowing and believing differed. Farnham waited. Moments passed, laden with excitement and dread.

"So be it," Farnham said. "Fire."

The gunner licked his lips and extended the igniter to the touch hole. A hiss, a streamer of smoke.

The cannon roared and bucked and rolled backward. The muzzle flashed orange and a cloud of smoke exploded from it.

The iron ball smacked into the tower, forty feet above the ground, slightly off center. Plaster flew from the wall, and limestone rained down. Cracks spiderwebbed the surface.

"Excellent," Farnham said. "But lower the arc. Hit the tower at its base and let the great weight of stone above help bring it down. Sponge, prime, reload, and ram."

Carter nodded. The exercise repeated, and Farnham again gave the order to fire. The roar and flash, the smoke, the metallic strike of iron on stone. The cascade of dust and rock from the tower house wall.

The pause. The wait for an answer.

None came. Perhaps Merriwether believed Farnham would exhaust his powder and shot and give up. He would be wrong.

The cannon roared again. The cracks in the tower house spread. Sections began to slough off in great masses. If the barrage kept on, the tower would soon collapse and kill all within.

From a window in the top floor, a pike extended slowly, a white banner hanging from it, and waved.

Merriwether had had enough.

FARNHAM WATCHED AND WAITED. He'd fought enough battles, seen enough treachery, to learn distrust. And those battles pitched civilized men against civilized foes. He would certainly not rush out with open arms to embrace a barbarian Irish foe, even one who was English.

The listless white flag withdrew. And still Farnham waited.

Carter, next to him, shifted restlessly. "Blast 'em again, Captain?"

"Patience," Farnham said. "They were lost as soon as the gun arrived. It just took them awhile to know it. There's no need to kill them all."

"Captain, they'll all hang, you know."

He knew. But that blood would stain someone else's hands.

AT LAST, Merriwether exited the tower house, followed by his wife. After them came a red-haired girl of about eleven years, and two old women and an old man limping along on a crutch. Fifteen men followed, poorly armored in the tradition of the barbarians, but unarmed and with hands raised.

The entire body trod through the collapsed gate of the low, surrounding bawn wall towards Captain Farnham. His men trained drawn bows and arrows upon the lot of them. At length, Farnham raised an outstretched palm and said, "Come no closer, traitor Merriwether. Kneel where you are, all of you."

The body paused, watching their lord. Merriwether studied Farnham for a moment and sank to his knees. His entourage followed suit.

"Very good, traitor. Have you weapons, any of you? Speak truly and seek our good graces. If we find even a knitting needle upon you, you will die on the spot."

"We have no weapons, English," Merriwether growled.

"That is good. Do not move while we put your claim to the test."

Farnham's soldiers searched the kneelers. One of the men, Mason, yanked the young girl to her feet. She screamed and he slapped her, knocking her back to the ground. "This one's got a blade!"

Merriwether sprang to his feet. "Get your English hands off her!"

"Stay put, Merriwether," Farnham snapped. "Little girl, withdraw your blade and cast it aside. Mason, careful. Release her and back away."

The girl whimpered and looked from face to face, her eyes wide.

"Do you speak English, girl?"

"Damn you, Farnham. My little girl is Irish, through and through." He turned to his daughter. "*A chaitheamh ar leataobh an lann, cailín.*"

The girl nodded, sobbing. From under her apron she withdrew a long-handled wood spoon and cast it aside.

Farnham sighed in relief. He turned to Carter. "Seize and bind the traitor."

"An' the rest, Captain?"

"Escort them under guard back to camp. Traitor Merriwether, is anyone left in this ridiculous castle?"

"No one that yet lives, ye English lackey."

"And Catherine Stokes? I know for a fact that she never left. Therefore it follows that you have murdered the King's own emissary. An unwise choice."

"Take it as ye will, lackey. Aye, the woman did not leave and does not yet live. If the King sends witches to do his work, he should not expect better."

"What do you mean?"

"The witch lies dead and mouldering in the dungeon, lackey."

Farnham considered this for a moment. Superstition ran rampant through the uneducated underclasses of Europe. Yet it never ceased to amaze him; and this traitor, Merriwether, came from a fine family and estate in Cornwall, and had received a gentleman's education. "Show me to the dungeon, traitor and murderer. The emissary shall be accorded a decent Christian burial. Perhaps you shall join her."

CAPTAIN FARNHAM ADVANCED step by careful step toward the tower house, his fist twisted into Merriwether's collar, pushing the traitor in front at arm's length, a human shield. He would not chance the possibility of a vengeful rogue or two still lurking about the place, committed to some suicidal last stand.

The swift Irish weather changed, a cold westerly wind sweeping over the land and driving a rain before it. Lightning flickered and the sky rumbled.

Farnham knew well the intricacies of tower house defenses, and Merriwether's stronghold likely incorporated them all. He took a moment to look the castle up and down once more.

Carter, in his youthful, foolish eagerness, strode past, sword drawn.

"Hold, lad!" Farnham snapped. "Caution is the order of the hour. Look up."

Carter stopped and stared upward.

Perched and overhanging the door niche, at the very top of the tower house, a dark rectangle of stone projected a few feet outward, directly above the entrance. The machicolation. Defenders above would simply drop things upon the intruders. Boulders, boiling oil. They could not be avoided, and bloody ends inevitably awaited some unlucky soldiers.

Nothing came raining down from above.

The great oaken door hung upon iron hinges, recessed sideward in a niche in the base of the tower wall. Directly in the back wall of the niche, two slits, one horizontal and one vertical, formed an elegant cross-shaped window that had nothing to do with Christian piety. The vertical slit formed a loop for arrows from a longbow, and the horizontal slit a loop for the launch of bolts from a crossbow. Anyone approaching the door could not avoid the line of fire.

Farnham shoved Merriwether against the crossed loops and leapt to the side of the niche, pressing himself against the wall, swinging his shield up protectively, and looked up. As expected, a dark opening graced the ceiling of the niche. The murder hole. Another ingenious defense against unwanted visitors. If one stood within the niche out of the harm of the machicolation, defenders could stab from above with long-handled pikes.

"I told ye no one left alive remains in the castle, lackey."

"And I trust you implicitly, traitor." Farnham swung Merriwether about and pushed the door open with him. "You still have value, it seems."

A small vestibule lay within, a heavy door on the left of it opening onto the kitchen. He turned to look up the narrow staircase that wound its way up and out of sight. "Up you go, traitor."

They climbed the five levels of the tower house, pausing to inspect each room, finding each untenanted. At last they reached the top room, the entertaining hall. Farnham knew that the dungeon entrance lay in the top room, the most inaccessible in the castle. He shoved Merriwether inside and released him. "The dungeon entrance, traitor. Show me."

Merriwether mumbled some gibberish curse, and crossed to the wall opposite the doorway. A niche, with window looking out, held doors on either side. One would be the entrance into the cavity within the double wall of the tower to the quarters in which occupants relieved themselves. Opposite it, a second narrow door also opened into the double wall. "Here?" Farnham said.

Merriwether nodded.

"Good. Carter, descend into the dungeon and fetch the prisoner."

"You may regret it."

"And why is that?"

"Why? The woman was a witch."

"'Was?'"

"Don't be a fool, lackey. We lowered the witch into the dungeon and left her. Four months ago."

"And I assume you gave her food and water."

"One does not offer sustenance to evil."

"Then it is as I feared. You have murdered the King's own agent and you will hang for it."

"James I is your king, not mine. He is my oppressor and his agents my enemies. I shan't weep over the deaths of enemies."

"And I shan't weep over you as I watch you squirm and kick when you drop from the gallows. Carter, open the trapdoor."

Carter shot him a glance, gripped the iron ring handle of the trap door, and heaved it up and open.

Captain Farnham stepped back, expecting a miasma of death and decay to assail him. Yet no stench of rotting flesh assailed him. Just a smell of ancient, musty nothingness.

"In you go, Carter."

Carter grimaced, and a look of fear shadowed his face. "Captain—"

"Oh, come now, Carter, afraid of the dark? You always claimed to be the bravest man in the King's ordnance. Don't disappoint. We cannot simply leave the remains of the emissary in this dungeon. She must be afforded a decent burial."

"Captain, I do not fear dying. But this—"

A sound, a muffled scraping, came from the dark depths of the dungeon. Carter backed from the opening. "Saints preserve us."

The scraping sound ceased, and silence reigned for a moment. And they heard a voice. A woman's voice. "I should like to be free now, if you please. Kindly toss a rope down and we will chat."

Farnham took a moment to gather his wits. "You down there . . . who are you? How did you come to be sealed with the King's emissary?"

"I *am* the emissary of His Majesty, King James I. A rope, if you please."

Dublin

FARNHAM PUSHED his way through peasants and laborers outside the gate of Dublin Castle. Thousands thronged and buzzed in anticipation, eyes wide with excitement. The crowds surprised him; but then, this trial stirred peasants and titillated nobles, making it the event of the season, if not the entire year, in Dublin. News of the great witch trial swept the province, and the few facts known and shared had taken on lives of their own. The defendant, it was whispered, prowled and pranced about on cloven hooves. Fur—or scales, depending upon the teller—covered her body, and her tail writhed and twisted like a serpent.

Farnham presented himself to the scowling guards. After whispered discussion, one of them ushered Farnham inside and escorted him into a broad, high-ceiled room, the great banquet hall. The room bustled with the movement and animated conversations of three hundred men and women. He spotted his wife, Mary, and nodded to her. She smiled weakly in response, her face drawn and pale.

The guard waved Farnham to the front of the crowd and off to the side. A vast table of oak occupied the center, with three high-backed chairs, all empty. After a few minutes, a quartet of soldiers marched in and positioned themselves, two to a side at the ends of the table. Three men swept in behind and took their seats at the table, and the crowd fell silent.

Farnham knew the men. To the left and right sat Sir Hugh Colby and Sir Charles Lytton. Between them sat Sir Edmund Godfrey, a small man made large by virtue of heavy red robe, black mortar cap, and permanent discontent. Godfrey motioned impatiently to a boy, who hurried to hand him a parchment. Godfrey placed the document upon the table before him and studied it at length, his face darkening. Presently he looked up. "Fetch the prisoner," he said.

Two soldiers hauled a woman in filthy rags before the table and pushed her onto her knees. Her blonde hair hung limp and tangled, and dirt smeared her face. Yet beneath the young woman's squalid exterior, her eyes belied a quick, observant intelligence. Catherine Stokes. The tower house prisoner.

Farnham glanced about. As half-expected, no one seemed to represent the prisoner. Her surname bespoke humble origins; most certainly she was not high-born and of generous means. Yet somehow this tradeswoman had been selected by His Majesty to represent his government abroad. That the King had selected a woman to send on such an errand was unheard of. That meant something, so one could not underestimate the woman.

Godfrey studied the prisoner, read a bit more from his parchment, and looked again at her. "Catherine Stokes, you stand accused of witchcraft, a most serious crime in the eyes of God and King. Care you now to confess the crime, that we may end this trial and get on with our lives?"

"I do not confess, Sir Edmund."

Godfrey nodded to a scribe, who wrote furiously with quill and ink on a small table to the side. "Very well. Mister Williamson, record every word, omit nothing. This trial's record shall speak truths to future generations." He paused. "I have read the report of Captain Farnham and the statement of the traitor Merriwether. Have you anything to say in response?"

"I have not read those documents. I cannot respond."

"You traveled to the country two day's north of Cashel, accompanied by one of the King's soldiers, to treat with the traitor, at the behest of His Majesty, King James I."

"I did."

"What instructions did the King provide?"

"The King directed me to implore Merriwether to end his reckless behavior and return to loyal service immediately."

"And His Majesty would then grant clemency?"

"His Majesty might then let Merriwether live out his days. In the Tower of London. But Merriwether's family would be spared, stripped of title, lands, and rights, and released to move west and perhaps live as Irish."

"You delivered the message as directed?"

"Yes. And more."

Godfrey raised an eyebrow. "Well then?"

"I delivered it as commanded. But King James had no intention of letting the man escape execution. I added alternative suggestions."

"You offered *alternatives* to the King's wishes?"

"I am the King's emissary. His diplomat. Diplomats seek ways to end impasse."

"And your suggestions—?"

"That Merriwether accompany me to Dublin and London, to explain to His Majesty that Ireland is not England, that it has its own history, its own heroes and villains, its own language, its own gods and demons, and that it should be treated as an equal partner."

"What unbridled rubbish! Have you not seen this land? It is not the equal of England. It is not even the equal of France, or Spain, or Portugal. It is perhaps, if one uses license, the equal of the savage New World."

"I have seen many countries, known many peoples, spoken many languages, Sir Edmund. It is why I am the emissary and not you."

"Let the record show that the defendant misrepresented the King. Criminally poor judgement at best, treason at worst. Trending toward the latter." He leaned back in his chair and tapped softly on the table. "Bring the traitor forward."

Guards shoved Merriwether closer.

"Traitor," Godfrey said, "understand that you are not on trial. But you *will* hang. Useful information rendered might, however, ease your journey into the next world, be that one of fire or one of light. God hates traitors to England, but smiles upon those who aid the war against evil. We, and our God, acknowledge that you imprisoned this woman or monster."

"I didn't know she was a witch when she first arrived. I didn't know that until the next day."

"You realize that you draw a breath and elude the hangman only insofar as you may bear witness against the accused witch, do you not?"

Merriwether shrugged. "I am a dead man either way. Timing concerns me little."

"So be it. What became of the soldier accompanying Catherine Stokes?"

"He was killed by one of my men."

"So I have read. Do you care to explain the murder away?"

"When she differed from the wishes of King James, her soldier flew into a rage, drew his sword against her. I commanded him stop, but he swung mightily downward and the emissary fell back to avoid the blow. The blade sliced through her collarbone and two ribs. A frightful injury. My men ran the murderer through and killed him on the spot. The woman was gutted yet seemed not to care. No cry escaped her, though her blood fell in a torrent and she weakened and stumbled. My women bandaged her tightly in great haste, but I did not expect her to live the night. We plied her with whiskey to ease her suffering and provided her warm bedding and locked her in an empty room to recover. Or to die."

"Most hospitable of you."

"There was little to be done for her."

Godfrey motioned to a guard. "Strip the accused's tunic."

The guard tore the garments from the prisoner, exposing her breasts.

Godfrey looked at her and then back to Merriwether. "She hasn't a scratch upon her!"

"Aye, now ye begin to understand."

"You claim she has healed completely in the three months since?"

"Ye *don't* understand. She didn't have a mark the *very next morning*."

"Rubbish. No one can heal that quickly."

"Therein she must be attained a witch. And in my terror, I committed her to the dungeon."

"And treated her well?"

Merriwether hesitated. "Your king sent a witch with frightful powers to bargain with me. I could think of no reason for James to do so other than to destroy me with black magic at little cost and no risk."

"Answer the question."

"We treated her accordingly."

Godfrey waited, his face darkening.

"I threw her into the dungeon to die," Merriwether finally said. "I did not need the agent of a despot in my house wielding the very powers of Satan against me. We gave her neither food nor water."

"You speak absurdities. The King's view of witchcraft is well known and his righteous attendance to the North Berwick trials bears this out. He will never allow a witch to live in his kingdom."

"Except perhaps to deal with Irish barbarians. A bad outcome for either is a good outcome for your king."

Godfrey scowled. "Captain Farnham. You freed the prisoner from the dungeon. What was her condition?"

"Filthy, yet healthy as now you see her. No signs of starvation or privation. No wounds. No bruises. Not even the slightest scar."

"Then you attest to witchcraft?"

"I attest only to what I report. I freed a woman who bore signs neither of abuse nor neglect."

"How do you account for it then?"

Farnham shrugged. "The simplest explanation is most always the correct one. Merriwether is a traitor to England and beneath contempt, and one must assume him a liar as well. I believe Merriwether treated and fed his prisoner well, and lowered her into the dungeon the very moment he saw our cannon arrive."

Merriwether snorted.

Godfrey tapped his fingers on the table. "And what, pray tell, does he gain by this? If he had treated the emissary as a guest, he might have somewhat mitigated his punishment."

"He is a clever fiend, no doubt. If he has half a brain, he knew defeat was imminent the moment we hauled cannon within range. He then hid the prisoner in the dungeon, bound and gagged, and planned to say that she had visited and left freely, never to return, or that perhaps she never even visited. Both lies are plausible, if we hadn't found the prisoner. Yet I am well-schooled in the architecture of tower houses."

Godfrey turned to Catherine Stokes. "And what do you claim to be the truth of the matter?"

"The good captain is correct, my lord. Lord Merriwether indeed treated me well, though under lock and key. I neither saw nor knew of a dungeon until the morning of the cannon's bark."

Merriwether laughed. "What a lying denizen of hell! What a damnable fiend!"

"But if such is the truth," Godfrey said, "it mitigates somewhat his crimes. He would have no reason to fabricate such a falsehood, so it rings true."

"A test of witchcraft, then! Take your knife. Wound her. Carve a 'W' in her forehead. I promise ye, by this time tomorrow there won't be a mark upon her, and ye'll have your proof."

"Slice up the hand-picked emissary of His Majesty? I think not. I have grown attached to my balls." Godfrey chuckled, and the audience joined him.

Farnham stepped forward. "If I may address this court?"

Godfrey gave the slightest nod of assent.

"I was quartered in Scotland those few years ago and attended the North Berwick trials," Farnham said. "I saw the King's justice and wisdom on display. And I have studied at length the King's great work of scholarship, *Daemonologie*." He paused. "We have reached a delicate point. We have one here accused of high treason and another of witchcraft. Which is the worse crime? One is treason against England, the other against God. That is for greater minds than mine to decide." He turned to face the rapt crowd. "My lords, my countrymen, the honorable judge is in a spot. If he finds Stokes guilty, he can by law claim her possessions and wealth as his own."

A silence and stillness filled the great hall. Farnham glanced at Godfrey, who regarded him through narrowed eyes. "This is the great beauty of witch trials," he continued. "A pestilence is stricken from the country and the presiding judge walks away a wealthier man. An enticing proposition. I'm told that the honorable judge has a taste for gaming, yet lacks skill at it, and manages frequently to find himself in substantial debt. Just as he found himself in the gaming rooms of Edinburgh. The North Berwick trials provided lucrative, fortunate timing indeed. Speedy convictions of dozens of witches, and speedy confiscation of property by the judge. Within days, his gambling debts had evaporated."

Godfrey slapped the table. "Careful what you say, man!"

"Yet Stokes is a woman of little means, in spite of her high posting. She seems to have accumulated little wealth during her service to the King. Still, she is bound to have some small amount of money, so even though our fine judge finds himself again in debt, he stands to gain from a witchcraft conviction and much-needed securing of money.

"Sir Edmund Godfrey was dispatched from London for one task alone; preside over the treason trial of Merriwether, gain a conviction, and dispense immediate and harsh punishment. Send a message to the wayward English lords in Ireland. Sir Edmund prepared for the quick trial and conviction, but received a surprise. Merriwether was delivered to him but so was another, this woman Catherine Stokes, the King's own, accused of witchcraft.

"I witnessed the North Berwick trials. They came swift and ruthless, as so many confessions had been wrung from the defendants through torture. Godfrey is not about to torture the King's emissary, who professes her innocence. Yet he cannot sidestep the trial. He is forced, it seems, to find the accused guilty; there are many witnesses, and even though they attest to the impossible, under the King's moral authority their testimonials must be held to be true."

"You approach treason yourself, Captain," Godfrey said. "The King himself presided over Berwick, and you hint that his divine guidance was less than honorable. He shall know of this."

Farnham glanced at Mary. Her face was drawn with fear, her eyes glistening, pleading to go no further with this. He wavered; the path ahead lay fraught with mortal danger, not just for him but for Mary as well. But the past and his own failure as a man had returned to confront him and demand reconciliation.

With effort, he looked back at Godfrey. "Ah, Your Honor, I dare not question the wisdom and motives of the King! I seek, rather, to simplify this case for all." Farnham strode toward Catherine Stokes, and stopped a pace from her. "We have heard the extraordinary claims of Merriwether. Claims of miraculous power." A sudden movement, a glint of metal, and Farnham produced a knife and slashed the face of the accused.

The prisoner winced and cried out. But her reactions missed a beat, the merest of hesitations. Something seemed untrue, as if the wound alarmed the prisoner not at all.

Blood welled and spilled from the cut on her cheek. A deep, scarring cut, to be sure, but not a dangerous one.

The audience cried out. Godfrey sprang to his feet. "Damn you, man! What are you doing?"

"Putting accused and accuser to the test. If the witchcraft be true, by Merriwether's assertion she will be healed by tomorrow. If the accusation be false, she will remain cut deeply. I have given her a scar to bear for life, but in doing so I have given her life. She is no witch. You would try her and convict her on the testimony of a traitor, and burn her at the stake within the week. I stood by and watched this in Berwick; I shall not stand by again."

A terrible quiet filled the hall. Godfrey fixed his dark, narrowing eyes upon Farnham. "Very well, Captain. The court shall reconvene at noon on the morrow to consider the wound of the accused. And know ye this: protecting a witch implicates the protector in the same wicked practices. Interfering in a charge of treason implicates one equally in crime. These are principles of God's natural law, and of all civilized men. You are herewith jailed until your own guilt or innocence may be decided."

FARNHAM PACED his cell in the New Gate Prison, thinking things through. It did not seem promising. He had put Godfrey in an untenable position, and no doubt the judge was concocting unpleasant outcomes for him even now. He had let the bastard off easy by making the decision for him, yet Godfrey would still demand his pound of flesh. The King would not abide a witch and would be satisfied with her execution. Godfrey could then count whatever small sums he would earn from the extinction of Catherine Stokes. Now, by Farnham's hand, Catherine Stokes stood at least a chance of release—scarred and bloodied, true—but her innocence intact. And if she were executed in spite of it all, the whispers of injustice would spread through the kingdom.

Both Farnham and Merriwether would hang.

So Farnham paced the inky blackness, unable to sleep. He stopped at the massive gate of crossed iron bars and tested it for the hundredth time, pulling it this way and that. It did not budge. Hannibal's elephants could not throw down this gate.

He reached through the bars and felt the keyhole for the lock. There would be no opening it. He withdrew his arm and sank to the floor, thinking of escape, going over the possibilities once more.

He'd searched every square inch of his cell. Useless. If there stood a chance of escape, it would be when someone from outside opened his cell or grew careless. So far that had not happened. The only time the door would be opened would be to escort him to his own trial and execution.

The cell possessed no flaws. In a century, perhaps, as the iron rusted and limestone masonry weakened. But he didn't have a century. He had at best three days.

He harbored no illusions on Godfrey's adjourning statement. The judge's eyes signaled an unsavory end for that transgression. Farnham had cast his lot with the fates of two prisoners. Either, and possibly both, would be found guilty of their crimes, and Farnham would be assigned their guilt as well.

If found guilty of treason, Farnham would be hanged or beheaded. If guilty of witchcraft, he would burn. No workhouse or hard labor punishments awaited, only death.

Why had he thrown himself into this position? His rashness consigned his wife to a life of misery. Poverty and scorn would be Mary's reward, alone in an uncaring world.

Why?

He had served to the best of his abilities. He'd fought the King's wars, spread the King's rule across growing lands and seas.

He knew why.

Scotland. Godfrey and James had presided over the trial of young Katie Williams of Edinburgh, his wife's sweet niece, in North Berwick. She, like James himself, hailed from Scotland. Yet the judge condemned her to the brutal punishments of the times. A mere thirteen years of age, and a witch, they called her!

For the crime of rebuking and revealing Godfrey's advances.

Sweet, innocent, murdered Katie, now a pariah in England and Scotland, cursed and excoriated as Edinburgh Kate.

The moment Farnham laid eyes upon Godfrey in Catherine Stokes's trial, he could not let the man repeat that crime. He'd cast his lot with the condemned, and now stood condemned himself.

The chill of the night crept into the cell and into his bones. A rain had commenced as he was taken to the jail, and still fell for all he knew. Drops of water plinked onto the stone floor. Despite the cold and wet, he felt his eyelids grow heavy and the world drift from him.

Something, a sound, startled him awake. Had the day arrived, the day in which he would be charged with capital crimes of his own? He shook the slumbers from his mind, tried to clear his thoughts. He needed his wits today.

There . . . the sound again. Down the way, slow and stealthy. He strained to hear. Yes, someone approached, measuring footsteps. That perhaps meant relief. His jailers would certainly feel no need for stealth. Someone else lurked there.

The faintest of light, a glow, appeared down the corridor, and a single candle appeared.

Mary Farnham emerged slowly from the gloom, carrying the candle before her, looking this way and that.

"Mary! I'm here!"

His wife gasped and ran to him, her eyes wide. He reached through the bars and pulled her close. "What . . . how did you get in here?"

She held her fingers to her lips. "Shush, my darling," she whispered. "We must be quiet and quick." She inserted a long key into the lock, twisted it, eased the door open with a grinding of rusty iron, and stepped inside. They embraced and kissed. He felt the tears on her face. She took his hand, squeezed it, and led him from the cell. He crept toward the exit, the direction from which she'd come. She stopped, held his hand. "No. Not that way."

He looked at her. "I know this jail," he said. "It's the only way out."

Again, she pressed fingers to lips. She turned and headed in the opposite direction, pulling him after her.

The corridor turned once, twice. And Mary stopped before a cell. Sitting against the wall, Lord Merriwether looked up, surprise filling his eyes. "What's all this?"

"My question exactly," Farnham said.

"Quiet, the both of you!" Mary turned to her husband. "We must free him."

"Nonsense! Let us make our escape and quit this place at once."

"We must free him. I have promised his wife we would, and we owe your freedom to her."

Merriwether gasped and sprang to his feet. "To my sweet Saoirse!" He pressed his face to the bars, trying to see down the corridor. "Where is she?"

"She is—" Mary hesitated. "She is with the night guard, My Lord. Keeping him busy. It was the only way to draw him from his post."

Merriwether pulled back and looked at her. "She is—" He turned away, and back again. "By the saints, what a woman! This, Captain Farnham, is why I chose my sweet Irish bride. Can you imagine such a love from an English lady?"

Mary turned the key and Merriwether stepped out. "We must hurry," she said. "Saoirse has him occupied but his watch is to be relieved within the hour."

"Well, Captain Farnham. It appears we cannot find common ground, but our wives can."

"That would appear to be the case."

"Come," Mary said. "We must be away now."

"Wait," Farnham said. "Catherine Stokes. Where is her cell?"

Merriwether grunted. "Heavens, man! We must go."

"Her cell?"

Merriwether shook his head. "Very well. She is around the next corner, a few paces farther. And she is a witch and cursed to hell anyway."

"There are no witches, you fool. She won't die for your superstition." Farnham took the key and pushed past Merriwether. In a moment he stood before a dark cell. He could dimly make the shape of a woman against the far wall. "Mary, quick, the candle."

She hurried forward. Farnham turned the lock and opened the door. "Catherine Stokes, you are free. Step lively, woman."

"My thanks, my lords and lady." She stepped forward into the light.

Mary drew a sharp breath.

"Damn you, you see?" Merriwether said.

The hideous, deep cut that yesterday marred the woman's face from cheek to chin, the cut administered by Farnham himself, had vanished. Not the slightest mark remained. Farnham raised the candle to the woman's face, studying her.

"Then it is true," he whispered. "True."

"All that is true, my lord," Catherine Stokes said, "is that I have a remarkable capacity for healing. That is all."

"*All*? That is enough! Are you not a witch then? Are you not mortal?"

"I am not a witch. I am not mortal, either. I am . . . older than I seem."

"Enough," Mary said. "Husband, do you bring this woman with us in escape or not? We cannot sit and debate it."

Farnham stared at Catherine Stokes, all certainty crumbling inside him. Magic was afoot here. There could be no other explanation. Yet as he looked into the intelligent, sincere eyes of this attractive young woman, and her impossibly cured face, he sensed nothing evil. Nothing. Just an unearthly . . . difference.

"Husband!" Mary said, squeezing his arm.

He must decide, and quickly.

"Catherine Stokes," he said. "Good fortune shines upon you tonight."

"My gratitude, Captain. I am indeed lucky and have led what you might say is a charmed life, having survived many a certain demise. Yet a burning at the stake would not be survived even by one as . . . durable as myself."

"Egads, fiend, I should say not," Merriwether said.

Mary waited no longer, and brushed past them all, headed for the way out.

BY THE TIME the guard discovered the escape, they had slipped down a dark Dublin lane, and hurried down the shingled beach of the River Liffey. There they waited silent tense minutes. A faint tap of two sets of footsteps came to them, stopping in the blackness mere feet away.

"John?" a woman's soft voice called.

"Saoirse!"

Merriwether sprang forward and squeezed and kissed his wife and child.

Mary said, "We have arranged a boat, hidden just ahead. We will be on the sea and under sail in minutes and Dublin will be far behind us by daybreak."

"And where shall we go?" Farnham asked. "England is lost to me."

"Where we land matters not, my darling husband, as long as we are together."

"It matters immensely."

Merriwether stepped closer, pulling his wife and child with him. "It would seem ye are now much like me, lackey. An Englishman no longer welcome among the English. Care to become an Irishman?"

"Not especially." Farnham regarded the man for a moment. Merriwether's treason long preceded any misdeeds visited by him upon Stokes. Guilt covered the man like a shroud. Yet his story of Stokes's magic now rang true. Witchcraft? Perhaps. Or something else? Either way, the truth mitigated in small measure Merriwether's guilt.

"My family will begin anew—as peasants, in truth—in the northwest of Ireland. It is a wild, untamed country there. The tyrant James and his Dublin lackeys are far too busy pacifying the south and middle to worry about that land. Come, join us. Ye'll make a passable Irish man and woman."

Farnham sighed. Ireland. "And you, lady?" He held his lantern to the face of Catherine Stokes.

The strange woman remained quiet and still for a moment, her eyes distant, as if lost in thought, or eavesdropping upon faraway conversation. A smile ghosted her face. "Burnt offerings seem quite the fashionable punishment in Europe for misfits like myself, Captain Farnham. I should like to visit the Americas, I think. Peoples of wildly differing science and philosophy are being thrown together into a cauldron of a wholly different sort."

She paused and looked to the west. "Worlds are in collision. I am compelled to witness them."

AUTHOR'S NOTES – KEN PELHAM

ALTHOUGH THE WITCH trials of Salem, Massachusetts, are rightly infamous in America, they pale in comparison to the persecution and slaughter that raged across Europe. It's estimated that more than 100,000 witch trials took place between 1450 and 1750, and 50,000 persons, three-quarters of them women, were found guilty and tortured and murdered by the authorities.

A charge of witchcraft was hard to beat and witch trials became institutionalized and lucrative for the accusers. An accusing judge could claim the wealth and possessions of the convicted as his own, and build up quite a fortune. So judges were incentivized to find guilt and extract accusations implicating others. Defending an accused witch often meant becoming the next target for accusation. Ireland had its own history with witch trials, the most famous being held in Kilkenny, but by far the greater number occurred on the Continent.

King James I—the very monarch that commissioned the *King James Bible*—did indeed initiate and oversee the North Berwick trials of Scotland in 1590, in which more than a hundred persons were accused as witches (at the time, he was James VI, King of Scotland, not becoming James I until England and Scotland were united in 1603). James built on his witch-killing expertise by authoring a tome on witches titled *Daemonologie*, a work that inspired the witches of William Shakespeare's *Macbeth*.

The New Gate Prison (later "Newgate") was an early *gaol*, or jail, originally built around the 12th century as part of the city wall, or gate, a short distance from Dublin Castle. Prisoners on or awaiting trial were usually held there or at a private tower nearby, Brown's Castle, also known as the Black Dog (no relation to the Led Zeppelin song). The first Newgate Prison was later replaced by another completed in 1781.

Europe is dotted with the remains of castles, and Ireland, although never a power on the order of England, France, or Germany, boasts more per square mile than any other country. Tower houses came into vogue as a later version of the traditional castle, designed as much as residences for the local lords as for defensive fortification. Nevertheless, they were ingeniously planned and built for defensive measures—the machiolations, the crenellated tops, the narrow, twisting stairwells, the murder holes, the arrow loops—as described in "The Tower House Prisoner." The dungeon might be a tiny cell in the base or below the castle while its entrance might be in the top floor, making escape impossible. A prisoner might be lowered there, bound, and left without food and water until he or she died. I had the exquisite pleasure of spending a few days in 2016 in one such Irish tower house.

Thanks for reading!

—*KP*

HER MIDNIGHT RIDE

Bria Burton

Listen, my children, and you shall hear
Of a lovely feminine Paul Revere
Who rode an equally famous ride
Through a different part of the countryside,
Where Sybil Ludington's name recalls
A ride as daring as that of Paul's.
—Excerpt from poem "Sybil Ludington's Ride" by Berton Braley

New York, August 1776

On the veranda of her family home, Sybil sat in a rocking chair, a musket in her lap. She wondered if tonight she'd need to use it.

Even in the twilight hours when the sun had dropped below the horizon, the heat made Sybil dab her damp forehead with a handkerchief. Like a sheen over her eyes, the humidity added a light glaze over the darkening landscape. Yet she kept her gaze sharp on the surrounding farmland and distant fir trees. At Sybil's feet on the piazza lay a pile of wilting daisies, the aroma as unpleasant as when they had been freshly picked by her younger sister, soon forgotten when Mother told Mary to leave them out of the house. Mary had chosen to toss them onto the veranda rather than carry them to the barn where the horses could've devoured them.

Sybil's father, Colonel Henry Ludington, was due home any minute. He led a local militia known as Ludington's Regiment, which gave him the privilege of spending more time at home than most men during wartime. But a young boy had stopped by the house only minutes before to warn them that a loud-mouthed Tory, Ichabod Prosser, was rounding up a mob. Prosser wanted to claim the reward on Colonel Ludington's head—three hundred English guineas were promised from General Howe himself to the man or woman who brought Ludington in, dead or alive.

Movement in the distance made Sybil sit up. The sawmill and gristmill stood yards away from the house. Months ago, they had erected the mills—the first of their kind in Dutchess County—with help from many of the local women while so many men were off in the fight.

Something—or someone—was moving back there.

It wouldn't be Father. He would come through the front door. Unless he had been tipped off to sneak home by way of the mill.

Sybil squinted, tightening her grip on the musket. She pressed the butt into her shoulder, raising the barrel and aiming the muzzle toward the rustling sounds.

"Hello, there," a man's voice called, loud and clear.

Sybil sprang to her feet. "Who's that?" She aimed back and forth, prepared for the intruder to leap out from behind either wooden structure.

The man's hands appeared first, raised in surrender as he stepped out from behind the sawmill. "I'm looking for a place to stay the night. Is this a home that welcomes strangers?"

"Why're you hiding back there?" asked Sybil, muzzle aimed a few feet in front of him. She would hate to shoot him by mistake, but what if he meant them harm?

"I'm trying to dodge the redcoats." He approached, not too quickly, and as he neared, she appraised him. He was of a fair height, but not too tall, and wore a black hat and deerskin coat. A bag hung over one shoulder. "Is this place hospitable for someone who would like to avoid any entanglements with the British?"

Sybil lowered her weapon. He knew the code phrase, the one that meant this stranger was a friend of Enoch Crosby's. Mr. Crosby was a patriot spy and dear friend of the family. The true test would come in the follow-up phrases. "We welcome anyone who gives us no grief and means us no harm."

"Then I shall have to show you my boots." That was the second code phrase. The man approached, walking up to the veranda and stopping before the steps.

She kept a firm grip on the musket. The young man was maybe eighteen or nineteen, which would make him three or four years older than she. Beneath the brim of his black hat flowed shoulder-length hair. His brown fur-lined coat looked heavy—strange for a summer evening. The bag on his shoulder seemed to be a fine leather pouch.

"A splendid cobbler repaired these for me." The young man pointed down at the ground. At the same moment, he lifted his tall black boot and balanced on one foot. The raised toe of the riding boot tilted back and forth in three successive movements. He repeated the familiar signal.

Sybil's relief flooded over her like a warm bath. "Oh!" she yelped, covering her mouth in embarrassment at her own excitement. It was indeed the proper sequence of phrases and signals. "Why, then you're most welcome!"

One of her sisters ran toward them, following the wrap-around veranda from the front of the house to the back. "Sybil, what's the matter?" It was Rebecca. At thirteen years old, she carried her own musket and had been at the ready all evening beside the front door. Archibald, her nine-year-old brother, was right behind her.

"Both of you need to stay at your posts," Sybil ordered. "This is a friend of Mr. Crosby's." Sybil motioned for the young man to climb the steps.

"Eek!" cheeped Rebecca. "What a thrill. Are you like him?"

"What a question, Becky. How can you be so impertinent?" Sybil scolded. She would have a word with her in private later. None of them should make implications that could expose Mr. Crosby, even with someone who claimed his friendship as a patriot. The rest of the world knew Mr. Crosby as a loyal Tory, so it was likely he had shared his secret before sending the young man here for safety. But until the stranger revealed what he knew, they would say nothing. "Back to your posts, both of you. Father should be here any moment."

Becky followed the piazza back to the front of the house.

"We won't disappoint him," said Archie, always eager to please.

"No, for we are vigilant." Sybil patted his cheek, and he gave her a smile before returning to his spot at a window facing east. "Do come in, Mister—?"

He removed his black hat, revealing the rest of his thick, dark hair. "Samuel Smith."

"Mr. Smith." Sybil curtsied as she held open the door. "You must tell us how you know Mr. Crosby."

That was the polite way of asking someone whether they, too, were a spy without giving anything away unnecessarily. All things relating to Mr. Crosby fascinated Sybil. He risked his life pretending to be on the side of the redcoats. He and Father had spent several evenings in deep discussion about the things Mr. Crosby was involved with, and Sybil sat at their feet soaking it all in. The signal that Mr. Smith had just proffered—the wagging of the toe of his boot back and forth three times—came about because Mr. Crosby was a cobbler by trade. He could show off his boots, as Mr. Crosby liked to say, while signaling to another patriot, and the redcoats would have no idea.

"Sybil, who's this?" asked Mary. She stood halfway down the stairs with baby Abigail in her arms. At eleven, Mary was much happier mothering than standing guard. Yet they all had a duty to protect their home, and especially to protect Father. Even Derick, who was five, had learned to fire a musket once it was loaded for him. He was on the floor building a fort out of wooden blocks, content with his imagination and needing no one else to play with. Mary could handle a weapon should the need arise, but someone had to keep three-year-old Tertullus and six-month-old Abby entertained while Mother was ill.

"This is Mr. Smith, a friend of Mr. Crosby's."

"Oh," said Mary.

"Remember what I said. Keep Tertie and Abby as quiet as you can so they don't disturb Mother."

"I'm doing my best." Mary carried Abby back upstairs, out of sight.

"I can take your things to our spare room," Sybil offered.

Mr. Smith gave her his coat, pouch, and hat. "A fine family, as Mr. Crosby said you would be."

When Sybil returned from the spare room, she lit a few candles as the evening settled in and overshadowed most of the remaining sunlight.

"He did, in fact, mend my boots for me," Mr. Smith said with a smile. The dim light of the candle softened everything about his features. Sybil realized she had never seen anyone so handsome. His hair was soft and dark, his complexion fair, and his nose the perfect shape.

Sybil was not very fond of her own nose, and she had no beauty to speak of, but it hardly concerned her. There were more important things, like the ability to ride and shoot well—both skills at which she excelled.

"Make yourself comfortable." Sybil gestured toward a bluc armchair. "I must return to my post." Mr. Crosby would not have sent him unless he could be trusted. She explained, "Our father will be home soon, but a mob may be after him. The British have put a price on his head."

"Can I help?" asked Mr. Smith. "I'm very handy with a musket."

Sybil hesitated. "I can loan you a musket, but I'll keep it until my father gets home." If being overly cautious made her seem rude, Sybil could bear it. Her father had a saying that even the most trustworthy man should not mind being haltered. If he gripes, that man should be hogtied. Father usually made the statement when he suspected a young man might come courting.

"I understand."

Pleased with Mr. Smith's lack of protest, Sybil picked up a spare flintlock from the closet. Out the back door, they sat in the wooden chairs on the veranda. Sybil leaned one gun against her chair and the other she lay on her lap. Twilight had given way to night. Frog songs erupted from a distant pond, the deep melody like a lament. The mills and the barn stood in darkness like towering shadows. Still no sign of her father, and she tried not to worry.

"I'm not sure what we'll do if we're overrun." She sighed. "I should've said something before I invited you in. I'm afraid this might not be the haven you were looking for."

"On the contrary. I've been in many battles. You have an advantage."

"You've been in battle?" Sybil couldn't hide her excitement. "Where? How many?"

"Too many to list, and in several colonies." A wry smile stretched across his face, not reaching his eyes. "Not many victories for the Continental Army in this war."

Sybil understood that Washington's Army was a ragtag group of farmers, tradesman, lawyers, vicars, and few trained soldiers. It was the same with Ludington's Regiment.

"And yet," Mr. Smith continued, his countenance brightening, "the last battle I was in, we won the day. It was a key moment when the men realized that for once the redcoats were on the run, and not the other way around." He grinned, this time his eyes smiling, too. "I've been in war before. There's a spirit of courage and hope in this one the likes of which I've never experienced."

"You're in the Continental Army, then." Sybil debated whether to ask questions. If so, why wasn't he with his regiment?

"Yes. When the war first broke out, I was on the other side," Mr. Smith confessed.

"Like my father," Sybil said. "It's nothing to be ashamed about. Everyone had to decide which side to choose when the lines were being drawn. It's a decision no man or woman should take lightly. The Bible says there is a time for everything, even a time to kill. But no one should take up arms without first reconciling with God and following his guidance. It's the only way to even attempt to make a right decision."

Mr. Smith stared at her for what felt like a long time. In the dim light from the candles inside, his expression was unreadable. Had she spouted off her beliefs to ears that did not welcome that kind of talk?

"I apologize if my religious leanings aren't to your taste. It's what I believe." She shrugged, suddenly feeling foolish.

"It's refreshing to hear you talk about making the right decision." His gaze glanced over the farmland before resting on her. "People make choices every day, some very mundane. Others can affect the course of history." He gestured toward her with the palm of his hand raised. "One act of bravery, and you could be a woman that history remembers."

A sound startled Sybil. Her sister called from the front of the house, "Father's home!"

Yet the shout alone hadn't made Sybil's heart pound inside her chest and her breath catch in her throat.

Mr. Smith held the musket that had been leaning against Sybil's chair. He knelt at the railing, aiming out toward the mill. It was as if he'd been there all along, not seated beside her unarmed only seconds ago. The transition seemed instant to her, his speed almost unbelievable and much more startling than Becky's shout. No one she knew could move that fast.

"Mr. Smith, I don't recall handing over the musket," Sybil said cautiously.

He rose, lowering the weapon to his side and facing her. "I heard something back there, but it was just a fox. He scampered off."

"Oh." Sybil had heard nothing, and for a split second she feared that letting Mr. Smith sit in reach of a musket was a terrible mistake.

Her father opened the back door to introduce himself to the friend of Mr. Crosby. Mr. Smith gave the musket back to her so he could shake her father's hand, and Sybil's fears vanished.

"Come in, both of you." Her father cut a fine form, tall and broad in his blue coat with gold buttons. "And explain why Becky greeted me with a musket at our front door."

"It's that wretched man, Prosser." Sybil followed behind Mr. Smith, carrying a flintlock in each hand. "He's been seen gathering a mob and they might come after you tonight."

"Are you sure?" The colonel shut the door, glancing out the window.

"Young Luke Chadbourn warned us. Prosser's a spiteful old skinflint who just wants to claim the reward." Sybil leaned the extra musket against the kitchen wall.

"Then I'll quickly put my horse in the barn. Load my Brown Bess and have it ready for me," he ordered, drawing his pistol and rushing out the back door.

"Becky, get his musket and I'll load it," Sybil urged.

Rebecca dropped her weapon with a clatter at the foot of the stairs before she scurried up them.

"Careful with your flintlock!" Sybil called out, sinking into one of two blue cushioned armchairs. Mr. Smith sat in the other chair. "My father will come up with a plan. Although it would be wise if we kept to our posts," she said, brushing a lock of hair out of her eyes. In moments, her sister returned with the Brown Bess, a powder horn, and a bag of musket balls. Sybil removed the ramrod, pausing in thought. "Maybe Becky and I could stand guard around the veranda, make them think twice about approaching."

"May I load it for you?" asked Mr. Smith.

Sybil hesitated, glancing at Becky. At the foot of the stairs, Becky reclaimed her dropped weapon. "Well, Mr. Smith," said Sybil, "I can't say that your behavior on the veranda made me terribly comfortable." She prided herself in speaking her mind. "Although you've given me no other reasons to distrust you."

"Please believe that I mean you no harm." He raised both hands in a defenseless gesture. "And call me Samuel. We are comrades in arms now."

Sybil smirked. His charm was disarming, but she would make him understand his predicament. "All right, Samuel." She gave the Brown Bess to him with the tools to load it.

Becky held hers at the ready as she stood behind his chair.

"Only a fool would try to outsmart two armed and capable young women who loaded their muskets hours ago," Sybil said.

"I give you permission to shoot me," he replied, "if you think me anything less than honorable."

"How do you know Mr. Cr—" Before Sybil could finish the thought, it stuck to the tip of her tongue. The speed at which Samuel loaded the musket was alarmingly rapid. His arms, hands, and fingers moved and shifted over the weapon at a fluid and seemingly effortless pace. It was like a swift dance. Stranger still, he spilled none of the gunpowder.

Archie left his post at the window and gaped. "Whoa! How'd you do that?"

Sybil pressed her hand beneath Archie's jaw, pushing his mouth closed. "Don't gawk. You'll scrape your chin on the floor."

"Like I said, I'm very handy with a musket." Samuel held Father's now loaded Brown Bess out to Sybil just as the colonel burst back in through the door.

Samuel redirected the flintlock, barrel down. "Here you are, Colonel Ludington."

"We need to prepare ourselves," said the colonel. He huffed, wiping his brow. "You girls hide upstairs—"

"Father," Sybil interrupted. "We're not hiding. They won't get near you without a fight." She gripped her musket, gazing over at the broom cupboard. "I know what we need to do."

SYBIL ASSIGNED Archie and Derick each a downstairs window. "This is your new post. You shall not leave it unless Father or Becky or I tell you to. Do you understand what you need to do?"

They both nodded.

"Mary, take the window in Mother and Father's room. Father will be at your bedroom window."

"I'll check on Mother's fever, too." Mary hurried up the stairs.

"Assure her everything's fine!" Sybil called after her sister.

Mother had been ill for two days and could do nothing to help except continue to rest and get well.

Father led Samuel out back toward the sawmill where the young man had offered to scout for intruders.

Sybil joined Becky at their shared post on the veranda. They both wore overcoats and hats borrowed from their father. Her sister paced like a sentinel on watch, musket held in the proper position, just as their father had shown them.

From the sawmill, Father jogged toward the house through the yard. He jumped up the veranda steps and stopped before Sybil, squeezing her shoulder. “By God, your plan might just work.”

When he disappeared inside, Sybil smiled as she fell into step with Becky, musket raised, but turned the opposite direction. At the corner, she followed the piazza as it wrapped around to the front of the house before circling back to Becky again. They made this their route, with Becky at the rear this time and Sybil at the front.

Naught but a sliver of moonlight hung low on the summer night sky. Stars shimmered above, an endless parade of glitter. The low hum of chirping crickets broke the silence.

And then the voices of men.

A COWBELL RANG out loud and clear from the sawmill, followed by the explosion of a firing musket. The signal from Samuel confirmed that intruders had been spotted.

An unmanly cry rivaled the sound of the cowbell. Samuel was true to his word. He could shoot and had hit someone.

“I am Colonel Henry Ludington, commander of the 7th Regiment of the Dutchess County Militia!” Father cried from a second-story window. “Any intruders within the sound of my voice will be shot. We will defend ourselves and take no prisoners.” He fired his Brown Bess.

Sybil knelt on the piazza, sweeping the barrel of her musket along the railing. From her vantage point, she still saw no one entering the yard from behind any trees or bushes.

"They knew we were coming!" a voice cried. "Look! The windows have all come alight."

Archie, Derick, and Mary had lit the candles and paced in front of the windows with their broomsticks—Archie with a musket—as instructed, bringing the darkened house to life with armed rebels.

"Ludington's Regiment is here!" someone else cried.

The ruse was working. In the dark, Sybil aimed the muzzle toward a copse of trees along the edge of the front lawn and pulled the trigger. The flintlock responded with the expected explosion of fire and smoke.

Seconds later, Becky fired as well.

A pair of men jumped out from behind the trees where Sybil had guessed they might be hiding. They rushed away from the house. "They're covering every angle!" one of them yelled. "Flee, men, flee!"

As Sybil predicted, they had seen her and Becky pacing and mistook them for watchmen of the regiment. While Sybil sat on the piazza reloading, another man behind a bush at the opposite edge of the front lawn sprinted away without a word.

"Prosser, you Tory coward, show yourself!" Father challenged. "Come and claim me, if you can."

The next shot must have come from Samuel, the only one of them who could reload so quickly. Sybil tried to hurry as she went through the steps, but she had none of Samuel's impressive skills. It took her some time.

No one else spoke. The scuffle and rustle of fleeing men died down quickly as the mob escaped.

Sybil placed her reloaded musket on the railing. She scanned the front lawn and beyond. No one was there. Stranger still, not one of the mob had fired off a shot.

"WHY DIDN'T they bother to fire upon us, Father?" Sybil asked once her exhausted brothers and sisters had collapsed into their beds.

Samuel sat in the blue armchair again while her father lounged in its twin. They both held goblets of red wine. Sybil was content on the floor where she could clean her musket. "I was in the loft above the rafters," Samuel said, "when I spotted someone coming into the mill. He didn't have a flintlock and took a musket ball to his kneecap."

"The ones who did probably hadn't loaded them." Father took a swig of wine. "Thought they would have plenty of time once they surrounded the house, expecting to catch us unawares. They didn't know we would be waiting." He grinned at Sybil, then suddenly smacked his armchair with the palm of his hand. "Goodness, Samuel, you must have reloaded in a flash to have fired that second shot. My regiment can't get two shots off in less than half a minute."

"I've spent a lot of time practicing." Samuel's tone held no bravado.

"Humility is the essence of a good Christian nature," Sybil said, "but you, sir, are remarkable in your abilities and your level of humbleness."

"It must have been God's will to send you to us for protection," said Archie. He ducked back into the hallway when Father gave him a stern look of reprimand. The boy was a minister in the making with his constant prayers and the blessings he spouted over everyone.

"To bed, Archie, and stay put," said Father.

"We are forever grateful to you, Samuel," Sybil said, echoing Archie's sentiment.

"And you, Sybil. Well done." Her father raised his goblet to her. "I count Sybil's capabilities the equal of any man's in my regiment," the colonel said, addressing Mr. Smith.

"Thank you, Father." His proud gaze was all the praise she needed. "Samuel can stay as long as he likes, can he not?"

"Of course. But I am curious. What is the nature of your acquaintance with Mr. Crosby?" asked the colonel.

"He had his boots mended. Isn't that right?" Sybil waited for his confirmation.

"There's a bit more to the story," Samuel admitted. "General

Washington was impressed with my skills on the battlefield. He introduced me to Mr. Crosby and asked if I would be willing to work with him. In his cobbler shop, Mr. Crosby told me the nature of his work as he mended my boots."

"You met General Washington?" Sybil bit her lip, intrigued. She wiped half-heartedly at the musket barrel. "Are you on a secret mission?"

"Sybil, he might not be able to tell us," the colonel warned.

"Yes, Sybil. I'm on a secret mission and I'm a spy." Samuel stared at her, a blankness in his face. "I can't tell you more." He sipped his wine.

Sybil gasped, although deep down she knew it must be so. "Did Mr. Crosby have any messages for us?"

Samuel raised his gaze skyward. "He did say his shoulder was feeling better after using the salve you made for him."

Sybil grinned, pleased he'd remembered to apply it.

"And he asked after your new horse, Star. He suggested the name, I believe?"

Sybil nodded, pleased. "He's the best horse I could've asked for."

"Mr. Crosby tells me you broke him in yourself," said Samuel. "Impressive."

"Did he say when next he would visit?" she asked.

"That he did not."

Sybil's shoulders dropped, not exactly in disappointment, for he must intend to come by soon. It was an honor to aid yet another patriot spy, perhaps one on a mission from Washington himself.

That night, Sybil couldn't sleep. She could do nothing but imagine she'd joined the infantry. She could picture marching alongside her fellow patriots and firing upon the enemy when Colonel Washington gave his orders. And thanks to her abilities, Mr. Crosby would beg Washington to send her to him. He needed a female spy for a special mission accompanying Mr. Smith. The revolution needed her.

She grinned to herself, shaking her head. Her imagination was running off, as Mother so often said. Right now, Father needed her. They did well to keep him protected at home.

And yet.

Sybil sighed. Who could say what would happen? At a time like this, anything was possible.

A girl could dream.

New York, December 1776

PATRIOT SPY MR. ENOCH CROSBY stood before the mantel warming his hands over the fire. Snowflakes dusted his hat and coat. Sybil had hung them on the hooks beside the door while her father handed him a dry black coat, which Mr. Crosby now wore over his white tunic. He turned to face Colonel Ludington. His average height and frame seemed small compared to that of Sybil's husky father. Mr. Crosby wore a powdered wig which made him look much older than his age of twenty-seven.

"Thank you," Mr. Crosby said when Becky offered him a steaming cup of tea. He sipped. "Ah, what pleasures I take in the small blessings. A hot drink for my cold throat." He grinned at her, his pleasant manner prompting Sybil's sister to curtsey in response.

The visit had been planned for some weeks, as Mr. Crosby and the colonel had revolutionary matters to discuss. Sybil was privy to many conversations between her father and Mr. Crosby. As her father would say, his eldest child would be responsible for the family should anything happen to him, and she should be about her father's business.

Mr. Crosby suffered the injustice of being hated by his former friends who believed him to be an avid Tory supporter. Their belief, and the confidence of the British monarchy, meant his work as a spy furthered the goal of American Independence. But at great cost. His own family had no idea he was helping the noble cause in which they believed, leading his father to confess shame for his son.

Perhaps that led Mr. Crosby to their house so often. He must've looked upon Sybil's father as a surrogate when he could not expose his true loyalty to his own.

Late into the evening, as Sybil sat wrapped in a wool blanket across from the two men, the name she longed to hear was introduced.

"Samuel Smith has been captured."

A lump formed in her throat. Unable to speak, she covered her mouth with her hand.

"But it is not what you think," Mr. Crosby amended. "He is not a true prisoner."

"What do you mean?" asked the colonel.

With bated breath, Sybil tried not to imagine the worst.

"It's all part of General Washington's plan. Mr. Smith has an uncanny ability to pick any lock. He is imprisoned at—well, best not to reveal too many details there—but his location is a prime spot for British intelligence. Whenever his guard falls asleep—a fairly regular occurrence throughout the week—he picks the lock and escapes to a designated location. A hidden scrap of parchment and a pencil are left for him to write anything he has learned. He returns to his cell with his sleeping guard none the wiser."

"But how do none of the other guards spot him escaping and returning?" Sybil had many questions, and this was the most puzzling.

"He is an expert at blending in, but I'm not at liberty to share any more details. I will say that he is the most extraordinary spy I've ever known."

Such praise from Enoch Crosby, a remarkable spy himself, meant Samuel Smith was the patriot hero Sybil had believed him to be from their brief encounter. When Samuel had left them, only a few weeks after his arrival, he hadn't divulged his secret mission. Upon his departure, he said he could never return to the Ludington Farm, but was forever grateful for their hospitality.

"When this war ends," Samuel had said, "I'm heading west to start over."

Now Sybil knew what had become of him, which left her satisfied that he was out there somewhere on his mission furthering the cause, just as she hoped to do someday.

New York, April 26, 1777

A HARSH KNOCK at the door startled Sybil. It was nearly nine o'clock in the evening, much too late for anyone to call. A storm raged outside. Ten claps of thunder in the past twenty minutes had shaken the house. In the rocker, she had lulled baby Abby to sleep while her mother put the children to bed. Now Abby wailed. Sybil rose to her feet, carrying Abby on her hip and shushing her.

"Who is it?" Sybil asked through the window.

"I'm a messenger!" cried a thin, sopping wet boy in a drenched coat and hat. On the steps of the veranda, he held his horse's reins. "Please, miss, I come with terrible tidings. The colonel is needed."

Her father came down the stairs. "Sybil?"

She surveyed the front lawn, and noting that the rider was alone, turned to Father. "He says he has a message for you."

Father met the young man on the veranda. The colonel nodded to Sybil through the window as the two of them spoke. He signaled with a wave that the boy was welcome. Father escorted his horse to the barn through the pouring rain. Sybil held the door open as the rider entered.

The messenger hung his hat on the hook by the door. In the kitchen, his boots left a trail of mud that would not please Mother. His trembling legs lowered him onto their wooden bench. He panted, peeling off his wet coat.

"You're exhausted. Let me take that for you." Sybil hung the dripping coat on the mantel. It dangled before the fire as she rushed Abby upstairs.

When she returned, he begged, "Water?"

"Would you like hot tea?" she asked. "The kettle won't take long to boil."

"As long as it isn't *English* tea."

Sybil would've laughed, but he seemed resolute on that point.

"We only make Liberty Teas from our own garden." She took a mitt and placed the kettle, sloshing with water, over the fire. "My favorite is a blend of raspberry and lemon balm leaves, peppermint, and chamomile. I had some earlier, so all the ingredients are here in the kitchen."

He nodded.

Father came inside. "This is Sybil, my eldest. I trust her with any information you would share."

"My name is Robby Freeman," the young man said. "There are some thousand or more redcoats destroying the patriot military storehouses in Danbury, burning them to the ground." He shook his head. Water flung from his wet hair. "When I left, a large group of the lobsters were drunk, brawling in the streets, and setting more fires. Any house not marked with chalk—where Tories lived—they're burning."

"By whose order?" barked Father, his neck flushed with anger.

"Far as I know, General Tryon's."

Sybil knew that name. "Isn't he the one who appointed you captain?"

"The very same." Father inhaled. His nostrils flared. "That was before I joined the revolutionary cause."

What kind of a man would do such a thing? Sybil knew her father had never thought highly of General Tryon, but this behavior was grotesque.

"I was sent to tell you that your regiment is needed," said Robby Freeman. "We need them now."

"My men are scattered over two counties and beyond. Most of them are farmers on leave to tend to their fields and crops during planting season." The colonel tapped his chin, thinking. "I'll need to get word to them to meet me here so we can plan our attack." He glanced down at the young man.

Robby visibly paled. "My horse is useless now."

"Yes, I did notice," the colonel acknowledged.

"I've come over fifteen miles in this tempest." Robby's ragged breath hissed through his teeth. "I was hoping to rest the night here."

"We've got a horse you can—"

"Father," Sybil interrupted. The boy's limbs still shook even as he sat. Could the colonel not see his bloodshot eyes? "He's in no state to ride again tonight."

"Surely you can manage a few more miles when it's this important," Father persisted.

"Colonel, upon my honor, I would, but I'm barely keeping my eyes open. I fear I would fail before I even began."

"You have not failed," Sybil said, clutching her father's arm. "You have done your duty, Robby Freeman. You need a bath, a bed, and thorough rest for all you've been through this night." She spotted Becky at the top of the stairwell. "Becky, draw the bath in the spare room. Finish making his tea, as well."

"Father?" Becky awaited confirmation from the man of the house.

"Go on, Becky." He nodded to Sybil, a half-grin rising up one cheek. "Come on, Robby. Allow me to help you upstairs."

"Thank you, colonel. God bless your generosity. And forgive my weakness."

"There's nothing to forgive." They lumbered up the steps, Robby's arm over Father's broad shoulders.

Sybil dashed to the closet, took out a cloak, and tied it around her neck. After pulling on a pair of boots, she placed a wide-brimmed hat on her head. She opened the back door and rushed to the barn, sloshing through puddles and mud.

Inside, the scent of hay blended with the strong odor of manure. She took one of the older saddles from the back corner of the barn and placed it beside Star. Riding side-saddle wouldn't do in this weather. Even as the thunder roared outside, the gelding stayed still, arching his neck to sniff her as she moved about him. The white snip on his nose brushed her face several times as she secured the hemp rope bridle on his head. After throwing a blanket into place, she lifted the saddle over his back. Before she'd finished fastening the girth straps, Father burst into the barn, shutting the door behind him.

He was drenched. "Sybil?" he asked, wiping his face.

"Father, I'm going to rally your men. I've joined you enough times to know the route by heart." She secured the final buckle. "You're needed here to receive your militia and ready them for Danbury. There's no time to argue."

Her father held out a bundle. "I'm not here to argue. I thought you could use these. Wool breeches to keep you warm and dry."

Sybil took them, her heart full and racing. She hadn't noticed the pounding in her chest until that moment.

Father turned away.

She slipped off her boots, hiked her dress up, and stepped into the breeches. "I promise I won't stop until I've completed the circuit: Carmel, Mahopac, Farmers Mills, Kent Cliffs, Stormville. And back here to Fredericksburg, of course."

"I know."

Boots on, Sybil led Star to the closed barn doors. She hoisted herself into the saddle and positioned herself astride. Star pawed a front hoof through the air as her weight settled on his back.

Her father gripped the ankle of her boot. "Kent Cliffs is before Farmers Mills."

She shook her head. "I misspoke. I know the route, I swear it."

"Forty miles," he said. "Sybil, it will be rough. And dangerous."

No threat could remove her from that saddle, not a storm, nor redcoats, highwaymen, thieves, wolves, nor any other wild animal. She was not afraid. It felt like a calling, something she was meant to do.

Only in her dreams had she ridden with haste for the cause of American Independence. And only in her dreams had she been wearing a white dress on a beautiful summer day, hair flapping like a banner in the wind. Beneath her, Star's hair had been braided with colorful ribbons. At the edge of a large saddle blanket, gold and silver tassels swung near the ground.

A flash of lightning lit up the cracks in the barn. It was as if the hand of Providence had touched her, reminding her that this was no dream, but a true mission.

"No point in taking a musket in this weather. Can't see how the powder will stay dry. Hand me that shovel?" she asked.

"I have a better idea." Father jogged to the opposite side of the barn and returned with a large but light stick. It was damp and one end was pointed. "Archie whittled the sharp end. It will help you ward off animals or, God forbid, any Cowboys or Skinners. But if you see redcoats, I suggest you hide."

"I'll take care, Father. I best get to it." Stick in hand, Sybil steeled herself against the realization that she would travel farther—much farther—than Robby Freeman. The weather wasn't giving an inch. If anything, the rain pelted the roof harder. A flash lit the barn's doors and crevices again followed seconds later by a clap of thunder.

Father reached up, beckoning. She lowered her face toward him. He stroked her cheek and gave the brim of her hat a tweak. "You've grown into a tenacious woman and I couldn't be prouder. But even at sixteen, you're still my little girl."

Sybil pursed her lips. No point in arguing, even though Father knew she loathed being called "little girl." He meant it affectionately, so she wouldn't despise him for it. Anyone else tried to call her that, she'd introduce them to the sharp end of her stick.

"Tell the men to come as quick as they can, no later than dawn." Father straightened up as he reached for the barn door. When he opened it, the rain poured onto him as if the heavens had been waiting to dump a bucket of water over his head. "Godspeed!"

Sybil ushered Star forward. As her steed broke into a run, she met the storm head on.

A TORRENT of wind crashed into Sybil. She braced her legs against Star, leaning forward. A gale lifted her hat off her head and she wasn't quick enough to catch it before it landed in a mud puddle. She gripped both the reins and Star's mane in her hands, blinking through the cascade of rain pelting her eyes. Star had always managed well through tall grass, dense forest, narrow dirt roads, and rocky, unmarked paths. She hoped he would prove as capable in such a storm.

"Well done, Star," she cooed as she slowed his trot to a walk through the maze of trees that would empty them out into Carmel.

The first soldier in Ludington's Regiment to receive Sybil's message was a farmer named Duffy. The urgency of the situation required unmistakable and swiftly given orders. There was no time to dismount. At the outskirts of Duffy's land, she and Star broke free of the woods and galloped onto the farm. The dull end of the stick would serve as the perfect knocker. Still astride, she halted Star and hammered the front door.

"The British are burning Danbury! Muster at Ludington's!" she cried.

A light brightened inside the house. Mrs. Duffy, Sybil presumed, peered out through the window in her nightcap.

Mr. Duffy opened the front door dressed in coat and trousers, as if expecting her. He held an iron candleholder. The flickering flame lit up his pocked face. "I knew someone would come. Something must be done about that atrocity." Mr. Duffy pointed behind Sybil.

She glanced over her shoulder. Where the woods ended, the distant glow of a burning city disrupted the black of night. Danbury on fire. Smoke rose high, difficult to discern in the storm even though the rain had lightened for the moment.

"Can you rally the Carmel men? I've got to alert the entire regiment."

He nodded. "Those cowards won't get away with this. We must stop them, whatever the cost."

"Get the militia in the vicinity to the farm before dawn." She urged Star forward, unable to take her eyes off the burning city until the recurrence of woods blocked her view.

There was no mistake in what Robby Freeman had said. The situation was dire, and she had to finish her task as quickly as possible. The next township was Mahopac. As she neared a small road snaking through the trees, the glow of fire from the south broke through the darkness.

Torchlight. Redcoats approached.

Being caught by the redcoats could mean death. She crossed the lane, slinking into the forest on the opposite side. Behind a thick tree, she hoped the darkness would do its work to conceal her and Star.

She waited. The troop marched past, torches raised high, armed with muskets and bayonets. No one so much as glanced in her direction. They continued in formation until they were out of earshot.

With the redcoats as good as gone, she pushed on, not concerned about the snapping twigs beneath her horse's feet. Sybil patted his neck. "Good work, Star."

Had she brought a musket, it would have been tempting to pick the lobsters off one by one. Probably for the best as she was on her own and didn't have time for it anyway.

When she reached Mahopac, the storm's forceful wind and rain had returned. She banged on several more doors along the way, delivering the same message, no longer stopping to chat. "The British are burning Danbury! Muster at Ludington's!" she repeated until someone in the house acknowledged her.

Sopping strands of hair slapped her face as Star galloped through the night. Many times, she had to slow Star to a walk through the pitch blackness, whether in the forest or through open fields. More than once, he slipped in the mud. It wouldn't do to push him to an injury.

All along her route, many women had answered Sybil's call with promises to alert nearby militia while the husband—or father, or brother, or uncle—readied for their own ride to rally others to Ludington's farm.

Near the township of Kent Cliffs, she had to dismount at Benjamin Gage's house. The blackened windows showed no sign of life. She banged on the door repeatedly. Finally, a flickering candle made its way from room to room toward the entrance. "The British are burning Danbury! Muster at Ludington's!" she cried.

Mr. Gage threw his door open, the large man as full of his temper as Sybil had remembered the last time she'd been there with her father. "What are you trying to do, torture my poor wife? She gets no sleep as it is, constantly having to nurse our new baby!"

"The British are burning Danbury! Muster at Ludington's!" she repeated, screaming it at him as she remounted Star.

"Why didn't you say so in the first place?" He slammed the door shut.

Riding onward, Sybil said a prayer, releasing her irritation to God.

The lightning and thunder moved away. Echoes rumbled in the distance. As the night wore into the early hours of morning, an ache rose from Sybil's hips to her lower back. Her legs felt like jelly. The storm had left her soaked through. While the wool breeches had kept her warm until now, the pattering rain slipped into every fiber of her cloak and dress. It puddled inside her boots and chilled her to her very bones.

Star panted. The wet sheen of his coat made him look black instead of brown. His mouth dripped with rain or spit, Sybil wasn't sure which. She stopped at a stream where he drank for several minutes. The nimble and agile horse was a credit to the Crocker farm where he'd been sired. His stamina rivaled the legendary Bucephalus, Alexander the Great's famous horse. The downpour might be relentless, but so were Sybil and Star.

A narrow, rocky pass ahead would require Sybil to lead Star on foot through the winding crags and crevices before she reached Farmers Mills. Upon dismounting, she stretched her arms and legs, relieving some of her tension and stiffness. Through the pitch black, she guided Star, gingerly stepping on slippery rocks. Star followed with the same care Sybil took. The rising and falling terrain of the boulders was difficult to perceive. Where Sybil thought she needed to step higher, the darkness tricked her. She slid but did not fall.

A branch cracked. Sybil's gaze darted toward the black woods twenty yards ahead. Had it been an animal? Or a weak tree limb that succumbed in the storm?

She and Star traversed the last boulder. They stepped off the rocks onto a pile of wet leaves. She walked Star forward, stick raised, pointy end aimed outward.

The tall trees held secrets they wouldn't share in the dark. Too wet and miserable to linger, she reached for the stirrup.

A pain lanced Sybil's shoulder. Something with fur threw her body to the ground. A wolf? A bear? The pile of wet leaves caught her, easing the blow of the fall and soaking her back through her clothes. She held up the sharp end of the stick as she scrambled to her feet.

The creature before her was no animal. It was a man.

Distant thunder rumbled. The rain slowed, the drops on the boulders and leaves like a hush falling over the landscape. Star retreated a few steps toward the woods.

The man's face was masked in darkness beneath a wide-brimmed hat. He wore what looked like a bearskin coat—the fur that had brushed her neck when he'd grabbed her, pushing her down. A glint of light flashed near his wrist, barely discernible, but Sybil knew what it meant. He was holding a knife.

She tensed. Goosebumps surfaced across her limbs. The joint in her shoulder ached. "Stay away!" she cried. "I'm not afraid to use this." In that moment, she was willing to do whatever it took to survive. "What are you, a Skinner?" she asked.

No reply. And no more sounds beyond the low whistling of the wind. A faint stench of tobacco reached her nostrils. He must be chewing it.

If he was a Skinner, he had no loyalty to either side. They stole from farms and families, selling the loot to the highest bidder whether they were British or Colonists.

Sybil pointed the stick at him. "I'm rallying Colonel Ludington's 7th Regiment. They are preparing to fight the redcoats who burned Danbury. You will get out of my way."

"Humph." The bear-like sound was deep and guttural. The man spit. "I aim to take what ya got. Startin' wi'that horse." He moved in lumbering steps and pointed his hunting knife at her.

Sybil swung the stick at his head. The wood smacked his skull above the ear, knocking off his hat. The moment she struck, the stick vibrated in her hand and she knew she'd hit him hard.

He stumbled, thrown off-balance, and groaned. His hand covered the injury.

Sybil ran, switching the stick to her left hand so she could mount quickly. Star waited between two trees. Startled, he moved off when she grabbed for the reins. Snatching his mane, she ran alongside him and then jumped into the stirrup, throwing her leg over the saddle with surprising ease. They'd ridden nearly thirty miles. She shouldn't have been able to leap at all.

Star galloped forward. Sybil glanced back at the Skinner nursing his head wound. The man had no horse. He couldn't possibly catch up. As they wound through the forest, she slowed Star to a reasonable pace. Twigs crunched underhoof as Sybil's eyes glazed over. Her hands clenched into fists as they held the reins and stick. When she relaxed, her hands shook.

"Thank you, God," she prayed, "for protecting us."

The last ten miles, she knocked on doors, rallied the men, and left Stormville through buckets of rain. When she walked Star into Fredericksburg, nearly home, her eyelids flickered. For hours she'd barely been able to keep them open. But as she glanced toward her family's farm, an astonishing sight made her halt.

Hundreds of men stood in the field. Invigorated, Sybil trotted Star toward her father, who barked commands to what must be the entire regiment.

Dawn's light peered through the gray clouds. The rain slowed to a drizzle until it stopped completely.

"Sybil!" someone shouted. "Huzzah!"

She had no idea who said it first, but soon the assembled militia was chanting in one unified voice, "Huzzah! Huzzah! Sybil! Sybil!"

The stick was still in her hand. She dropped it, dismounted, and ran into her father's arms.

"My brave girl." He wrapped her in a tight embrace and stroked her soaked hair. "All four hundred arrived because of you."

"What?" She pulled away and gasped. Her parched throat made her response sound like a whisper.

"Every last one." Colonel Ludington puffed out his chest with pride.

The resounding echoes of the regiment's chant wrapped a second hug around her heart.

Sybil stroked Star's neck before burying her head into him, not caring that the gelding's wet coat was slick with mud. She held back tears.

"Sybil?" Robby Freeman approached. "You did it." He blinked bright blue eyes at her. "You're remarkable."

Her pride swelled again, and she resisted the temptations of vanity. She rubbed Star's chest. "God was with us," she said in her hoarse voice, giving credit where credit was due.

"You both deserve a good meal and rest," said Robby. He stroked Star's mane.

"Goodness!" Becky rushed toward them from the house. "Sybil, you're shivering. And filthy."

Every stitch of clothing was wet and streaked with mud. Sybil's hair and face were surely mud-splattered, too.

"I'll take care of Star," said Becky. "Mother has your bath ready. She's making a pot pie, too." Becky took the rope and led Star toward the barn.

"You must be starved." Robby offered his arm.

"I am." Sybil took it. The sopping wet boy she had seen last night didn't seem to be the same young man escorting her now. She glanced at the regiment. Several of them waved to her, and she waved back her goodbye.

"Have you ever heard of a man called Samuel Smith?" Robby asked.

"I might have." What a surprise to hear his name. Sybil had thought about Samuel a few times during her midnight ride. One courageous act, he had said, could mean that history would remember her. When she thought of his work as a spy, she realized history might never know the debt it would owe to him or to Mr. Crosby. She gazed at Robby. "It's a common name, isn't it?"

"Sharpshooter. Brown hair like mine about this long." Robby released her to remove his hat. He held his hand at shoulder length. His hair was almost the same brown color as Samuel's, but not as long. "Wears a black cocked hat."

Just before the veranda, Sybil halted. "Can we sit?" She lowered herself onto the first step. Her sore legs and backside made her sigh. "Why do you ask?"

Robby sat beside her. "I heard he came through Fredericksburg. Thought you might've met him with your pa being colonel over the local militia. You see, Samuel and I were in a battle together. I wanted to introduce myself to him, but he was gone before I had a chance. It was strange the way he seemed to disappear. I was even worried he might've deserted. Which would be disappointing since he's sort of a hero of mine."

Sybil knew what Robby meant, thinking of how Samuel had aided her family against the Tory mob. The amazing young man could fire a musket better than anyone she knew. She admired everything about him. "I do know he's a true patriot who fights for the cause of independence. I'm not sure where he is, though."

"Oh?" Robby knit his brow.

"I've probably said too much. I'm sorry I can't say more." It wasn't her place to tell anyone about her family's connection to Samuel or any other patriot spy. "I was very impressed with your ride, too," she said by way of changing the subject.

He seemed to understand. "Thank you."

"Will you march to Danbury with my father's regiment?"

"Yes. I should join the ranks." He rose, bowing to her. "Miss Ludington."

"Call me Sybil." She rose, shaking his hand. "You're always welcome in our home."

Robby smiled as he backed away. "You know, your achievement just might've turned the tide of this war in our favor. I'll be sure to tell General Washington about you."

Sybil tilted her head, unsure if he was teasing. Did he know General Washington? She waved as he turned and rushed toward the militia. The idea of meeting the general thrilled her, but as she slowly took each step up onto the veranda, she realized something.

Acclamation and applause had never been important to her. She hadn't ridden forty miles in a thunderstorm for the recognition. Just like the men she had summoned, who answered the call of duty without question, so Sybil had answered the calling God laid on her heart. Someone had to take the ride. Why not her?

The exhaustion that swept over Sybil nearly knocked her over. She couldn't wait to lay down, let sleep overtake her, and dream sweet dreams.

AUTHOR'S NOTES – BRIA BURTON

WHEN I FIRST READ ABOUT Sybil Ludington, the fearless sixteen-year-old revolutionary who outrode Paul Revere by an estimated twenty-six miles, I immediately wondered why I had never heard about her in American History classes. It could be that what is known about Sybil began as oral history, later to be documented in an article by her great nephew, Lewis S. Patrick (in some places spelled Louis). Which brings up the fact that there is some confusion regarding the spelling of Sybil's name. Variations include Sibbell, Sibyl, Sebal, Sebil, and Cybil. The most common spelling given to her now is Sybil, and therefore I used that in the story.

While "Her Midnight Ride" is indeed fiction, I took as much historical fact as I could find and infused it into the story. That includes her brilliant idea to fool the Tory mob seeking to kidnap her father for General Howe's promised reward of three hundred English guineas. Her siblings marched in front of the windows with muskets and broomsticks to make it appear as if the local militia was protecting Colonel Ludington. My hope in writing this story is to increase awareness about Sybil's amazing feat and bring her to the forefront as a true American Revolutionary heroine worth celebrating.

For readers interested in learning more about this fascinating young woman, I suggest starting with the many websites dedicated to honoring her legacy. One site claims to be her personal blog: www.sybilludingtonblog.weebly.com. It includes a short animated film that aired on PBS Kids TV. And here is an article from Equitrekking that acknowledges her and her amazing horse, Star: www.equitrekking.com/articles/entry/sybil-ludington-and-her-horse-star-heroes-of-the-american-revolution.

—BB

REMUDA

Elle Andrews Patt

True love stories never have endings.
—Richard Bach

Goodnight-Loving Trail, New Mexico
October 1886

Ranger stared down at the groaning horse as it lay on its side, heaving in great drafts of breath. He had lassoed it in the dark after it began to roll within the tight confines of the rope corral, causing the other horses to mill about, snapping at one another. Now the pale grey light of pre-dawn brightened the sky as the other cowboys started stirring around the chuck wagon. He gripped the lasso in his hand still, although most of it lay in a loose coil on the torn-up grass.

Surging into action once more, the horse thrashed at the churned ground, kicking its hind legs out and writhing until it flipped itself over again, legs paddling through the air, neck and head stretched back and eyes rolling as its nostrils flared.

"Shoot it," the deep voice of the trail boss said from behind him. A rifle appeared in Ranger's peripheral vision, Bobby's hand wrapped tight around it.

Ranger nodded. It was his job after all, the care of the remuda, the herd of horses that enabled the cattle drive to happen at all. But he'd never shot one before. It happened to be his favorite of the ranch-owned stock, one of the three horses he'd reserved for his own use.

The Jacobs Cattle Company was small, but Luke "Old Man" Jacobs had gained the reputation of a master breeder. His pedigreed Longhorn herd brought large profits in sales to other ranches, as well as good money for those cattle culled for meat. Every fall, the old man paid well to move his prized herd from their leased and fenced Colorado summer range to his ranch in Texas for fall calving.

Paying well drew the most experienced cowboys, who brought their own horses. But more were always needed, due to injury or temperament or mishap. And someone had to oversee the care and security of the full remuda. That was him.

"Go on, boy," Bobby said in a mild tone. He'd been trail boss on this run for the past seventeen seasons, since 1869. Longer than Ranger had been alive.

Ranger took the rifle. He had the revolver his dad gave him tucked at the small of his back, with his belt cinched tight to hold it there, and five cartridges in his pocket, but those were strictly for emergencies. He walked around to the front of the horse's head, Bobby following him a couple of steps back. He cocked the rifle and then had to crouch to line the shot up properly. The horse tossed its head, lifting its nose from the ground and then flopped it back down in a better position as if it knew what was coming and welcomed it.

Taking advantage of the luck, Ranger visually marked an "x" on the horse's forehead, drawn from each ear to the inside of the opposite eye. He shoved the muzzle of the rifle within inches of a point just above the midpoint of the "x" at an angle in line with the horse's neck and pulled the trigger. The rebound sat him on his rump from his awkward position, but the horse died instantly. The horses in the corral wheeled as one from the report. They clustered at attention on the far side of the small area, heads raised to watch the men, nostrils flared.

"Good job. I'll tell the old man you did fine," Bobby said and held his hand out again. Ranger held up the rifle. Bobby took it. "Looks like the boys are headed over," he continued.

Ranger glanced toward camp. Three of the cowhands were coming to collect their mounts. He scrambled up onto his knees, loosened the circle of the lasso around the dead horse's neck, and worked it up and off the head.

"I'll be wanting my little bay mare," Bobby said.

"Yes, sir," Ranger said and if his throat was a little tight, his voice a bit thick, they both ignored it. Coiling the lasso into his hand, he walked on stiff legs to the corral. He roped Bobby's bay mare and held her while Bobby slid her bridle on over her ears.

"Stumpy for me today," one of the hands called out as soon as Ranger slid the rope off the mare's head.

One by one, Ranger roped the horses up, waited while they were bridled, and then moved to the next as the cowboys led their chosen horses back to camp to care for and saddle them. He eyed the remaining horses. Seventeen of them wore the JCC brand on their hips. A few of the older ones had a lot of cow-sense and were only ridden when cattle needed to be roped for hands-on care or riders were sent out to find strays.

Most of the rest would be traded out during the day as fresh mounts. Which left a spooky grey gelding that only settled after a couple hours of riding and a young chestnut mare with a big blaze and a wall eye. No one wanted to ride her, including Ranger. She was barely broke.

He glanced over at the steady mount lying dead on the ground and sighed. Roping up the mare, he examined first her brown eye and then her blue. Both were clear and bright. She flipped her head and snorted, spraying snot on his chest. He gave her a cursory brush, checked her feet and legs, and tacked her up as she sidled from side-to-side, turning her head to try and watch him as he worked around her.

When he was done, he left the rope over her neck while he

checked and released each of the other horses to graze and broke down the simple corral. By the time he was finished, Cookie already had his four mules hitched and was driving the chuck wagon in his direction. The cook seemed a good guy, a little older than usual, but he was strong and energetic. The hands were a bit quieter around him than on the other two drives Ranger had been on. This Cookie was unusually even-tempered, even cheerful sometimes, and not much of a talker.

He watched, though. He always knew when a cowboy needed an extra biscuit or a hand on his shoulder. His rare comment could lift the spirit or cut through an argument before it escalated. He called to the mules. Their ears flicked back before he lifted the reins and halted them. He wrapped the reins around the long handle of the brake. "Sorry about the horse, son," he said, holding Ranger's gaze. His eyes were warm, his expression solemn.

It eased Ranger's heavy heart to be verbally acknowledged, but made his throat ache with a sudden wave of grief. Not trusting his voice, he nodded. The cowboys all loved a horse or two over time, had a favorite they would tear up over at the campfire while telling the story of how the horse endeared itself to him, but daylight hours were working hours. No time for tender hearts or sympathy beyond a sideways glance of recognition and the steady beat of routine to keep one on track.

Cookie climbed down. He handed Ranger his breakfast in a bandana. Two biscuits, a bit of bacon tucked inside each if the heady smell that made Ranger's stomach growl was anything to go by. Ranger stuck the bundle inside his shirt for eating while he rode.

Together, he and Cookie piled the forked corral stakes between boards nailed along the wagon's right side, then slung the coiled lines of rope on top. "See you at mid-day," Cookie said, climbing back up to the driver's seat.

Ranger pulled the lasso off over the mare's head, pulled her head around to the saddle, and stepped up into the stirrup. He waited there while she blew sideways, talking nonsense to her and never letting go of her head. When she calmed, he gave her a little slack and then slung his leg over. She bowed her back up under him as his weight landed in the saddle. She jerked her head down, yanking the rein through Ranger's glove, and then bucked.

He leaned back into it. His head smacked her rump before she plunged downward straight-legged and leapt into the air again, letting her hindquarters rise into another big buck. As she landed again, Ranger snagged the left rein in both hands and pulled with all his might. Stymied, she spun in circles for a couple of minutes before she stopped, blowing hard.

Ranger eased the rein out as his toes found the stirrups and he slid his feet back into them. She bowed up, but moved off when he gave her a little boot with his calf, making sure to keep his spurs clear of her sides. When she decided to trot off, he allowed it, figuring forward was better than up any day. She didn't neck rein, but by turning his head in the direction he wanted to go and pulling on either rein, he could steer her. Posting up and down in the saddle to her rapid pace, he took her in a wide loop around the outermost horses of the grazing remuda, which had paid no attention to her antics.

Knowing the drill, trained to follow the cattle, the horses lifted easily off the ground as he called to them and swung his coil of lasso up, smacking it down on his thigh. They trotted along, headed for the tail end of the disappearing herd. When Ranger caught up, whatever cowboy was assigned to him today would break free and help him by riding at the front of the remuda to lead them alongside and past the slower cattle so that they could meet Cookie at the short mid-day break and be ready to switch out horses for the cowboys riding herd.

THE GREEN-BROKE MARE dumped Ranger on the unforgiving ground twice during the day with hard, twisting, unexpected bucks. And then she evaded his attempts to corral her with the rest of the remuda after the evening graze. Resigned to giving up some of his precious sleeping hours to find her, he volunteered to help locate missing hand Willy, and the five slower, heavily pregnant cows Willy had been minding.

People whispered about Old Man Jacobs' backwards methods, breeding for spring and fall calves, not moving his herds by trains the way he could, but his success couldn't be argued. His trail-tested cattle were hardy and long-lived, their offspring proving themselves as reliable producers at other outfits across a wide-range of operations. By the time Ranger was nine, he was catching JCC calves for branding and fell hard for the life. He'd already decided his future, and it wasn't as a lawyer like his dad. He wanted Jacobs Cattle Company. What was a few lost hours of sleep compared to that?

If he dedicated himself to doing the best job he could for his grandfather, learned the operation from the ground up, he could take over running the ranch by twenty-five. By thirty, he could name his price to stay on. That price would be a hardy stake in JCC, which would give him a leg up on any interest his cousins might take in it later and equal standing with his uncles, who were already mumbling about the "end of an era" and how the railroad and feedlots were going to make companies like JCC obsolete.

But those feedlots would still require calves to fill them, right? And those calves had better be tough and able to handle early weaning, which meant JCC's breeding lines would still be in demand. And no one knew Granddad's formula for choosing which bulls to cross on which of his cows. Not even Uncle Bradley, who was in-charge of most of the day-to-day business operations.

Ranger rode Bandit, one of JCC's seasoned geldings, down the dark, cold, back trail of the herd now grazing just beyond the chuck wagon under the watchful eye of the night shift. The tough grass was still spare, but would improve as they neared the Pecos River in the next few days. Even on a moonless night, Bandit wouldn't need the unlit lantern hung from the saddle's horn.

Under the half-moon, despite the clouds obscuring it, Ranger didn't hesitate to let old gelding have his head, knowing the surefooted horse knew his job. When Bandit's pace quickened or he began to meander, there'd be time to light the lantern so Ranger could either alert Willy to his presence or direct Bandit in the most promising direction to search for the wayward cowboy and the pregnant cows in his charge.

For the moment, he watched the darker shapes of the rugged landscape and far hills against the dark sky, looking for shapes that did not belong, listening for Willy's voice, or the low bawl of a cow separated from the main herd. The night sky seemed far away, the trails of stars sprayed across it a map of a land he could never visit.

Not that he'd ever had an interest in travel. All he wanted was the ranch. And the cattle. Before this drive, he'd not even taken much interest in the horses or much appreciated their contribution to the work. He'd argued, in fact, that he'd learn nothing on a drive he couldn't learn on the ranch and especially not if he were in charge of the horses and not working the cattle directly.

But now he could barely remember why he'd objected so. He could never travel the stars, but maybe he'd go to New York someday. Or go to Scotland to pick out and import his own Aberdeen-Angus bull like the one he'd seen at John Farwell's ranch when he helped deliver twenty JCC longhorns for a cross-breeding trial. That might be something.

Bandit snorted, drawing Ranger's focus back to the trail in front of him. His breath rose before him in the still night. They were on a widely-trampled part of the trail. Ranger could just make out the trickle of running water. The landscape opened to his right into the arroyo where the cowboys had let the herd drink before proceeding to the start of the grassy valley where Cookie had set up a dry camp for the night. It seemed a promising place for Willy to have pushed the strays into for water or protection or calving if it came to that.

Ranger lay the left rein on Bandit's neck and the horse turned right into the steep-sided gully. When the footing became rockier, he picked his way along, Ranger concentrating on keeping his balance in the middle of Bandit's back to make the horse's job easier. Where the slope started back up again, Ranger stilled and lifted the reins. The horse stopped. Ranger listened. Nothing but the sound of the creek and the bite of the cold September night on the skin of Ranger's face and ears.

They made their way back out and further down the trail at a comfortable jog. About ten minutes later, Bandit lifted his head, his ears pricked forward. Ranger muttered to him in acknowledgement. Within a couple of minutes, Willy's distinctive Irish voice drifted over a low hill to the left as he sung to the cows.

Bandit headed that way.

"Hallo," Ranger called out when he could make out the cows strolling along ahead of Willy.

"Who goes there?" Willy said.

"Ranger. You get all five?"

"Plus one," Will said, pride creeping into his voice.

Ranger scanned the cows, along their sides, and sure enough, a little, independent shadow bobbled along in the middle of the pack. "Looks hearty," he said.

"Fine lass from a well-matched cow," Will agreed. "Easy birthing."

"You see a chestnut horse out here anywhere?"

"That wall-eyed mare you were riding today?"

"The very one."

Willy poked his thumb back over his shoulder. "Thought I saw her lurking along the ridge just there. I wondered if she got loose from you again."

"That she did."

"There's a nothern' one with her."

"Another horse?"

"All I could see in the dark was a snip and a sock. Probably some handsome fella out to steal her."

If it was a bachelor mustang or a loose ranch stallion gone feral, then Willy might be right. Ranger would have to approach with caution if he could find her.

"I got these girls, if you want to go have a look. At least you can tell the old man you did'na just wait to see if she would be back at sunrise."

BANDIT DROVE each hoof into the loose shale for a toehold in more solid earth. Ranger stood up in his stirrups and leaned far forward to keep his weight off the working horse's back as he climbed up the steep, rocky slope. At the top, they stopped a moment and surveyed the view.

The moonlight lit only the flatter portions of ground. The undulations and the drop-offs over the sides of the ridge remained in deep and shifting shadow. A rabbit crouched a few feet from them, hoping it hadn't been seen. Ranger nudged Bandit forward and the rabbit leaped forward to Bandit's left and off the cliff in front of it. Pebbles tumbled down the rock in the wake of its wild flight.

Something larger moved off below. Ranger urged Bandit over the edge to see what he could see. The shadow of a horse moved off, but it carried a rider. "Hey," Ranger shouted, regretting it even before he finished the single word. How stupid was he?

He wheeled Bandit around on the thought and the horse scrambled back up onto the ridge line. Ranger trotted him along the top a few yards, knowing whoever rode below could hear him. He halted. Bandit tossed his head in protest. The unknown rider continued to pick his way downslope. One of Willy's strays bawled from far below on the other side.

Ranger dismounted, leaving one rein over Bandit's neck and holding the other. "Hup," he said in a soft voice, commanding Bandit to stay. Essentially tying the horse to the ground, Ranger dropped the rein he held. He strode to the cliff edge, scanning for the rider before he squatted to watch.

The horse was careful, almost balky, placing a foot at a time, but the rider remained patient, leaning back and facing forward, seemingly unconcerned about Ranger.

The rush of Ranger's blood in his ears calmed. Behind him, Willy's faint song and the shuffle of the cows faded into the distance between them. Bandit shifted, his foot scraping on the hard ground and the leather of the saddle creaking before he stilled again. Only the quiet footfalls of the horse below remained for several long moments. Then the furtive movements of the small critters living along the ridge picked up again.

Ranger stood. The clouds shifted, dropping light onto the horse and rider. All he could tell was that the horse was dark-colored. And the rider rode bareback. He could be an Indian. The horse turned, skirting a boulder in its winding path, revealing its build before it swung its head and the big white blaze on its face shone.

Yep. That horse was his. "Dammit," Ranger spit. The rider was wearing some sort of boot that caught the moonlight as well. Maybe that was what Willy had seen in the dark. Assuming a bachelor mustang was a better guess than a random horse thief alone and on foot out here in the dark. But he wouldn't get away with it. That mare belonged to JCC.

Ranger caught Bandit's dangling rein on the run and swung up into the saddle. The older horse plunged fearlessly downward onto the arroyo slope once more. Ranger pointed him on a straighter path that would intersect the thief's at the base of the canyon. They scrabbled to the bottom in a rattle of shale, the frigid wind buffeting Ranger's face, causing him to squint against the tearing of his eyes, and deafening him to anything but his own progress.

The slope steepened right at the bottom. Bandit sat hard, Ranger leaning back against his rump, and slid the last ten yards. Gathering himself at the last moment, he made a powerful half-leap onto level ground and galloped forward, ears pricked, focused on the mare. Ranger gave him a little check. Bandit responded by slowing the slightest amount, so Ranger let him go again, aimed straight at the thief.

The mare shied hard away from Bandit, nearly unseating the thief, and then bolted. The thief hunkered down low over her neck. Ranger gave chase, leaning low himself, part pissed about a run through the dark on stony ground that could reach up and cripple anyone of them at any second, part exultant, thrilled at the hard, short bursts of Bandit's muscles rising and falling beneath him, the pump of his own heart, the wind in his face.

Within a minute, Bandit caught up to the mare as she slowed to let him come alongside, her instinct reminding her that safety lay in the herd. They galloped along shoulder to shoulder for a few strides, and then Ranger eased himself straighter in the saddle. Bandit slowed under him and the mare slowed beside him.

Ranger glanced over at the thief. Two strong, small hands

gripped the mare's mane. Long hair tangled and whipped over the thief's hidden face and hunched back. Knees gripping hard, the thief's white boot angled along the horse's dark, heaving sides. Slower, slower, both horses broke to a rough trot. Ranger posted up and down. The thief jounced on the mare's back.

Ranger just caught the move from the corner of his eye, the thief performed it so fast. The white boot flashed in the light as he straightened his leg downward, then drew his upper body back before flinging himself forward. His boot swung high over the mare's rump and then the thief was gone. Ranger sat down in his saddle, pulled up hard on the bit, and whirled Bandit around right into the path of the mare. She slid to a stop, flinging her head up.

The thief had landed on his feet and run. Ranger could just make out the white boots, headed into deeper shadow, and then around an outcropping of rock and mesquite.

The mare snorted. Bandit whuffled his breath on her as they brought their heads close together. Ranger tugged on Bandit's head and kicked him away before the squeal and kick he knew would come in the next second. The mare tossed her head but held her ground. Ranger reached to the saddle behind his leg, his experienced fingers finding his rope in a second. The mare shifted, ready to run. With a small deft flip, Ranger settled the big loop of rope he'd already formed over the mare's head just before she spun away.

He held tight. Bandit, well-trained, felt her weight in the rope and lowered his butt against it, backing up to take up the slack. The mare recalled her own small amount of training and stopped her move into headlong flight, bouncing at the end of the rope, and then spinning herself back around to face Ranger.

"There now," he said. "Good girl."

He gathered the rope, drawing her alongside them on his right as he asked Bandit to walk forward. He lifted the annoying lantern, lashed the rope around the saddle horn, and replaced it. Searching the outcropping as he moved the horses forward, he saw no movement. He picked his way over anyway, the mare bumping up against his left leg every few steps.

He halted them once he rounded the rocks. It was a bit of a

wash. Level where he stood, the ground climbed steeply beyond it and on either side. No movement. No clatter of stone. No lighter-than-the dark boots giving the thief's movement away. The horses' breaths filled his ears and the air, visible as white streamers rising along their faces. He had the horse. He should just go on.

He studied the wash. The mare shifted. She lifted her head high, her ears perked forward. Bandit followed suit. Ranger could see nothing.

He should go.

As if of its own accord, his hand rose to his mouth, the glove already half-off. He pulled it free with his teeth and found one of the loose matches in his canvas coat pocket. After dropping the reins on Bandit's neck, he tugged his glove back on and used both hands to light the lantern. The match shook. He shoved his fear down, waved the match out, and dropped it to the ground at Bandit's feet.

The small, bare hands, the long hair.

Something wasn't sitting right with him.

Lifting the lantern in his left hand, he took up the reins with the other and nudged Bandit forward. Each hoof-fall seemed to boom in the still quiet. They weaved their way through and around fallen boulders and hard sand hillocks into the wash. He sent the light into each crevice and dip and alcove, the shadows skittering and skidding and sliding away. There. Someone walking forward now, coming to meet him.

Ranger drew Bandit to a halt. Leaning forward, he pushed the lantern out in front of himself. A young woman wearing white boots and a rabbit skin coat walked into the light. Her wind-blown dark hair fluttered and shimmered over her shoulders and chest, crossing her face in tangled steams. She lifted a bare hand and pushed it away, tucking it behind her ear.

This was his thief.

Remembering himself, Ranger straightened in the saddle, drawing the light back. She followed it in, reaching out to caress Bandit's nose before she stopped by his right shoulder, close enough to touch Ranger's knee if she wanted. She tilted her face up to study him. Her eyes were as dark as her hair. Her straight, wide nose led to slightly parted full lips. She was still.

Even her breath, as it rose to greet him, seemed calm.

Ranger blew out his own deep breath at her appearance in a noisy rush. "Who are you?"

He was surprised when she answered, aware then he had not expected one, or maybe not one in English. She was clearly a half-breed. Close to his age. "Sophie DuBois," she said, holding his gaze.

Every thought fled him at the lilt in her voice.

"I am lost," she continued.

Unable to find his tongue, Ranger unwound the loop of lasso over the saddle horn. He offered her the tight coil of rope. The mare skirted away from him at the sudden movement. Sophie soothed the mare with her hand upon the horse's shoulder as she accepted the rope. She loosened the loop over the mare's neck. Sliding it up, she twisted it to form a loop over the mare's nose before tucking the whole coil back through the neck loop. Now the mare wore a halter of sorts.

Ranger took the lasso when she handed it back to him. Only when he closed his fist around it did he finally shake himself out of whatever had come over him. "You're out here by yourself?" he croaked through his inexplicably tight throat.

"No," she said.

He looked up then, the lantern swinging, wild light springing away into the dark. He'd let his guard down. And blinded his night vision. Fumbling with the lantern, burning his hand on the glass, he doused the flame, plunging them into darkness.

A CLEAR, tinkling laugh penetrated Ranger's panic. It rose through the night, as if the girl herself was growing taller or floating. Something soft and lingering brushed across his face and Ranger could only think feather. An image of the girl with wings spread, an angel come to Earth, hovering above the rocky ground before him rose unbidden in his mind's eye.

The mare moved off. Ranger pulled back on the lasso in his

hand by instinct. The mare closed the space between them again, bumping against his leg, her head crossing over Bandit's withers, bumping the hot lantern. Something warm and hard fetched up against his thigh. Sophie's hand closed on his forearm and she laughed again. Her hair brushed his shoulder.

She'd swung up onto the mare, that was all.

His eyes were adjusting. He let the rope slide a little and toed the mare away. "Who's with you?" he said, his voice coming harder than he meant.

"You," she said in her heavy accent.

Surprise opened his chest and he took his first true breath in what felt like hours. Maybe days.

"This horse found me," she said. "And brought me you."

Maybe it'd been years since he'd truly breathed. Maybe his whole life, Ranger's heart whispered. He filled his lungs with the crisp, cold night, scented now with a sweet musk he couldn't identify, but must be the girl. It made him settle in a way he'd never known before. He didn't even know he'd been restless, before, just that it seemed now he could stop right here and be satisfied to never leave again.

A coyote yipped, somewhere close. And then another. Sophie looked over her shoulder. "They were following me before I found the horse."

Ranger booted Bandit's sides with a gentle heel. The mare followed along. Out of the wash, Ranger turned Bandit's head back the way they'd come. They listened to the coyotes talk to one another in occasionally yips on their back trail.

Sometime later, after watering the horses at the arroyo and reaching the start of the long valley the herd would travel along for three or four days, Sophie began to hum. Ranger lost himself in the pretty melody and sway of the saddle as Bandit walked.

The sounds of the herd were just night-time sounds until they grew loud enough to spill over and then they were the herd's, spread out before them. The shift of heavy bodies, low murmurs of bellies grumbling, the rip of grass and steady grind of teeth, the occasional bawl of a disgruntled or lonely cow.

"Find her?" Willy said as they rode up on him where he sat on the herd's left flank. And then, "Who you got there? A kid?"

"A woman," Ranger said. "Sophie Dubois."

Willy pushed his hat back. He opened his mouth, but then closed it again.

The cows nearby lifted their heads, staring back the way Ranger had come. "Coyotes," he said.

Willy nodded and lifted his reins. He'd sweep the backside of the herd, make sure the stragglers came up. A few weeks ago, Ranger would've asked where Willy was going. The last few weeks seemed like a lifetime. Although he hadn't wanted to come, his grandfather had been right. He'd learned more about the cows than he thought he would, but more importantly, he learned a lot about the drovers he'd have to manage someday.

They were a strange breed of cowboy, working without sleep, in the rain, through the danger of fording rivers, lightning strikes, the possibility of death that every small injury or illness brought with it on the trail, for less than any of them could make doing ranch or railroad work. And, for the most part, they did it with great cheer, no matter how dirty, wet, or tired. He couldn't fathom why, but also knew the next time his grandfather asked him to work the drive, there'd be no backtalk. He'd saddle his horse in a heartbeat.

Ranger and Sophie moved on. Instead of disturbing the camp, Ranger rode straight for the remuda. The only other drover they saw on herd gave them a nod, but said nothing. Near the remuda, a horse in the herd nickered. The mare whinnied in response and surged ahead of Bandit.

At the corral, Ranger sent the wrangler he shared night watch with to bed. Sophie slid off the mare before he could help her. She stood to one side while he released the mare into the herd and untacked Bandit.

When he turned from laying his saddle aside, he found Sophie rubbing the sweaty saddle marks from Bandit's coat with a handful of grass. He did the same on the opposite side and then returned Bandit to the herd. Not sure what to do next, he gestured towards the banked fire where the wrangler lay prone, already asleep or close to it.

"Water?" she said.

Oh! He snatched up the water skin lying next to the lantern. It hadn't occurred to him to offer it earlier. She drank her fill, followed him to the fire where he dropped his pad and saddle, and rolled up in the thin wool blanket he gave her like she'd done it every night of her life.

Ranger sat and watched her sleep.

In the distance, a coyote barked and then howled, soon joined by its brothers.

ROPING a horse up in the corral, Ranger missed the initial stir Sophie's entrance caused after she woke and made her way over. In the breaking light, her dark skin seemed luminous as she regarded the cowboys standing in a tight cluster and staring back at her.

"Uh," Ranger said. The horse he held stamped its foot, breaking the stand-off.

"She's a half-breed, ain't she?" a tall cowboy named Gus said. He turned his head and spit on the ground.

"You speak English, girl?" another said and the man beside him said, "Got a name, sweetheart?"

She looked between them and then held out her hand. "Sophie Dubois."

The cowboys drew back as one, like she might be speaking in tongues.

Gus recovered first. "I'm Gus. Where'd you come from?"

She cocked her head with a slight frown before her expression cleared. "That way," she said and pointed back towards the hills.

"You French or Indian?" Beans drawled from the rear of the group.

Sophie smiled, causing another physical stir. "Oui," she said.

"You're We?" he said. "Never heard of that type Indian."

"It means 'yes' in French," Bobby said, walking up behind them.

The cowboys startled. Stepping on each other, they parted,

letting the trail boss pass between them. Bobby nodded at Ranger. "Gus, take your horse," he said. "I'll take my bay mare again today, Ranger."

"Sir," Ranger said while Gus slid his bridle over the horse's head. "She was on the mare, sir, when I found her."

"Horse thief?"

"Opportunity, I think." He flicked his lasso off over the horse's head when Gus was done. "But she was riding her without tack, not even a rope."

"How'd she catch her?"

"I don't know, sir."

"That makes no sense, Ranger. Fetch my bay. Who are you, ma'am?"

Ranger backed away, reluctant to leave.

Sophie held out her hand. "Sophie Dubois."

Her hand disappeared in his when he took it. "Bobby Gafford. I'm in charge here."

"Oui," she said. "I was lost. Now I am found."

"Glad we could help with that," Bobby said, holding her gaze. "Ranger, get my horse."

Sophie glanced over at him. "Ranger?"

"Yes?" Ranger said.

"That is your name?"

"That's his name all right," Bobby said, dropping her hand. "Go now, boy."

His tone remained the same, but Ranger knew he'd pushed the boss as hard as he could without earning himself a serious punishment. He spun on his heel and dove into the herd in search of the small bay mare.

When he returned, Sophie quirked the side of her mouth up at him.

Bobby bridled his horse. "We'll talk about this later," he said to Ranger as he lifted the lasso loop over the bay's fine ears and off her head to shove it against Ranger's chest with a stern look. Shifting his gaze to Sophie, he said, "Come with me."

She shrugged and followed Bobby and Gus away toward the main camp.

RANGER COILED the last of the corral rope and laid it atop the pile of stakes. Shielding his eyes from the low morning sun, he could see the chuck wagon pulling away from camp, Cookie in the driver's seat and Sophie beside him. Ranger had saddled another of JCC's old geldings for the day, but roped the mare up as well. He wasn't sure why. He let his hand drift over the lasso around her neck, but then stopped before lifting it. Giving the mare her freedom after chasing her down the night before wasn't a mistake he wanted to make twice.

The chuck wagon trundled like a cloth-backed beetle over the short distance. Bobby wouldn't refuse hospitality to a woman by herself in rough country, but Ranger wasn't sure if he'd place a half-breed in the category of "Lady". He didn't know what Bobby'd ask of her in return for bed and board, even if was just a bit of hard ground and some beans. Twice already along the journey, they'd had women come out of nearby towns to keep company with them.

Ranger had kept his distance. He was meant to stay with the remuda, anyway, so it hadn't been hard to keep his head down and ignore the more blatant fumbling under cover of darkness and nothing else. Would Bobby expect that kind of service from a half-breed as a matter of course?

Sophie's happy voice, although he couldn't understand her above the rattle-creak-groan of the wagon, seemed familiar although they'd not talked much. It eased his worries, and settled him in the same way he settled a horse with a kind word. She chattered at Cookie, who was grinning so wide that Ranger moved a few steps away from the piled corral gear for fear Cookie's cheeks had blinded him.

Sophie beamed at Ranger and jumped down from the wagon as soon as the mules stopped. "Hello, Ranger," she said, but ducked past him to go to the mules' heads and coo to them. Cookie said something that Ranger couldn't quite catch. Sophie answered and again, Ranger missed what she said.

Cookie climbed down, talking as he did. Ranger knuckled his ear. They continued to chat as Cookie made his way around the wagon, collected Sophie, and walked over to him. He stared at Cookie and his mouth for several seconds before his brain recognized that they weren't speaking English. It must be French, given Sophie's name and the commotion at the corral earlier.He'd never heard it spoken before.

"You know French?" Ranger asked Cookie, unable to think much past that. No one he knew spoke French. Spanish, of course, but not French. He'd heard the accent once, when a French-Canadian cow poker spent a few days at JCC.

But Cookies only spoke English, and maybe a bit of Spanish. None of it proper. It was all drawls and slang and shortcuts, although less so with this Cookie, come to think of it. This Cookie also talked differently to him than on the rare occasion he talked to the other hands while slinging dinner in camp. But French?

"Oui," Cookie said, which Ranger only knew meant "yes" because Bobby had said so this morning. "And Sophie here speaks very little English."

"Oh." He'd thought their silence mutual as they rode. Maybe he thought she'd been afraid, between the dark, cold, coyotes, and him. Although she hadn't acted afraid, come to think on it. "Why is she out here?"

"Her papa died. He raised her in a cabin in the Sangre de Cristo hills after her mother died when Sophie was six. He did all the hunting, and traded horses for their supplies, while she stayed behind to care for the stock. So after his death, she was unable to fend for herself. She hid when some men came through and raided what little food remained. After three days, they were still there, though, so she left, with just what she was wearing at the time."

Ranger's mind blanked. He'd never heard so many words from Cookie at one time. And Sophie's father left her alone while he went off into the woods? While he went wherever and bartered for supplies? Ranger grew up on the ranch. He couldn't think of a time when he hadn't been within a few hundred yards of someone he knew. Even now, on the drive, someone would come looking if he were gone too long. "Wait. Where was she going?"

"Abilene. Her father had a lawyer there and there's a bank account. There's family in France."

"But they lived alone? There's no one here?"

"Her mother was Jicarilla Apache. She said she remembers visiting with the tribe, but then they stopped going. She doesn't know how to find them."

"But—"

Cookie grabbed the ropes on top of the stakes. "But what?"

"She's gorgeous."

He laughed and slung the ropes on their hooks. "And what does that have to do with anything?"

Heat filled Ranger's face. He hated how easily he blushed. "Nothing, just—"

"Actually, that might just be why he hid her away."

Sophie came back to help them. They took turns loading stakes onto the wagon. When they were finished, Ranger said, "She's headed the wrong way."

Cookie laughed again and then spoke in rapid French. Sophie smiled and shrugged. "*J'ai dit j'étais perdu.*"

"Yes, you have," Cookie said, then to Ranger, "She says that she's already said she was lost."

"Is she riding with you?"

Cookie asked her and she answered.

"She'd like to ride the mare."

"She can ride Buck, here," Ranger said. "The mare's green-broke."

"I heard Sophie rode in on her."

"Yeah, but—"

"I'll pull the spare saddle. And there's a hemp bridle under the wagon seat."

Ranger just nodded. It was true the mare hadn't objected the night before, but that didn't mean she'd be the same under saddle. He could maybe ride her out first. He bit his tongue, though, watching Sophie's swift, confident actions as she swung the pad and saddle up and on and cinched the girth up with a smooth efficiency that seemed to stun the skittish mare into complacency.

It certainly stunned him.

"Biscuits," Cookie said from his elbow, holding out the greasy bandana that Ranger delivered back to him every day at the noon meal. "Use 'em to close your mouth."

Within a minute, Cookie had the mules leaning into their harnesses and the chuck wagon pots rattling again while Sophie bridled the mare without so much as a by-your-leave. She patted the mare on the neck and took up the near rein, letting the far side loop to the level of the mare's knee. Grabbing the mare's mane in her left hand, she swung up before Ranger could shout out a warning.

He grimaced, waiting for the coming disaster as the mare bowed her back up.

His stomach dropped when Sophie thrust her hand forward, giving the mare her head and kicked her forward, stirrups dangling loose. The mare ducked her head down, preparing for an explosive buck. Sophie urged her forward again, rocking her hips with the effort, and put her hand further forward. The mare froze.

"Watch—" Ranger yelled.

The mare heaved a big sigh and stepped forward. She took another short, sticky step and then walked on, her back relaxing, her nose nearly on the ground.

". . . out," Ranger finished, the word trailing off on the surprised huff of his breath.

He glanced to the chuck wagon, but Cookie never looked back.

BY MID-DAY, Ranger had trouble tearing his gaze away from Sophie long enough to do his job. Keeping the mare with her, she'd wandered off by the time he finished helping the cowboys switch out their mounts for the afternoon. With a sigh, he saddled the spooky grey he'd been avoiding. Ghost. The name was all wrong since it was the grey who was afraid of anything that moved. Or didn't move. He was hard to predict.

Ghost held his head high on a stiff neck, his ears swiveling and eyes everywhere as Ranger led him over to the chuck wagon to grab his meal. Sophie turned at his approach, and then gave him a big smile. Cookie was standing on a box with a cowhand in front of him with his head tilted back and mouth wide open.

"What's he doing?" Ranger said.

Sophie raised her eyebrows.

"What's he . . ." Ranger circled his finger at Cookie and the cowboy.

"You're fine," Cookie said. "Sit over there a second. Ranger, these cakes getting cold over here are yours."

Ranger took the offered plate of sourdough pancakes warmed up from breakfast, Ghost sidling sideways at his sudden movement. He wolfed the pancakes down, watching Sophie watch Cookie.

Cookie ground a bit of dried root up and poured boiling water from the kettle over it before he started packing up to race down the trail to the next camp site, far enough ahead of the herd to get the evening meal ready. Sophie tied the wall-eyed mare to the side of the chuck wagon, something Ranger had never seen Cookie allow before. Then she set about helping him pack, talking to him with ease in her own language.

The cowboy Cookie had been examining sat where he'd been placed, seeming mesmerized, his eyes glued to Sophie. Ranger dropped his plate in the wreck pan behind him. Ghost startled, shying away from the loud clatter, and ripped the rein from Ranger's hand.

He took off.

Sophie laughed.

Cookie cussed, ranting about stupid cowhands bringing their horses to breakfast as Ranger chased a few steps after Ghost. He stopped, watched the horse veer around the nearest of the lead cowhands, who flapped a hat to scare him off the herd.

If Ghost started the cows running, Ranger would really get it from Bobby. He craned his neck to see where the horse was headed. Back to the remuda, it seemed. The wrangler watching them graze managed to get out in front and slow him to a trot before Ghost ducked around him, but at least the runaway didn't disturb the remuda or the herd.

After slowing to a halt, Ghost stood to the side a moment, snorting and shaking his head, and then tried to go to grazing as if nothing had happened. The second rein was wrapped loosely around Ranger's saddle horn. He bobbed his head a few times and the rein pulled free, allowing him to get his mouth down into the scrubby grass. Damn horse.

"I'll take him," Sophie said, coming up beside Ranger.

"What?"

"I ride him," she said, pointing at Ghost.

"If you can catch him," Ranger said.

As Ranger rode away on the mare, Cookie shouted after him, "You should be walking, boy, this girl is being too nice to you!"

Ranger agreed.

He had the wrangler help him bring the remuda up trail ahead of the herd, cringing every time Ghost's dangling reins wrapped around a foreleg or he stepped on them and then flung his head in the air to free himself. They found a good spot and Ranger dismounted. He handed the mare's reins to the wrangler.

Ghost eyed him. Every time he advanced on the grey close enough to rope him, the wary horse hid behind another. He'd have to wait until they set the corral up to trap him. Ranger remounted the mare when the chuck wagon caught up to them.

Cookie slowed to keep the remuda from scattering, but the horses were grass-starved after several days with little forage and a night corralled. They showed no interest in the mules or wagon clattering by. Pulling the mules to a halt, Cookie let Sophie leap off. "Don't want to see her walking into camp," he called out.

Ranger gave him a salute. Cookie shook his head and slapped the reins on the mule's butts, clucking them back up into a trot, the pots and pans rattling against each other.

Sophie dusted off her buckskin leggings. Her white deerskin boots were dirtier from riding the day before in the cloud of dust the herd raised, but still bright. She threw a questioning look Ranger's way. He swept his hand at Ghost in invitation. They still had a bit of time before the lead hands caught up to them with the head of the herd.

She skirted around the remuda, getting behind the grey before approaching. But then, although she waded bravely into the herd, she still didn't go for him directly. Instead she headed for a chestnut gelding, who raised his head to watch her. She plucked a bit of grass and held her arm out to offer it to him. With plenty of grass around him, the chestnut still reached out to pluck the offering from her flat hand. She stepped in and petted him.

Another chestnut ambled over and snuffed at her shoulder. She spoke to him and petted him, too. She turned away and both horses followed her as she walked over to a rangy bay with three white socks and made another friend. Now several horses had shifted, a couple still grazing, but all focused on her as she wound her way through the remuda offering words and pats.

Ranger tensed as she came closer to Ghost, on the far side of a bony chestnut named Fernie. Sophie patted Fernie's shoulder and then stroked his side. He turned his head to smell Sophie's hair, stepping over with his hind feet to keep his nose next to Sophie's head and pushing Ghost aside. It was only as the horse stepped around that Ranger could see Sophie had a hand on Fernie's far-side cheek and was asking him to turn with her. When she had turned the horse all the way around, she switched hands, asking him to turn the other way, putting her back to Ghost where he stood watching her.

She ignored him. And although she released Fernie, she remained there beside him, talking to the appreciative horse, stroking his thin neck and rubbing his ears. The other horses gathered close to them. Behind her, Ghost bounced his head, the reins flapping. When she continued to ignore him, he stretched his neck out and nuzzled her back.

Ranger willed her to whip around and take the loose reins, but instead Sophie greeted Bandit, who had managed to insert his head next to Fernie's. She leaned in and kissed Bandit's nose. Ranger wrinkled his own nose. Really?

Ghost had had enough and stepped forward to put his head over

Sophie's shoulder. She reached one hand up to rub his face while she continued to talk to Bandit. Ever so slow, she eased around and said something to Ghost. He bounced his head. She kissed him as well and then slid her hand down his neck as her other came up to his cheek and she turned him like she had Fernie.

Without touching the reins, she changed his direction, turning him the other way. She started rubbing him with both hands and rubbed and stroked her way back to his rump. Ranger thought she'd stop there, but she went right around him, scratching his big rump, and catching his tail in one hand, letting it slide from her fingers as she patted and scratched and rubbed all along Ghost's opposite side as well. Ranger could just see the top of her head.

"Holy cow," the wrangler said.

Ranger started, the mare bunching up beneath him. He'd forgotten there was anyone beside him. "You ever seen anything like that before?"

"Once," the wrangler said. "During the war. A Calvary officer, a furner. He done that."

A foreigner. He slid his gaze sideways at the black wrangler. His name was Andrew, but everyone called him Sticks. "Were you free, before the war?"

"Naw," he said still focused on Sophie. "Worked cows on a plantation in Virginia. Joined up when the Union burned it down. You know, wish I could remember that man's name. She has the same look about her, ceptin' she's dark and dark haired. He had the goldest hair I ever seen and as wall-eyed as that mare there. Looky there, just look at that."

He'd missed it. Sophie was just settling in the saddle, Ghost standing stock still, his head turned to snuffle her leg although both reins were looped low. She shifted all over his back, wiggling and swinging her legs, reaching back to pat his rump with either hand and then leaning forward, her hair swinging to pet both sides of his neck. She stood in the stirrups and stretched to reach both his ears and scratch around them. She rode him through the remuda, and around the outside, and then back through the middle.

"Let's go," Andrew said. "Herd's coming."

Sure enough, the leads were within calling distance, the head cows shuffling along behind them. He gave Bobby a wave and then he went to the left and Andrew to the right, lifting the remuda with Sophie on Ghost in the middle of it, and took them further aside to let them graze a bit more.

They'd keep the horses a bit back of the head, near the second swing rider, in case anyone needed to change horses. When they settled again to await the second swing, he glanced over at Sophie. As if she could feel his gaze on her, she looked back at him just then and gave him another of her brilliant smiles.

Just like that, he knew he loved her.

THE NEXT WEEKS passed as if Ranger were dreaming; the warm, work-filled days, the cold nights under the stars, the rain like a blessing, finally bringing Sophie against him, huddled together for warmth that burst to flame. She shared none of the reservations of the girls he knew, having not been brought up under the strict rules of Texas matrons and southern culture. Both uneducated and lacking any skill, they reveled with unrestricted passion by the privacy of the remuda fire.

They were happy.

And Bobby was happy to have an extra wrangler, freeing a hand for herd duty.

Ranger learned more from Sophie than he ever thought there was to learn about working around the horses. The wall-eyed mare became a reliable mount. Ghost, although still sensitive, bloomed into the best kind of working horse, one with cow sense and utter focus—as long as his rider kept his focus on the job.

Cookie got an apt pupil as he professed to teach English to Sophie, but Ranger suspected she knew more English than she was letting on, she picked it up so fast. He added her to his future plans. With her knowledge of the horses and his love for the ranch, Jacobs Cattle Company would become known across the globe. They could breed and train JCC-branded horses to sell alongside the breeding stock cattle.

But then they hit the Rio Grande.

SAN FILIPE DEL RIO was dust, a couple of bars, a church, a general store, a post office, and a coach service east to San Antonio where Sophie could catch a train to Abilene. Bobby and Cookie bid Sophie good-bye and good luck. Cookie placed a hand on Ranger's shoulder and squeezed before he let go. They made their way to the general store, leaving Ranger and Sophie standing on the boardwalk outside the coach office.

"I don't understand," Ranger said. "I'm offering you a home. Anything you want. You don't know that your father left you anything in Abilene."

"I trust in him, Ranger. Here, I'm a half-breed. I listened to your cow boys while I helped Darrien cook. I will be out cast here."

Darrien. Ranger had never even asked Cookie's name. He was just Cookie. "Not at JCC."

"JCC is not the world, Ranger. And there are many places and many horses and I want to see them all."

"But I love you. I want you here, beside me."

"Come with me. Don't you want to see the ocean? Paris? The River Thames? The Parthenon? The pyramids?"

Ranger shook his head. He did want to see those things someday, maybe, but right now he couldn't imagine not waking to a rope in his hand, the bawl of cows in his ear, a horse underneath him. It was simple, repetitive, but changed every moment. It required his brain and his body, every moment. Sitting on a train? Trapped on a boat? He could imagine the hell of that.

The ranch was all he wanted, besides Sophie. He wouldn't get it traipsing off to Abilene on some goose chase after lawyers and bankers. The thought of lawyers made him think of his dad, sitting behind a desk for hours on end. No.

The only way to win JCC as his own one day was to be there working it. He needed his grandfather to know all he'd learned on the drive. He wanted to ask if he could concentrate on the horses, maybe breed a little. Maybe his interest would show his grandfather that he could handle learning the old man's secrets for matching cows to bulls for the famous JCC brand. If Sophie found nothing waiting for her in Abilene, maybe she'd come back here to him.

"Ranger?"

"I'm sorry, I can't."

"Then we are here."

"Yes. We are." He drew her into him, closing his arms around her. Her tears wet his shirt. He pretended his weren't dripping off his chin, but ruined it by dragging a hand across his face when she lifted her head and turned her face up to him.

They laughed a little and then he kissed her again. A kiss to last a lifetime. She deepened it.

"Oh, my," a woman's voice said in passing, renewing Ranger's awareness that they were standing in public in the middle of a very small town.

They broke the kiss, but only for a second before they shared yet another. Deeper than the first, he remembered every moment they'd shared, imagined her rearing above him, the blanket dropping to her bare waist, the flicker of fire shadows painting her. The kiss eased into something gentler, like their lovemaking always did. Their lips parted and he rested his chin on her head, pulling her in tight before he let her go.

He turned, his chest aching, and walked to where Ghost and the wall-eyed mare waited for him. He looked back to see Sophie disappearing into the office to wait for her coach. Taking the mare's reins in hand, he mounted Ghost, hardly able to breathe. He looked again at the now closed coach office door. Spinning Ghost away, he kicked him up into a full gallop, the mare's head bobbing at his knee as she kept pace, and let the cold wind dry his tears.

Jacobs Cattle Company, near San Filipe Del Rio, Texas
May 1901

"HEY'YUH, BOSS," Willy said, poking his head through Ranger's office door. "That grey mare just foaled. Brawny black laddie."

Ranger leaped to his feet, eager to see JCC's newest addition to their working horse operation. They walked out together to the new thirty-stall broodmare barn and leaned on the new mother's door. The black colt twitched its short bushy tail as it nursed, wobbling on its long legs like it was balancing on stilts.

Only time would tell if the colt would stay black or fade to grey. Ranger had been trying for three years for a black stallion to use as his next foundation stud. Hopefully, they could increase their chances of throwing more black foals in future, a color that always commanded higher prices, without losing the physical build and temperament that JCC branded horses were now known for. His mind wandered back to that first cattle drive, when he had learned to appreciate the working horses for all they did on the trail as well as on the ranch.

And as those kinds of thoughts always did, they led him back to the memories of Sophie and those amazing weeks along the Pecos. There'd been other women. And he'd almost gotten married once. But then he'd let the ranch interfere, took any distraction he could, to try and turn his thoughts from comparing those women to his first lover and the dark months that followed while he held onto his dream of owning the ranch with both hands to keep from running to Abilene and chasing her down.

"Why do you do that?" Willy said.

"What?"

"Always think about her when we're looking at the horses. You were a kid, Ranger. It probably was'na as great as you remember it. Not so great as to be throw'n your life away after your heart."

Ranger flicked his hand at the colt. "I'm not throwing my life away."

"Kids are better'n a colt any day, man. Put yourself out to stud."

Ranger laughed. "Is Lizzie pregnant again?"

Willy grinned as he stood up tall. "That she is," he said with pride.

The old man came down the center aisle.

"Sir," Willy said, tipping his hat. "I'll go check the yearlings' water, Boss," he said to Ranger and moseyed away.

Luke Jacobs settled in beside Ranger. "Nice colt," he said.

Ranger had thought he'd dabble in the horses until he could convince his grandfather he was the one who would carry on the legacy of JCC's cattle breeding. But that honor had gone to Uncle Bradley. And as Ranger could see now, Uncle Bradley had always been the natural choice.

But the old man had encouraged him in his work with the horses. Now he not only trained and bred all the ranch's working stock, he also trained the horsemen that sought him out once they'd ridden his stock.

"Who'd have ever thought?" Ranger said.

"Me," the old man said.

Ranger chuckled. "Thank you, sir."

"You're very welcome. Now, there's someone waiting for you at your dad's office in town."

"Who?"

"You'll want to go now."

Mystified, Ranger said, "Right now?"

"I believe so," the old man said. "I'll keep an eye on this fella for a while."

"Yes, sir."

THE RIDE into town wasn't far. His father had brought in two other lawyers over the years as Del Rio's borders pushed out in all directions. Riding down main street, Ranger nodded to several people he knew on horses and in wagons and then the owner of the most prosperous saloon, who was driving one of the three cars in town. He tied Ghost to the hitching post at the law firm and greeted a woman and her daughter as they passed by him on the tree-shaded boardwalk.

He opened the door to the law firm.

His heart leapt as he heard a voice he'd been listening to in his dreams for the past fifteen years. "Sophie," he shouted, joy cracking his voice.

"Ranger," she said, flying out of his dad's office and straight into his arms. "I have dreamed of you!"

Without thought, he kissed her, but she kissed him back with every bit of passion he could remember. Some part of him worried about a disappeared husband or lover in the midst of that kiss, but once again he settled into his heart and mind, more at home in that moment, that kiss, than he'd been at the ranch these past fifteen years.

Someone cleared their throat.

Ranger raised his head to tell his Dad to clear off, but the eyes that met his were a stranger's. A young stranger's, yet his face had a familiar shape. Sophie turned in Ranger's arms, reaching out to grab the young man's arm and tug him closer.

Ranger let her go, running a hand up to smooth his hair, very aware of the heat in his face. He hated that he blushed so easy.

"This is my dear Lucas," Sophie said, stretching the "u" sound. "Your son. He wants to get to know you. And I've found that everything I've been searching for, I left behind. Here. I've been lost. But now I've found you, both here, and"—she placed her hand on her chest—"here. Will you have me?"

Ranger studied his son. He was Jacobs through and through, but darker skinned and darker eyed. His gaze shifted to Sophie's hand on her chest. Over her heart. On her heart. God, he'd missed that hand. "Always," he said, his throat tight, his own heart patched and bursting. "Always."

Hotel d'Aubusson, Paris, France
September 1901

HONEYMOONING IN PARIS, they lay together in bed. Sophie had taken him to see the home where she had raised Lucas, into Notre Dame, to the Louvre. Eiffel's Tower rose to majestic heights outside their open hotel window. Tomorrow they would begin their journey to Aberdeen, to look at horses and choose an Aberdeen-Angus bull for the old man and Uncle Bradley just as Ranger had dreamed of doing all those years ago.

"If it hadn't been for Cookie knowing French, you would not have known what happened to me," Sophie said. "I would not have been able to speak with you. Do you think it would have been the same between us?"

"I don't know. It's only because of him that I let you ride that wall-eyed mare, so maybe not."

"You only love me for my riding skills," she said and pooched her lower lip out in a pout.

"I loved you already," he declared, rolling up onto his elbow to look down upon her face. "I told Cookie you were gorgeous after he told me about your father."

"What did that have to do with anything?"

Ranger laughed and then kissed her. She was still gorgeous. When they broke for air, he said, "That's what he said."

"Where is he now, Darrien, do you know?"

Shaking his head, Ranger ran a hand up under her hair. He hadn't remembered the cook's name until she said it. "Nope. We asked him to come back for the spring drive, but he never showed. Never saw him again. I asked around a little the following year, but none of the cowboys coming in had seen him or knew where he might be, although he was good at the work. No one seemed to know him at all."

"He was educated," she said. "Maybe he went to work in a restaurant. Maybe he's here in Paris right now."

"He'd be an old man, by now. Maybe he sold that sourdough starter he had and made a fortune. Those were the best biscuits I ever had."

"Ever?" Sophie said.

"Ever."

"How'd you like the best croissant in the world, ever?" she said.

"Do you know where those might be?"

She sat up. "I do. Let's go."

Ranger pulled her back down, her black hair falling like a curtain around his head. He studied the bright, happy gleam of her dark eyes. She was older, of course, but age hadn't dimmed her beauty or lowered her zest for life. "I'd marry you every day, you know?"

"I know," she said.

"I would've waited a lifetime for you."

"I know," she said and took him down again into that glorious world that they first made in the long tough grass along the banks of the Pecos, with the bawl of the cattle and distant howl of coyotes singing to them in the dark, flame-streaked night.

AUTHOR'S NOTES – ELLE ANDREWS PATT

THE ACTUAL EXISTENCE of the American "wild west" was quite short. The cattle drive era lasted a bare twenty years. Following the Civil War, the country was beef-starved, except for Texas, where Longhorns had been wandering feral and breeding more of themselves. Longhorns could be purchased for as little as four dollars a head. Enter the cattle drives to other markets for stiff profits. Once railroad lines began to spider-web across the country, providing employment for thousands, transport of cattle became the cheaper alternative to sometimes dangerous months of slow walking and night-time grazing of spooky large animals.

And what of the horses of the west? Without the unsung wranglers on the drive, the cowboys who handled and cared for the horses, cattle drives would be impossible. As with many other progressions, the Europeans ushered in gentler ways of handling and riding horses well before the "West" as Americans know it existed. The cowboys who heeded their own intuitions, learned a few "tricks" from Native Americans, and had some knowledge of the techniques of "schooling" developed by the French and Spanish riding academies gave rise to the modern American methods of "Natural Horsemanship" after a couple of savvy cowboys capitalized on the techniques they learned from older horsemen who had lived on horseback. The dissemination of this information to the wider public keeping horses for recreation has greatly enhanced the lives and welfare of many, many horses in the Unites States and around the world.

History.net, texasalmanac.com, historytoday.com, and ncbi.nlm.nih.gov are good starting points for delving into the history of cattle drives and modern horsemanship.

—*EAP*

KNOWLEDGE IS POWER

T.L. Woolsley

I

1922, New Orleans

The cold air blowing off the Mississippi River would have chilled Lily had she been susceptible to such. As it was, she drew her coat tighter around her to mimic the actions of others nearby.

"Watch it, sister!" someone snapped as she stepped onto the streetcar and squeezed in. The car was packed with people bundled in bulky coats. Lily murmured an apology and wriggled into the only empty spot she could find. The vehicle started with a lurch and a ringing bell. Lily swayed to one side and struggled to stay upright. No one moved aside to give her room, so she resorted to a tenuous grasp on an overhead rail she could barely reach.

She rode until the conductor called out a stop and the car jolted to a halt. Lily decided to walk for a while. No one moved, despite her desperate pushes, until she placed her heel on a leather-covered instep and shifted her weight onto that foot. The owner of the foot yelped, but moved away. A path appeared, and she exited just before the doors closed.

She stepped off on a wide boulevard with no sidewalks. It was paved, in a way, in hard crushed shells. Motor vehicles and horse-drawn wagons shared the road. Lily joined the other pedestrians, careful to avoid both.

Sweeping his hat off, a man on the path stepped aside to allow her to pass. She moved past him, eyes wide. Belatedly, she remembered to bob her head and cast her eyes down to appear grateful. Everyone else ignored her. Lily took in the sights and the sounds of the city as she strode. *Need to understand. What is this place? These people—what are they like?*

Most of the people she saw looked very much like those she had seen over the centuries—small, thin, some of them stooped over and hobbling from a life of hard work and pain. Some, though, walked with energy in their steps. A man tipped his hat merrily at a group of women passing him on the sidewalk, and young women in their short dresses, draped in gaudy jewelry, giggled together as they entered an alley.

The community, though—so different from Europe! Many of the cities she had seen across the ocean were still devastated by the Great War, with scattered rebuilding efforts. The countryside had been cleaner and largely untouched, although France's great meadows and fields were still chopped up by deep trenches that zigzagged for miles.

Now she was here, in this new place. New Orleans. It was very unlike old Orleans when she had lived there. So much was different. *I am to observe. Do not interfere unless absolutely necessary.*

She had watched the Bartletts board their train. Although Mr. Bartlett had made a good living lecturing in Europe before he died, Mrs. Bartlett would now look after her own children while living with her sister in Vermont. Herman and little Muriel had given Lily fierce goodbye hugs, Herman trying hard to be a "big boy" and not cry, while Muriel's clasp left telltale moisture on Lily's coat shoulder.

Now Lily, too, had to move on. What was this country, this city like now? She had decided to remain a young woman. The United

States would give her a different perspective on the life of a young woman at this time.

The architecture reminded her of France. The people were more casual than the French, but the rice boiling, beans simmering, and bread baking still harkened to a different culture.

Her shoes crunched clumps of dried mud along the street's coarse path mile after mile, her heart uncertain of what she searched for. She would recognize it when she saw it. Houses and small shops filled some blocks, while other tracts of land were turned to vegetable gardens. Every mile or so, the feel of the place shifted ever so subtly, and Lily understood that she had left one neighborhood behind and entered another. She knew she walked a suburb of New Orleans, but had lost track of which one.

Then she found it. She went into the office front of a hulking building three stories high and pointed to the sign in the window.

The woman at the counter nodded. Her hair was cut short, in a style called a "bob." A flowered dress hung well above her ankles in what would have been a daring fashion statement less than ten years prior. Makeup, including penciled eyebrows, dark red lips ringed in a bow-shape, and heavy rouge on white powder, defined her face. "You want ta see Mistah Thomas—uh, Mistah Thomas Alexandre. Not here right now."

"I'll come back later," As Lily turned to go, the woman said, "Ya can wait for him, if ya want ta. Just went ta lunch. Back before long." She smiled, but her neatly shaped eyebrows drew down and she glanced from side to side. Lily caught the briefest emotion—agitation? Fear? It was hard to tell. Lily decided to act as if it were the latter.

She smiled back at the woman and remembered to open and close her eyes rapidly. "Thank you, I will stay." She held out her hand. "I'm Lily Brown."

The woman took Lily's hand in hers, and Lily felt cold, chapped skin covering delicate bones. "Helen O'Neill." Helen's smile was shy this time. "I do some of the deliveries for Mistah Thomas. Just the light stuff—taking bills ta people, or packages ta the post office or the train station."

A door at the front of the office opened with a bang and a man marched through. He looked, Lily thought, like an exclamation point: broad shoulders and beefy arms, but narrow hips and tiny feet clad in small black boots. His wavy black hair stood at ends from the wind outside. "Beat it, bitch," he growled to Helen. "Sam's got a deliv'ry for ya."

Helen paled and exited through a back door without another word. *Ah, the source of fear.*

Lily stood and stuck out her hand. "Mister Alexandre?"

The man laughed, revealing a mouth full of crooked teeth and breath redolent of tobacco, onions, and garlic. "Ain't hardly. Who are you?"

"Lily Brown. I'm here to apply for the bookkeeper position."

"Ha! Mistah Thomas ain't gonna hire no broad. Need a man who can do numbahs. You go home, now. Ah tell him you was here." He opened the back door through which Helen had disappeared.

Lily sat in one of the wooden chairs lining the wall. "I'll just speak to him myself, thank you."

The man whirled back. "Ah tol' you ta scram!" He stood over Lily, hands clenched into fists.

Lily lifted her chin, a move she'd seen Herman make once or twice when he was being defiant. She said nothing, and stared into space.

The lobby door behind Lily creaked opened. Lily and the brute turned from each other to see a slight man with grey hair step in. Steel-rimmed glasses did not hide brown eyes crinkled at the corners with crow's feet. "Here now, Del! What's going on?"

"Nothin', Mistah Thomas," he said as he turned to the newcomer. "Jus' greetin' a guest."

Mr. Thomas caught the big man's eyes with his. "Sure you were," he said softly. "Now go out back and help Sam unload that truck. Tell Helen to come up to the office when she's got the papers."

After Del left, the man turned back to Lily. "I'm sorry about that

—Del doesn't usually work up front. I'm Thomas Alexandre. Can I help you?"

She stood and offered her hand. "My name is Lily Brown, and I am here about the bookkeeping job."

His eyebrows rose a bit and he shook her hand. "If you would, please follow me."

The door in the back of the office led to a warehouse. Deep, wide wooden shelves were bolted to each wall. Ropes dangled to the floor from pullies affixed to the rafters above. A rough staircase to the right led to a third level. Two wide, barn-like doors led outside.

Mr. Alexandre turned left and motioned for Lily to proceed ahead of him onto a flight of stairs along one wall. He followed until the second-floor landing, then opened the door for her. The office, lined with windows overlooking the cavernous space below, ran the width of the building.

An older black man swept the floor in the office. A boy in his teens nodded at Mr. Thomas and mumbled, "Good afternoon, sir," before moving further into the office, a sheaf of folders in his hand. Mr. Alexandre guided Lily to one end of the office where a cluttered wooden desk sat, cordoned off by dark wood filing cabinets. *His office staff is entirely male. And yet, they are all different—in size, in color, in social station. Humans always group themselves in predictable ways.*

"Now then, can I get you a cup of coffee, Miss Brown? No? If you don't mind, I'll get one for myself, then." He shuffled toward a narrow table. "This wind and wet weather goes right through me this time of year."

His saucer and cup perched on the edge of the desk, Mr. Thomas settled into his chair. The coffee aroma permeated the office and gave it a welcoming atmosphere. "What kind of experience do you have in bookkeeping, Miss Brown?"

They talked a bit, centering on Lily's business or manufacturing experience. No, she had never worked in a shipping business before, but she had done bookkeeping for her uncle's pharmacy. She made it a point to add that she could take dictation and had excellent penmanship.

Mr. Thomas waved these skills away. "That won't be necessary for this position, Miss Brown, but thank you. I need someone who can keep up with payments and invoices and balance the books." *Interesting. Mr. Thomas only seems concerned about whether I can do the job. Wonder why Del thought otherwise? A threat to his position?*

He cocked his head to one side and pursed his lips. "Why don't we give this a try for a week or so? If we both think it's a good match, you've got the job. If it's not right for you, then just say so, and we can part on good terms."

"You have a deal, Mr. Alexandre."

"Call me Mr. Thomas—everyone does. And welcome to Alexandre Shipping."

LILY GLANCED AT THE CALENDAR. February in New Orleans was warmer than February in most of Europe and much of the northern hemisphere, for that matter. Perhaps 1922 would simply be a warmer year.

"Here ya go, Lily," Helen said, handing a wad of money to her new co-worker. "From Mistah Houlihan over in Gentilly."

Lily rifled through it with the sure hands of someone with long practice. "Helen, this is wrong." She shuffled the money again, this time taking the time to arrange the bills by denomination and ensuring that they all faced the same way.

"What do ya mean?" Helen stared at her. "Del gave it ta me. Said he got it from Sean, the driver."

"Three dollars are missing," Lily said slowly. "Here's the invoice." She unfolded the paper that had been wrapped around the money. "See? We were due sixty-three dollars and twelve cents, and we credited Mr. Houlihan's twenty-dollar deposit ..." Lily's index finger traced the figures at the bottom of the invoice.

Helen did not even glance down. "If you say so, Lily." *Can she count? Why would she take my word on such an important matter?*

"Go ask Del if he counted it when he got it from Sean."

Lily glanced up. Helen's lips were set tightly. "Not me. I want ta live. I got me a date ta go dancing this Saturday."

Lily grasped the invoice and the money tighter. "I'll go ask him myself."

Helen put a hand on Lily's arm, strong, rough hands holding fast. "Don't. Ya don't know what he's like. Wait until Mistah Thomas gets here. He'll ask Del."

Lily pulled her arm away and turned away without a word.

She found Sean in front of the flatbed truck, sleeves rolled above his elbows. He had just grasped the starter crank when she strode up. He stood and swiped strawberry blond hair out of his eyes. "Eh? Can I help you, miss?"

She held out her hand. "Lily Brown. I'm the new bookkeeper."

Sean wiped his hands off on his overalls before gingerly pumping her arm up and down. "Sean Mallory."

"Did you bring in the shipment and payment from Mr. Houlihan over in Gentilly?"

"Yes, ma'am." He jerked a thumb over his shoulder at several men unloading barrels. "Got that stuff for Mr. DeCorte to make his dyes."

"Did you count the money when you received it?"

"Oh yes, ma'am. Mr. Thomas told all us drivers to do that when we're right in the customer's building. That way there ain't no mistakes." He looked up at the rafters for a moment, where dust motes danced in the beams of light coming through the big warehouse door. "Let's see. Mr. Houlihan owed eighty t'ree and twelve, 'cause Mr. Thomas said Mr. H paid twenny when he placed the order." He faced Lily and bobbed his head as he named figures. "So I counted sixty t'ree and twelve when I picked up today—t'ree twennies and t'ree ones, plus a dime and two pennies." He smiled through the blond-and-red stubble on his face. "I got a good mem'ry."

Lily smiled back. "Thanks, Sean."

She made her way back upstairs, careful to avoid the loading dock where Del might be working.

II

"Put ya finger here," Helen commanded.

Lily obeyed. She watched, eyes wide, as Helen tied string around the package and knotted it above Lily's finger.

"Okay, when I get it close, you pull ya finger out real fast."

Lily nodded. In seconds it was done.

Helen gave Lily a quick smile. Lily blinked, then smiled back. She had settled well into her new job, she thought. After having been there for more than a month, she had made friends with some of her coworkers. *Observe and evaluate. What is 'absolutely necessary?' How will I know, here in this new place?*

"Just a minute," Helen said. "I can't forget the letter. Goes under the string." She took a sheet from the table and glanced at it. "Oh, no. Mistah Thomas misspelled Mistah Brunnann's name again. He always forgets the second 'n' in the middle." As she glanced up at Lily, Helen's blue eyes narrowed. "Would ya re-type it for him, please? Package has ta be delivered today, and I'm ready ta take it."

"Sure." Lily placed three sheets together: letterhead, carbon paper, and onion skin, then rolled them into the big Underwood perched on a table.

Heavy footsteps thudded on the stairway, the vibrations more noticeable than the sounds in the second-floor office. Del stepped in, odors mingling from his unwashed body and the short, fat stogie jutting from his mouth.

Him again.

"You got them papers?" The wave of air from four mere words bore a smell of grain alcohol and tooth decay, mixed with smoke from the stogie. He grabbed the finished letter from Helen's hand.

"Wait! That's not the paper ya need!"

Del held it above his head before she could grab it. "Who says? What'll happen if I take it to da pharmacy wit me?"

"Nothing will happen. They'll just wonder why ya gave them the wrong papers. They're almost ready. You'll have ta wait just a minute."

Del pushed his face up to hers. Helen leaned backward as far as she could. "I don't *wanna* wait. I gotta deliv'ry to make."

Helen swallowed and turned her head aside.

Perhaps I could say something. Lily typed as fast as she could. "Here," Lily said to Helen, yanking the finished paper from the typewriter. "Here's the letter you need." Helen managed to slide away from Del and glanced over the letter.

"What about Mr. Thomas's signature? He won't be back until tomorrow."

"Ah can sign it," Del announced.

I doubt that.

He snatched the letter from Helen and crossed to a nearby desk. Del jerked a drawer open and grabbed a pen. "Where do the signatooah go?"

"I don't think …"

"O'course ya don't t'ink." He grabbed Helen by the hair and pulled her to the desk. "You a moron! Now where does the signatooah go?"

Is this 'absolutely necessary?' He is hurting her.

Her hair still in his fist, she stood on tiptoe to relieve the pain. She pointed. Del released her hair with one hand, only to snap a blow directly onto Helen's face with the other. She flew backwards and crashed to the floor. Lily rushed to Helen's side.

"'m aw right," Helen mumbled from a lip that still bore the marks of Del's knuckles. Blood coated her teeth.

Del focused on the paper in front of him and grasped the pen. He set his teeth in the stogie, then narrowed his eyes as he drew the signature. Mr. Thomas's signature was plain, consisting of only a few loops. Del exhaled and set the pen down. "See? Don' that look like Mistah Thomas write it?"

Neither woman spoke. *He can draw well enough to mimic that signature. But is he literate at all?*

"Now get me mah papers!" Del ground out from around the stogie.

Helen clambered to her feet. She took the papers off a desk and thrust them at him. Her eyes caught his and for a moment Lily thought the other woman would say or do something. Then Del turned and left the office, his heavy boots telegraphing his movement down the stairs.

Observe and … In the echoic silence left behind, Lily spoke. "Why do you let him hit you?"

"What can I do? He's bigger than me."

Lily considered that for a moment. "Does Mr. Thomas know?"

"Don't think so. Del's sneaky. Mistah Thomas ain't around most o' the time."

"What about the other men?"

"They never around when Del comes up here. They stay in the warehouse." She brushed by Lily, her lip swelling. "C'mon, we gotta get this invoice ready for the pharmacy. They gotta new shipment coming in next week, and Mistah Thomas won't send it ta them if they ain't paid this one."

Helen helped Lily fold letters and invoices, insert them into envelopes, and seal them. They worked side by side, speaking now and then about their work.

Lily noticed Helen's bruises blooming on her face, the swelling lip growing in size.

Helen paused at one point, hand on her darkening cheek.

"Does it hurt?" Lily asked.

The other woman started, as if caught by the question. "No—no, it don't."

"I'm sorry he hit you."

"'s okay, I tell ya."

"Mr. Thomas seems like a nice man. If you only tell him—"

"Leave it alone, will ya?" The edge in her voice had an undercurrent of pain and embarrassment.

Too much. Must be more delicate. "Of course."

After a moment, Helen sighed. "Ya right, of course. Mistah Thomas would do something, if he knew. But I think Del's related ta him or something. He never gets in trouble for anything he does. A lotta time Mistah Thomas don't even know. Nobody tell him."

Lily was silent for a moment. *Ah. More information. Familial relationships imply …* Lily took a breath. "Do you think someone is being mean to Del?"

Helen's eyebrow's rose into her dirty-blond hairline. "Him? Nah, I think it's the other way around!"

"Maybe he's being mean to you because someone has been mean to him."

Helen smirked. "He was born mean."

"No one is born mean, surely …"

Helen shook her head. "I dunno, Lily …"

"I wonder if someone was nice to Del, would it change him?"

This time Helen snorted. "I think the only thing that will change Del is a priest, or maybe a … a bigger, meaner man than him!"

Lily said softly, "Maybe. It seems to me that he might be a different man if someone cared about him."

"Huh! No fear of that happening. I wish he was dead."

Lily stared at her. "Do you mean that?"

"Yes, I do! He's a brute, and I'll bet I'm not the only one he abuses. The world'd be better off without him."

Lily blinked. *Observe and study. Absorb. Understand, if possible.*

III

"THAT SMELLS GOOD!" Helen said, "Smells like spring."

"What does?" Lily was just coming in for the day as Helen emerged from the warehouse in the back. Lily breathed deeply. She smelled sweat and sawdust, the exhaust from the truck just backing in, the outhouse in the back yard, and a sharp, plant-like smell. "What is it?"

"Wintergreen," Helen replied. "Mistah Dunn, the pharmacist, orders it sometime. He makes medicines with it."

Lily blinked. "I see." She climbed the staircase to the office, Helen following.

"Got such a clean smell compared to some of the other things we get 'round here. Too bad it won't be spring for a couple of weeks yet."

A distant voice caused them both to turn. Del ran across the warehouse floor, yelling. He tripped and would have fallen if he hadn't caught himself on a support post. "I'm going to get you!" he roared at the top of his lungs. His dark hair was soaked, plastered against his head.

Him again. He has a bigger presence than his position would imply.

The men unloading the truck scattered as Del lowered his head and ran at first one, then the other. His fists balled tight, he took a swing at the biggest man, but his blow missed by so much he overbalanced and fell to the floor. Del lay quiet for a moment, his chest heaving.

"Is he … ?" one man asked.

"I dunno."

"I ain't get close enough ta find out," someone else called down from a crate on which he'd taken refuge.

"What's going on here?" Mr. Thomas emerged from the second-floor landing. His voice carried throughout the warehouse.

"Del got ossified again," a man explained.

Mr. Thomas descended the stairs slowly. "Anyone hurt?"

"Nossir. He passed out onna floor heah."

Del's prone form snored softly. Mr. Thomas shook his head. "A couple of you fellows need to get him up. Put him in the usual spot so he can sleep it off."

One man stooped down and gathered a handful of straw that had fallen off the truck. "We'll draw straws to see who gets the honors this time."

Casting lots. Apparently, the one with the shortest straw must do the unpleasant task.

"Not me," someone said as Lily and Helen followed Mr. Thomas back up the stairs. "I did it las' time an' he almos' get me in da jaw when he wake up halfway dere."

THAT EVENING, a stream of people flowed from the streetcar and trudged down the road with a gait common to workers everywhere. Now and then a truck or a horse passed them. Lily placed her feet carefully on the crushed oyster-shell road so as to preserve the leather on her shoes as long as possible.

She considered Del's interaction with Helen—why did she not

defend herself? Yes, the man was larger, but all humans were vulnerable if one simply knew and exploited the weak points. *Observe. But what if I do not understand?*

Lily thought of Helen's ladylike hands and marveled at their strength. She had seen the woman help the men load and unload trucks in the warehouse when needed. Helen delivered papers and packages in all sorts of weather without complaint; there was no question about her physical stamina. *Here, now, females can compete with the males on almost every task. And yet they do not seek to do so. I wonder why? Does this have anything to do with being a 'lady?'*

Lily cleared her mind as she mounted the steps to the Seiler house, where she and a few others took room and board with an older couple. Old Mr. Harrod had just risen from a chair on the wide porch and held the door for Lily as she approached. He smiled and nodded. "Miss Brown." He shuffled toward the dining room.

"Not yet, Mr. Harrod," Martha Seiler said to him. "Supper will be at six o'clock sharp, as always." Then she bustled back into the kitchen.

Undeterred, Mr. Harrod stood in the dining room consulting his pocket watch. He peered near-sightedly at the grandfather clock in the nearby parlor and worked to reset his watch.

Lily trotted up the stairs to her third-floor bedroom to change. Martha Seiler had firm ideas about women wearing "work clothes" to the evening meal. "Always dress like a proper lady at each meal, Miss Brown," Mrs. Seiler had said. "You must woo your husband over every day, if you wish to keep him close to home."

I must fit in. The tiny bedroom felt close and stale. She opened the lone small window to let in fresh air. By the time she emerged and descended to the dining room, other lodgers had also returned from work or errands and prepared to dine as well. She heard the grandfather clock chime six times as she glided into the dining room.

A Negro woman set a large tureen on the table next to the ladle. Martha Seiler glanced around the table and nodded once sharply to the Negro. *This dark-skinned woman cooks, but Mrs. Seiler prides herself on her meals. How much cooking does Mrs. Seiler actually do?*

The dark woman trundled to the parlor and announced, unnecessarily, "Dinna!" The assembled lodgers who had lounged in the parlor, waiting for the announcement, made their way to the dining table.

Mr. Seiler spoke a ritual prayer, to which some of the boarders chanted along.

Cooked kidney beans filled the tureen nearly to its rim. A ham bone peeked out, its bony color changed to light tan from the hours of cooking. A deep aroma that spoke of onions, bell pepper, and celery wafted throughout the lower floor. Lily had learned, from her first unfortunate encounter with the dish, to look for the bone and the occasional bay leaf. *Not edible, only for flavor,* she had noted.

Lily added a scoop of rice on the top of the beans, as the others did, and accepted a serving of greens as well. *Brassica oleracea, Acephala group. A relative of cabbage and broccoli. High in nutrients and fiber.*

She forced her mind away from the nutritional analysis and focused on the conversation around the table.

"How was your day, Miss Brown?" Mr. Ellis asked. He was the only single male under the age of 60 who lodged at the Seiler's, and Lily had an inkling that he was interested in her on a social level beyond their shared lodging. She suspected that it had much to do with the fact that she was the only single female under the age of 60 who lodged at the Seiler's. *Observe. Do not interfere unless absolutely necessary. Although a sexual liaison would certainly give me more opportunity to observe.*

"Someone at work was ossified—er, drunk, today." *Must remember which group uses which terminology.*

All conversation stopped. Mr. Harrod froze, his hand still poised with the ladle for his helping of beans.

"What happened?" Mrs. Seiler said at last.

"Oh, he lost consciousness. The men in the warehouse had a place where he could sleep until he wakes again."

"How disgraceful," Mrs. Seiler said. "To make anyone work with a man who is weak like that. I'm so glad that alcohol consumption is illegal now. So many families have been ruined by that devil's brew." *Devil's brew. Interesting.*

"I suppose he will be fired," Mr. Seiler said slowly.

"I do not know. Apparently he has done this before."

Mrs. Seiler shook her head. "Perhaps someone could encourage that man to come to mass once he has sobered up. It would do him good to be among good Christians."

"Unless he takes Communion," Mr. Ellis pointed out.

"That is *sacramental* wine," Martha Seiler replied. "It has the presence of Jesus Christ Our Lord, and as such is not an intoxicating substance. If anything, it could turn that poor many away from drink forever."

Does she really care about Del? About his soul? She has never met the man.

The Negro woman burst back into the dining room, causing the door to the kitchen to swing wide. She whispered urgently into Mrs. Seiler's ear, hands death-gripping the chair back.

Mrs. Seiler drew away from the dark woman. "Yes, go," she said with a casual flip of her hand. The other woman swept back out of the room. Martha Seiler caught Lily's eye, then nodded once. "Lily, I shall require your assistance in the kitchen after supper."

Lily blinked. "I . . . I will do what I can."

Mrs. Seiler shrugged. "You only need to help wash the dirty dishes. It shouldn't take too much time."

"I . . . don't know how."

Mrs. Seiler stared back at her. The sounds of cutlery on plates, shuffling feet, and quiet conversation stilled. The other boarders stared at Lily.

Feeling the gazes on her, Lily continued. "I—when I traveled in Europe, we . . . ate in hotels. I don't . . . know how to wash dishes."

The other diners studied their plates. No one spoke.

Martha Seiler put up her chin. "Then you shall learn tonight. You will need to know if you should ever get married, Miss Brown. Some day you will be the lady of the house."

Why me? Because I am female? Or because I am the youngest?

"WHERE THESE GOIN'?" Del stood in the office, his grimy shirt buttoned to the neck. His ever-present stogie was unlit, but firmly in place to one side of his mouth. His unshaved face bore a sheen of sweat that rose to a shiny forehead. He appeared sober, but pale and uncomfortable. Now and then his forefinger rose to tug at the collar of his shirt.

Lily, the only other person in the office, glanced at the papers in his hands. "Give them to Sean. He can take them when he drops off that shipment of paint down at the port."

Del waved the stogie. "Nah, ahm sp'osed to go downtown an' pick up the money from da pharmacist. Wass'is name? Dunn, dassit."

Lily took the papers back. "Helen will do that. Mr. Thomas said you're to deliver from now on, or go to the postal office, but not pick up any mon … thing," she amended quickly. *Careful.*

Del flushed, first red, then purple. Lily had heard that he had been a terror downstairs after he awoke from his drunken rage four days earlier, but once the hangover eased he had turned into a model citizen—"At least, as close to it as he ever gets," Sean had confided to her. "He does this alla time. Gets all tanked and causes a ruckus, den once he gets sober—really sober—goes to mass an' confesses and cleans up for a while. Mr. Thomas, he big on givin' people second chances. If he wasn't Mr. Thomas' nephew, Del'd be gone." Sean had paused a moment before muttering, "I'd tossed his ass—s'cuse me—bee-hind out a long time ago."

Sean is good at amending his words and actions for the situation.

Del leaned over Lily, his breath thick with the smell of the stogie. "Ah . . . go . . . where evah . . . ah . . . want, bitch!"

She looked him in the eye. He had blue eyes—cold as steel. Her voice, even and quiet, nevertheless had force behind it. "No." *He will react. I must be ready.*

In the corner of her eye, she saw him draw back a fist. Her own small hand reached his body first, her stiffened fingers finding their mark at Del's solar plexus merely inches from her. His belly was soft and doughy and yielded easily to her strike.

"Ooof!" He folded in half, arms cradling his abdomen. Del staggered backward on impossibly tiny feet, fighting for air, mouth opening and closing like a fish. His face paled, then turned red on its way back to purple again.

Time to diffuse the situation. "I do have a delivery for you, though." Eyes still on Del, Lily took a stack of envelopes from a nearby desk. "These need to go to the postal office today." *Give him a chance to recover his dignity.*

He uncurled a bit, still gasping, his hands feebly taking the bundle. His glare promised trouble later, but Lily remained calm as he left.

Helen bustled in a half hour later, wearing a plain grey dress and a lace veil on her head. "What did I miss?" she asked as she peeled off white gloves and put her handbag down.

I must not tell Helen that Del tried to attack me. She will be even more frightened if she thinks I am vulnerable—and she will be ashamed if she knows I defeated him. "I sent Del to the post office to pick up the mail."

A grin spread over Helen's face. "Oh, goodie."

"Why?"

"I thought I'd find out for certain if Del's been taking some of the payment from the mail. You know how old Mistah Hall like ta mail cash? A friend of mine works for him, so she put together a thick brown envelope with his latest payment." She lifted one shoulder in a casual shrug. "We put a little gentian violet on the glue holding the envelope shut. If he breaks the seal and tries ta lick the glue ta re-stick it, we'll know."

Unbidden, information from her distant past came to mind. Once, a long time ago, she had learned some basic chemistry. *Gentian violet. Crystal violet. How odd. It is not made at all from gentians, crystals, nor violets. The name refers to its colour, being like that of the petals of a gentian flower. A slightly yellowish crystalline powder in its pure state. Blue-violet colour when dissolved in water. Or, most likely, saliva.* "What will you do if you catch him?"

"Tell Mistah Thomas."

"What will he do?"

Helen's chin rose. "Fire him, I hope."

. . .

LILY LOOKED up from a ledger as Mr. Thomas came in, humming to himself and sporting a toothpick in one corner of his mouth. He settled behind his desk to read the newspaper before tackling his usual paperwork regimen.

A few hours later, the office boy, Henry, came in. After a short greeting to everyone, he took a stack of papers and stationed himself at the filing cabinets, criss-crossing the office as he filed them. *Henry is Caucasian. Mr. Thomas is Caucasian—everyone here is Caucasian. Why?*

The only sounds in the office were the tick of the clock and the shuffle of papers. Occasionally Mr. Thomas sighed, then scratched his pen on paper. Henry quietly sorted papers on a desk while Lily reviewed the ledger from the previous month.

Helen broke the tableau when she stepped into the office, a swirl of cool, crisp air surrounding her. She strode behind the wall of filing cabinets and handed a bundle of papers to Mr. Thomas.

Back in the main room, she took her coat off, rubbing both hands together. "Got cold again last night!" she remarked to Henry and Lily.

"Yeah, it's sp'osed to be spring," Henry replied. "Nobody's ready for baseball with this kind of weather."

"It's just a blackberry winter," Helen reassured him. "Warm weather'll be here before ya know it."

"Hope so." Henry filed another sheet of paper and moved to the next filing cabinet.

"What is a blackberry winter?" Lily asked.

Helen shrugged. "Just that last gasp of Old Man Winter, when it gets cold late in the spring. Forces the blackberries to bud."

Mr. Thomas came in the main room and took his coat from the coat rack. He clutched a piece of paper and an envelope in one hand. "I've got to go away for a few days on a family emergency. I'll be back as soon as I can." His hands shook as he tried to draw on his coat with the letter still clutched in his hand, then put the letter down to slide his hand in. From across the worktable, Lily's glance showed only a few neatly handwritten words after "Dear Brother." One word was familiar to Lily: "consumption."

Then he was gone.

Helen stared at Lily and Henry. "Hope everything is all right."

Lily only nodded.

"Who will pay us at the end of the week?" Henry asked.

"It's only Wednesday," Helen said. "He may be back by then."

"Yeah, but what if he isn't?"

"I'll go ta his house and ask Mrs. Alexandre, if she hasn't gone with him," Helen replied.

The afternoon wore on in a slow grind. Henry finished his tasks and left for the day. Sam, the manager, locked the office for them and Lily took her leave with Helen, chatting as they descended the stairs along the warehouse wall to the first floor. Below, Sean and the others moved crates around so they could close the big doors for the night. Lily inhaled the smell of sawdust and the faint cooking aroma from homes near the warehouse. A part of her wondered if she would receive another 'homemaker' lesson from Mrs. Seiler tonight. *There are Negro servants, but she wants me to learn domestic skills. How interesting. And what does it truly mean to be a 'lady of the house?"*

Sean laughed, his voice ringing through the rafters of the warehouse. "Nah, 'm savin' mah pay to get married," he called in answer to someone's question. "Gonna get down on one knee one o' these days. Hey—" he broke off to speak to another man smoking a cigarette. "—take that outside. We got too much sawdust and hay in here fo' you to smoke in here."

"And alcohol," someone else said, pointing to a barrel behind him marked METHANOL with chalk.

Another time, another place, Lily remembered making a salve in a chemist shop. *Methyl alcohol. Wood alcohol. CH3OH in chemical terms. Many industrial uses, including making dyes and topical preparations with wintergreen, for pain relief. Toxic, even fatal, when ingested.*

The smoker nodded and strolled outside, sliding between the doors and the truck still parked halfway through the door.

Helen turned to slide through after the man; the space between the truck and the door filled with shadow. Then the shadow moved into the warehouse.

Helen took one step back, then another. The shadow followed.

Helen bumped into Lily. The shadow grabbed Helen by the coat and threw her to the packed-dirt floor.

"You," Del roared. "Get outta my way!" He glared around the warehouse at the men. "Who done it to me? Somebody *poisoned* me." His voice echoed off the crates and filled the spaces in the warehouse.

Him again.

Helen scrambled to her feet. Del grabbed her arm, swung her around. Through clenched teeth he growled, "Where you goin'? Ah need a doctor. Ah could be *dyin'*."

Observe. Do not interfere unless absolutely necessary.

Helen's head shook as she fought to get away from Del's rage.

"Stop it, Del," voices cried out. "Leave her alone."

Lily stepped around Del as men gathered around, but couldn't get close to him. Several men clawed at Del's arms, trying to get him to release Helen. Instead, he threw her down again. She landed hard, crying out after her head hit the floor.

"What are ya doin'?" Sean demanded, thrusting his face up to Del. "Ya don't do that to a lady!"

"Ah need a doctor, ah tell ya! Got poison all over my face! Somebody get me a doctor." He stepped into the waning light and tipped his head up so that the others could see the telltale purple on his chin. He stuck out his tongue to show that it, too, was a deep shade of purple.

"You ain't poisoned," Sean scoffed. "It's jus' ink or sometin'. You sure ain't dyin'." The other workers chimed in from a safe distance:

"Can't go around hittin' a lady."

"Ain't right, a man hurtin' a little lady like dat."

"Gotta ack a gentleman."

Lily gently cradled Helen's head. "Are you all right?"

Helen lay still, gulping air, then nodded slowly. Lily helped her sit up. Helen's breath steadied as she filled her lungs again.

Del took another step toward Helen, but several guys blocked the way. "Go home, Del," someone from the back called. "Sleep it off."

He whirled on his impossibly small feet. "Ah'm not drunk." A large hand waved dismissively at the crowd. "Ah, what the hell do you jays know, anyway?" He strode off.

IV

IN THE DARKNESS of the pre-dawn the next day, Lily trod carefully down the stairs from her third-floor room, coat draped over one arm. The other lodgers at the Seiler's home were not up until much later, and she did not want to wake them. *If I am quiet enough . . .*

She stopped at the front door to don her coat when a voice hissed at her.

"Miss Brown!"

Mrs. Seiler, dressed and in full make-up, bustled toward her. "Let me see your dress," she snapped.

Astonished, Lily stared. "I ... I beg your pardon?"

Agitated, Mrs. Seiler threw her hands in the air. "I see girls going everywhere in this city, wearing their dresses way too high, and putting on too much makeup—thankfully, you don't do that, dear—but I won't have any lodger of mine going out in those shameful dresses." She bent and checked the hem of Lily's frock under the coat, then stood, hands on her hips. "Well, I don't like it, but it's not too bad. You need to look for dresses that are longer, Miss Brown. You must be ladylike in your attire." She wagged her index finger in front of Lily's face. "It's not seemly for a young lady like you to wear something that. You need a dress that will cover your—your *limbs*, dear. You mustn't allow men to see them."

Lily wondered, idly, how much caffeine Mrs. Seiler had had that morning. "Thank you for your concern, Mrs. Seiler, but I am quite capable of choosing my own wardrobe. Many women are wearing their dresses above the ankle these days." *Much higher, in many areas of the world.* Lily realized that her tone was sharper than she had intended, but it did cut off the flow of words from the older lady.

Mrs. Seiler tut-tutted. "Well, as I said, I don't like it, but at least it's below your knees. Now when I was a young girl—"

"I really must be going, or I shall be late to work."

"Of course, of course. Maybe we can talk again tonight. You might consider sewing something …"

Thankfully, the door closed on any more remarks. Lily felt the tension leave her shoulders.

Lily met up with Helen as they made their way to Alexandre Shipping. Helen walked with her head down and her coat wrapped around her.

"How is your head?" Lily asked softly.

Helen shrugged. "Fine."

"What are you going to do?"

"Everyone saw it. Maybe Mistah Thomas will finally fire him."

They walked for a while in silence.

"I heard someone say that Del is Mr. Thomas's cousin," Lily said.

"I heard nephew." Helen paused. "Does it matter?"

"I guess not." Lily repeated the phrase she had heard someone else use.

The two women stopped at an intersection for a vehicle to pass. "If Mistah Thomas doesn't fire Del," Helen said—almost as if she were talking to herself—"I quit. This is too much." *Helen is willing to risk being unemployed for her own safety. She has found her limit.*

They greeted Sam as he unlocked the front door for the day, and made their way through the office. Both stopped at the bustle of activity in the warehouse, so odd for such a time of day. Unfamiliar men loaded trucks with barrels that sloshed as they landed in the bed of the truck.

Lily spotted Sean's familiar face. "What's going on?"

"Oh, uh—Hi, Miss Lily. Helen." Sean wiped his hand down his face, producing an audible rasp against a day-old beard. "We're, uh, moving some cargo for Mr. Thomas."

"How come ya so late today?" Helen demanded. "Ya usually here b'fore the sun."

Sean made a face. "Bulls all ovah th' place. Just got clear."

Lily cocked her head. "What are … bulls?"

"Miss Lily—this is a private shipment, you see—"

Helen grabbed Lily by the arm. "I'll explain. Sean, ya go take care of what ya gotta do. C'mon, Lily."

"But—but, Helen, I want to—" *Observe.*

"No, ya don't."

Upstairs, Helen dumped her coat and handbag on the big worktable. "Lily, pretend ya didn't see that stuff."

Lily stared, her face passive. "What do you mean?"

"I mean," Helen replied, her attention on pulling files out of a cabinet, "sometimes Mr. Thomas ships private merchandise out of here, and we don't butt our noses where they don't belong."

Do not make changes unless absolutely necessary . . . .

"Private merchandise?"

"That's all ya need to know."

Contraband, no doubt. Black market goods. Likely grain alcohol, from the sound of those barrels. Lily remained silent and bent to her work.

Mr. Thomas came in late, his face pale and gaunt. No one spoke to him beyond the customary, "Good morning." He took no lunch, but continued working.

When Del entered the office in the early afternoon, Mr. Thomas did a double-take at his appearance. "What happened to you?"

Del grunted. "Poison."

"How the hell did you eat poison?"

Del swelled up, his forehead reddening. "Ah was tricked!"

"Jesus!" Mr. Thomas stood and grasped Del's chin in his hands, moving it so the light showed the stains better. "Made you sick?"

"Naw."

"How'd you get it on your mouth? What'd you eat?"

"I doan know." Now the flush filled his cheeks. His eyes were glued to the floor.

Helen turned to the mail she had been sorting, her hands shaking.

Something is happening.

With a tick of impatience, Mr. Thomas let go of Del's chin. "I think you *do* know; you just don't want to say. Remember when you were three and got sick because you snuck in the pantry and ate too much of your momma's cake? You lied then, too, as I recall."

"I doan 'member."

"Hmm."

"Muh-maybe," Helen said in a low voice, "it came from the envelope ya opened."

"What?" Mr. Thomas and Del stared at her.

Helen raised her chin and spoke with more confidence. She looked Del in the eye. "Ya know, that envelope from Mistah Hall."

"Mr. Hall sent another payment?" Mr. Thomas's dark grey brows drew in over his glasses.

"I doan know wha' you talkin' 'bout!"

"Sure ya do," Helen purred. "That brown envelope that was glued shut. Ya picked it up the day before yesterday."

Del shrugged, the picture of innocence. "Bunch o' stuff in the mail."

Mr. Thomas looked expectantly at Helen. She gestured with her chin. "Mistah Thomas, ya must not have gone through the mail yet. It should be on ya desk."

He pawed through the small mound of paper. "Brown envelope …? Here's one from Mr. Hall." He flipped it over.

"Check the seal," Helen commanded.

"It looks . . . well, it's not sealed well—"

"Open it, sir," Helen said softly.

Mr. Thomas slid a finger between the flap and the envelope. It gave way easily. He tipped it up and a piece of paper and some paper money fell out. He glanced at the paper. Lily could read the scrawled note in Mr. Hall's familiar looping handwriting, "payment on account."

Mr. Thomas counted the bills. "Forty-two dollars."

"How much did he owe?" Helen asked.

Lily answered, "Eighty-two dollars."

"So? This proves nothing."

Silently Helen licked her forefinger and ran it along the envelope flap. Then she held Mr. Hall's note with one hand while she traced a line down the paper. A faint purple smear appeared behind the finger's path. *She is clever without appearing to be so.*

Her boss turned to Del. "Well?" His voice rumbled in a threatening tone. Del said nothing.

Mr. Thomas spoke to Del in a low voice. "You're a piece of shit, you know that, don't you? Not good for anything. Can't read, can't write, can't do anything. Worthless. Can't keep a job on your own, th' only reason you're eating is you're my brother's boy, so I'm stuck with you." He slid the paper from Mr. Hall across the desk toward Del. "Go ahead, tell me what it says. You can't can you? You know why, Del? Because you're stupid, that's why. Couldn't put brains in your head if we had a barrel o' them and a funnel. Just would run right out o' your head."

This explains a lot.

Del hung his head and slouched, coiling into himself as if he expected blows. "Ah—ah . . ."

"Shut up!" Mr. Thomas snarled. "Do you still have the money? Or did you drink it all?"

Del shook his head several times, the motion causing his whole body to shudder. Reluctantly he dug into his pocket and pulled out a wad of damp bills, which he thrust at Mr. Thomas.

"You piece of shit," his uncle said. "I should have drowned you long ago. Get out of my sight." Del slunk out of the office, closing the door with a quiet click.

Observe.

Mr. Thomas turned to the other workers. "Everyone get out. I can't deal with this right now. Get out of here and come back some other time." He made shooing motions as Lily and Helen filed out.

Outside the office, Helen grasped Lily's arm as they descended the stairs. "I'm buying ya a drink!"

"What? Why?"

"Cause we won!"

"He didn't get fired."

"Not yet. But Mistah Thomas is on ta him now, and it's only a matter of time. Maybe he'll leave us alone."

The two stepped out of the office and headed down the avenue. "Where do you want to go?" Lily asked. "There's a coffee shop on the corner."

"Not that kind of drink," Helen chuckled. "A *drink.* A real drink."

"I thought alcohol consumption was illegal."

Helen grinned. "I know a juice joint."

They walked several blocks before coming to a restaurant that was clearly one step above the cafés and diners that seemed to inhabit every street corner.

The maitre d' sat them at a small table. Lily noted that the ordinary workday dresses she and Helen had one were not remarkably different from what the other women wore. The men largely sported suits. Helen picked at her simple frock. "Wish I was wearin' my glad rags. We could go dancing."

Everyone seems to be having a good time.

They shared a small hand-printed menu. "Let's have the 'Lady's Afternoon Special," Helen told the waiter. She winked at Lily. "Friend of mine brought me here once."

Shortly the waiter came back bearing a plate covered in crackers and two kinds of sliced cheese. He placed a small coffee cup—a demitasse—in front of each woman.

"Eat a cracker and cheese first," Helen instructed. "It helps."

Lily did as she was told. Helen made a face as she did the same. The cheese was ordinary, the cracker slightly stale. "Well," she remarked, "We ain't here for the food."

Each took a tiny sip of the liquid in the cup. Lily found it to be much stronger than she had expected, and flavored with a hint of fruit. *Cherries, perhaps?*

Helen smiled at her. "Whadda ya think? Ain't this the cat's pajamas?"

Lily blinked. "It's . . . nice."

The other woman raised her cup to Lily. "A toast. Ta … justice!" *Is that what you call it?*

Lily copied the action as she had seen others do in the past. "To justice," she repeated. She looked around. "Is this where you went on your date?"

Helen shook her head. "Nah. He was a real flat tire. No money ta really paint the town red. I'm looking for someone who really knows how to treat a dame. Say—maybe ya want ta go out with me some Saturday. We'll find ourselves a couple of guys, have a real gay time."

Lily took another sip, felt warmth spread throughout her chest. "I don't know, Helen. My landlady is very strict."

"Like how?"

"Well, she made comments about how long my dress should be, and—"

Helen laughed, and the crockery jumped as she slapped their food tray, drink in her hand. "Go on."

"And, excuse me, but she told me I mustn't wear any makeup, and my hair—"

"Oh, a real bluenose, eh? Yeah, I once had a room with a girlfriend of mine. Her mother was an odd bird like that. Mrs. Grundy had nothing on her, let me tell ya. Don't let that type get ta ya. Ya got ta go out and have yaself a good time."

By the time the drinks were finished, the restaurant was crowded. Smoke hung under the ceiling, and the two women had to shout to make themselves heard.

"We bettah go," Helen said in a loud whisper, her words only a little slurred by the drink. After paying, the two made their way outside. The cool evening felt clean and crisp.

V

THEY WALKED ONLY HALF a block before Helen stopped suddenly, one hand on Lily's arm to stop her progress. "Oh, no!"

"What is it?"

"I left my wrap at the office. I have to go back."

Lily stared at her. "Do you think Mr. Thomas is still there? Or Sam? I have no key."

"No idea. He been workin' like crazy ever since he come back from visitin' his sister. But I gotta get that wrap—it's not really mine. I borrowed it from a friend and she needs it tonight. She takin' the early train ta visit her mama an'—I just gotta get it back. C'mon."

Snatching up the skirt of her dress, Helen trotted as fast as she could along the sidewalk. Lily hurried to keep up.

Dusk was falling as they approached the office, crickets singing and mockingbirds chirping to one another as they sought a place to rest for the night.

Panting, Helen tried the front door. "Nuts! It's locked. We'll have ta go 'round the back and see if the warehouse is still open."

The sand road that ran beside the building was tricky to navigate in their office shoes, but they made it to the back with nothing more than some sand clinging to their stockings and a little down their shoes.

One of the delivery trucks was parked in the warehouse, and the warehouse door stood ajar. The women slipped in.

"'lo, Sean." Helen stood in the semi-darkness of the warehouse. "Thank goodness you still here. I need ta get into the office."

"Where y'all been?" The lanky man held his hat in his hand. "I was jus' gettin' ready to go home."

"Th' big cheese let us out early. I just remembered I left my wrap in the upstairs."

Sean gazed impassively at Helen. "Miss Helen, I don' have a key to dat office up dere. I jus' have th' one to this warehouse here."

Helen stamped her foot in frustration. "Oh, nuts. I don't wanna go find Mistah Thomas ta unlock it, especially in the mood he was in this afternoon."

Sean brightened, his face half-obscured in the shadows. "Mebbe th' key to th' warehouse works on th' office door, too. I nevah tried it."

"Would ya try it, Sean?" Helen asked. "I'm going ta stay down here long enough ta get the sand out of my shoes." She leaned on a support column as she worked one shoe off her foot with the other hand. Lily held her steady as Helen shook the offending grit onto the hay-strewn dirt floor.

Sean's heavy work books echoed as he tromped up the stairs. In the quiet of the warehouse, broken only by the faint sound of Sean's keys jingling as he tried one after the other, the two heard a distinct scraping sound.

Helen finished putting on her shoe. "What was that?"

"There's someone else here," Lily murmured to Helen as she brushed more sand off the sole of Helen's stocking-clad foot.

Lily peered into the shadows that darkened the wall that held deep shelves full of goods for shipping. Something moved.

"It's—" Lily strained to see. "It's a man!"

The movement increased until a figure separated from the gloom. The dim outline showed broad shoulders where he sat on the edge of a shelf, then hopped down. Del approached the two women, staggering a little.

Him again. I have observed him enough.

"Th' bitches," he said tonelessly. "Bitch A and Bitch B." He nodded at Helen first, then Lily. "Come ta ruin mah life some more."

Helen and Lily backed up, keeping Del in sight. Unseeing, Helen backed into a support column. Del's hands shot out to clutch her delicate neck. His face turned purple as he held his breath and squeezed. *Do not make changes unless absolutely necessary …*

Helen's hands clawed at Del's face, leaving a trail of blood as she scratched him. Her face blue, her neck displayed white outlines where Del's fingers pressed against her skin.

This is necessary. Lily tugged at one of Del's arms, but it wouldn't budge. She shrieked, "Sean! Sean!"

Sean's boots thunked down the stairs. "Miz Helen, none of these keys—"

The keys jangled as he dropped them. He dashed to where the three grappled. "Del!" Sean pulled on Del's fingers, trying to pry them away from Helen. "Stop it, Del!"

As if in a daze, Del did not seem to notice. "Ain't got no more money. M' uncle took it all away," he ground out from between his teeth. "'m stupid, he says. Got no brains, so I got no *money*!" He shook Helen as he said the last few words. Her eyes rolled up into her head.

Lily reached over Del's broad shoulders, grabbed his hair and pulled hard. *This is necessary.*

Del released Helen and whirled on Lily and Sean, face

contorted with rage. His eyes, blood-shot but rimmed with white, shone in a lone pale beam from the fading sunlight. "Don' *touch* me. I don' *like* it when people touch me."

Helen slumped to the floor.

Del lunged toward Lily, but one long side-step brought Sean in front of him. "Back off, Del!" His roundhouse punch knocked Del backward. The big man's head hit a support post with a dull thud and he lay still.

Sean stood over him, breathing hard, while Lily knelt and touched Helen's arm. Hair awry, Helen's every breath was a wheezing, tortured sound that moved the strands in front of her face. Color flooded her countenance.

"Is she all right?" Sean asked.

Lily nodded. "Him?"

"Jus' unconscious." He looked around. "Let's get outta here afore he wakes up."

Lily helped Helen to her feet, and the three made their way outside the warehouse door. Sean closed the big doors and locked them with a padlock. "That'll keep him outta trouble tonight, anyway." Sean set his battered newsboy cap on his head. "You ladies need help getting home?"

"No, thanks, Sean," Helen wheezed. "You go on."

By the time the two women made it to where their paths diverged, Helen was breathing and talking better. "No, really, Lily, I'm fine. There's no need to see me home."

"If you're certain …" Lily cocked her head to one side.

"I'm sure. See ya tomorrow."

Although still shaken, Helen's gait was steady as she made her way down the street.

I can no longer simply observe.

THE NEXT MORNING dawned hot and humid, with no breeze to cool things down or to keep the mosquitoes away. Lily spent most of her commute swatting and scratching. She imagined each blood-sucking insect as another of Mrs. Seiler's comments about her "lifestyle" and the argument she'd had with the woman the night before. Apparently, day-drinking and being out unaccompanied beyond dark was unacceptable to the older woman. "You smell of smoke," Martha Seiler had said, with an sour expression on her face. "Have you taken up smoking? Women should never smoke in public. It's not ladylike."

Splat. Lily brushed the crushed bug off her arm. *It might be time to consider moving on again.*

Helen seemed unbothered by the mosquitoes as she joined Lily for the last two blocks. Silent, she walked with her head down. She had tucked her hair behind her ears, and little makeup graced her face. The eyebrows appeared more natural, the rouge just a suggestion of healthy skin. *She is different than when I first met her.*

"How are you?" Lily asked.

"I'm all right, I guess."

"Last night sure was scary."

They stopped at a cross street. Helen gazed into the distance. "I gotta get a new job. That man is going to kill me if I don't."

"I can't blame you."

They crossed the street and entered Alexandre Shipping. A knot of men in the warehouse drew their attention right away.

"He got corked again," one of them said.

Lily and Helen pushed through the bodies and saw Del still lying on the ground.

"Move the palooka out of the way," Mr. Thomas said, his tone harsh. "We've got work to do. Soon as Sean gets here, have him run the truck over to the filling station."

Several of the men got Del to his feet. The lines on his face were already scabbing over where Helen had scratched him and a bruise bloomed on his jaw from where it had hit the support post. "Don' like bein' touched," he muttered, but clearly he was in no condition to struggle. They got him onto one of the deep shelves where he rolled over and lapsed once more into unconsciousness.

Mr. Thomas barked out orders. "You fellas, get ready for a delivery today. The rest of Mr. DeCorte's order is supposed to come in and I want the whole shipment in his hands before tomorrow."

He caught sight of Helen and Lily. "Oh, good morning, ladies. We have a lot to do this today, including all the work we didn't finish yesterday. Miss Brown, we need to invoice some customers right away." Lily nodded and started up the stairs. She could hear Mr. Thomas below her directing Helen.

"Miss O'Neill, we need to have those invoices in before the noon post, so I'll need you to deliver them a little later this morning. In the meantime, you check inventory on the Kipner order. That one will be going out tomorrow and I don't want the warehouse boys searching all over for the items that should go together. Last time we delivered to him, two barrels of crackers were left behind."

"Yes, Mistah Thomas."

"I'LL HELP YOU, if you like." Lily's smile was a welcome sight to Helen.

The items for Kipner order were, indeed, all over the warehouse. Helen found the missing cracker barrels on the very top shelf, three levels above the warehouse floor, and arranged to have them lowered down. The tinned food was on the second level, and Lily spotted the enormous jar of pickles that had just been delivered parked on a first-level shelf. She noted the pickles' location for the workers who would fill the truck for the next day's delivery.

The Kipner order was complete. "What did Mr. Thomas say was going out today?" Lily asked.

"Mr. DeCorte's order," Helen reminded her. "The bolts of cloth are coming in late today." They had been holding much of his order for weeks, only because he had paid in advance.

"Oh, there are the spools of thread," Lily called, pointing.

"Good." Helen made a note on a piece of paper.

"What else do we need for Mr. DeCorte?" Lily asked.

"Let's see. That stuff."

"That stuff" was the small barrel sitting one shelf above where Del where he lay softly groaning to himself. The chalked word METHANOL on the side was slightly smeared where hands had maneuvered it onto the shelf. It was not much bigger than the huge jar of pickles for the Kipner order.

"What does Mr. DeCorte use it for?" Helen asked.

"Most likely, to make dyes for the cloth he buys," Lily replied.

An incoherent shout from Del interrupted them. He seemed unaware of the noise he made, and once more lapsed into slumber.

Lily caught Helen's eye. "It's very handy, you know."

"That stuff?"

"Yes." Lily's gaze went to the deep shelves. "It has many uses, but some people mistake it for grain alcohol."

Helen said nothing.

"The problem is," Lily said softly as the two of them turned and walked away from the shelves, "it is poison. Methyl alcohol can cause nausea, blindness, delirium—even death."

"Oh?" Helen appeared to be mildly interested. "Sounds awful."

"Yes," Lily agreed. "It is a terrible way to die."

"HEY, SEAN!"

The lanky man ambled over. "Miss Helen," he said with a respectful dip of his head. "Are you feeling better today?"

"Yeah, Sean, thank ya." She pointed to the spools of thread. "You gonna deliver Mistah DeCorte's order this afternoon?"

"Yes'm, once the cloth come in. S'posed to be on the afternoon train."

"You goin' alla way ta Westwego tonight?"

"Yes'm. But it ain't no trouble."

"If you take it, you'd have to come all the way back here jus' to get back home, wouldn't ya?"

Sean shrugged. "I done it before."

Helen looked up at Sean, her bobbed hair falling away from her face. "Send Del with it."

Sean stood a bit straighter and his brow furrowed. "Del?" He glanced at the man lying supine on a deep shelf, rubbing his head.

"He lives out that direction."

Sean scratched his head. "Yeah, well, I nevah thought about

him takin' a delivery."

"He's sober enough. It'll get him outta ya hair and get the deliv'ry to Mistah DeCorte. He can drive the truck back here in the mornin'."

Sean glanced back at where Mr. Thomas stood, talking to other warehouse workers. "I guess I could …" He turned to go.

"Oh, Sean—"

He turned back briefly.

"Just make sure ya got all th' order on the truck before it leaves. Mistah Thomas'll have mah hide if you leave anything behind."

Sean's eyed the shelves stocked with merchandise. "Mr. DeCorte's order …" The barrel of methanol stood on the shelf directly above Del.

Sean caught Helen's eye. "Sure thing, Miss Helen," he said somberly. "I'll check it m'self. Wouldn't want you ta get in trouble."

VI

THE NEXT DAY dawned clear and humid, the moisture oppressive to humans and animals alike. Only a few birds sang as Lily trudged to the corner where she and Helen met.

"Hoo, it's hot." Helen fanned the skirt of her dress away from her body.

"Mrs. Seiler says that it will get worse."

"Yep. Summer in N'Awl'ns is like that."

When they entered the warehouse, a few men milled around, talking.

It felt emptier than usual. "Where is the delivery truck?" Lily asked.

One man shrugged. "Nobody knows. Sean musta took it to deliver to Mr. DeCorte yestiddy. He ain't here yet."

Helen opened her mouth to correct him, but at that moment Sean stepped in through the back door.

He saw the situation immediately. "Where's tha truck?"

"We thought you had it."

He shook his head. "I sent Del to Westwego. He's supposed to be back here this mornin'. We need to get the Kipner order out."

"Well he ain't here."

"Maybe he's just running late," someone offered.

"Yeah, that must be it," Sean said. "Give 'im a few more minutes."

Mr. Thomas arrived shortly and the information was repeated for him. He clenched his teeth. "Hope he didn't go on another bender. He could be anywhere down th' river."

"What about the Kipner order?" Sean asked.

Mr. Thomas gestured through the warehouse door. "See if you can get it all into my car, Sean."

In the office, a fan stirred the hot air and did little to cool the room. No breeze came through the open windows. In between balancing the ledger and typing out invoices, Lily fanned herself as she'd seen others do. The close room smelled of sticky humans and the peculiar odor of Mum deodorant. The hours dragged on.

Helen and Lily were discussing an upcoming order when Sean burst in. He stopped to close the door behind him, but went straight to Mr. Thomas's desk. His breathless words were loud enough for everyone in the office to overhear.

"He's dead, sir," Sean said.

"Who?"

"Del." The words were flat, with no inflection.

"How do you know?"

"After I delivered the Kipner order in your car, I went by his house. The truck was there, so I knocked on his door. No answer. I figgered he was jus' drunk, so I tried the knob. It wasn't locked—his front door, I mean—so I went in, callin' his name. Didn't want to surprise him. He was laid out on his bed. I thought he was jus' sleepin', Mister Thomas, I really did. But he wasn't. He was dead."

Mr. Thomas's voice was hushed. "I wonder what . . ."

Sean broke in. "It was that methanol, sir. He never made it Mr. DeCorte's. He had that little barrel of methanol next to the bed and about a third of it was gone. He must've drunk it."

All movement in the office stopped. Lily and Helen exchanged a glance.

"Why did you send Del to Westwego, anyway, Sean?"

Bony shoulders moved up and down. "He been givin' the ladies trouble, Mr. Thomas. I wanted ta get him as far away from them as I could. Mr. DeCorte paid for his stuff in advance, so I knew Del wouldn't need ta pick up any money. I never thought about the stuff in the barrel."

Mr. Thomas's fingers drummed on his desk for a moment. He sighed. "I'll go back to his house with you, Sean."

Mr. Thomas led the way out of the office. Sean stopped before exiting and caught Helen's eye. For a moment they just regarded at one another without speaking. Then Sean turned away and followed after his boss.

BEFORE SHE STEPPED onto the train, Lily turned and waved goodbye to Helen, who kissed her hand and waved it back at her. *I shall miss her, I think, but she is strong enough on her own.*

As she settled into her third class seat, she thought over her time in New Orleans and how she had come to leave.

Mr. Thomas never did make Mr. DeCorte happy. The man got his order—most of it—a day late, but had to wait for a new shipment of methanol. Mr. DeCorte accepted the methanol and canceled all his future orders with Alexandre Shipping. Mr. Thomas was not happy, but took the loss with a shrug and little grumbling.

Lily quit her job a few weeks later. "I would like to see more of America," she told Helen. The reason had the benefit of being the truth, although she also did not remember all of America being this hot and humid.

Helen seemed to understand. "Maybe I'll take a trip myself, one of these ol' days," she told Lily with a twinkle in her eye. "In the meantime, I'll stay with Mistah Thomas and Sean and everboddy."

I suspect she will stay there for quite a long time. She does not take risks easily.

Lily waved one last time through the window at her friend as the train lurched to a start. America awaited.

AUTHOR'S NOTES – T.L. WOOLSLEY

KNOWLEDGE IS *Power* was inspired by Bargain by A.B. Guthrie, Jr., which I read in eighth grade, I think. The story stuck with me, and when I got the opportunity to write as a part of this anthology, I remembered the story.

This story is set in the same "universe," if you will, as *Whisper Sister*, the novel I am currently re-writing. Prohibition, flappers, and a clash of cultures makes for rich storytelling.

—TL

HIGHBALL

Kristin Durfee

I

Chicago, Illinois, 1929

It started simply enough with a dog, appropriately named Highball.

James had been in Chicago for less than a year, but long enough to know his stay here would be short. He felt a pull to remain, but he pushed back against it.

He'd lived too long, seen too much. Knew how places like this fell from grace. The people walked through their city as if they were invincible. The fire that had burned them to the ground a mere fifty-eight years ago a forgotten memory. They walked on ashes without a second thought.

He didn't have such luxuries.

A series of shouts and calls drew his attention down an alley to his right. Five men in knee-length coats just like the one he was wearing were kicking a man on the ground with no coat. James doubted the man's lack of outerwear was the cause of the scuffle, but at this point, he didn't put anything past these humans.

He once saw a Neanderthal kill another because one moved rocks in an improper way. Maybe not having a coat was a grievous offense here. He took note just in case.

The calls intensified and were soon joined by the barking of a dog. The creature couldn't be seen from the street, but it sounded distressed.

James called out to it from a place deep in the back of his throat. The call was met by a yelp, deep growl, and more yelling.

He tried again.

Out of the alley a three-legged dog emerged, ears flattened against its head.

German Shepard. *Deutscher Schäferhund.* Developed in 1899 by Max von Stephanitz. Revered for their strength, personality, and herding ability.

He'd met von Stephanitz once, though found his incessant talking about his dog Horand to be quickly intolerable. He did not stay in that region of Germany long for that very reason.

The dog's tail was tucked between its legs, and it licked its lips as James continued to speak in a low voice. As it came up to him, he saw in fact it had four legs, but the right front was pulled up protectively under its body.

"You hurt bad?" He thumbed the collar around its neck. There was a golden bone dangling from it, the words "Highball" in block lettering across its surface.

"Come on, let's get you fixed up."

He picked up the dog in one movement, careful to avoid the injured leg. The cries behind them fell away in the cold air as they walked the short distance to the clinic.

James opened the veterinarian clinic soon after he'd moved to the city, but business had been slow. His accent had labeled him an outsider, and even though he now had a passible southside drawl, first impressions of him stuck. People went all the way to the other side of town to treat their animals rather than bring them to him. The city was wearing on him almost as quickly as his money was running out.

He wasn't sure which end point would be reached first.

He flipped the lights on, illuminating the stainless-steel exam table. Highball trembled as James lowered him, nails trying unsuccessfully to grip the surface.

"Shhh," he hushed. The dog relaxed, allowing the large pads on his three good feet to steady him.

"That's a good boy. Now, let's see what's going on."

James gently felt the leg and moved it closer to the light. The metallic smell hit his nostrils before he saw the blood. It bubbled around a large sliver of brown glass embedded in the middle paw.

He hummed low to relax the dog further and used a pair of forceps to remove the glass. It smelled like blood and whisky, the latter conjuring up a memory of the burning liquid.

After running saline over the paw until the liquid ran a healthy bright red, he used twelve stitches to close the wound and wrapped it with fluffy white padding.

James ruffled his fingers through the dog's neck fur, enjoying the softness of the surface while noting the muscular power beneath. A musty smell rose, and he breathed it in deeply. The room reeked of cleaning products and lack of use. Having an animal finally inside suited it well.

He thumbed the collar again and re-examined the tag. He did not see a phone extension on the flipside, but what was printed there was just as good.

In the same block letters as the dog's name was a single word.

"Bugs"

It all started falling into place. The men down the alley. The brown glass that smelled like whisky. This dog belonged to the bootlegger North Side Gang, run by crime boss Bugs Moran.

And now James was unwittingly involved.

II

HIGHBALL DOZED in the middle of the floor on a comforter James brought down from the apartment upstairs. The room came along with the building lease, and he was glad for the proximity of home comforts. James opened the fridge to cook up some dinner when he realized that finding Highball had interrupted his trip to the corner market.

"You all right if I run out to get food?"

The dog's lack of response was taken for consent.

He hurried to the store and picked up a few items that would probably get the pair through at least until the next day. James was halfway home when he sensed the footsteps behind him, matching his pace. He quickened and slowed just to confirm. Yes. He was being followed.

He was about to turn around when a hollow, round object pressed into the back of his head.

"Don't turn around, keep walkin'," the rough voice grumbled.

A new feeling bubbled up in him, bringing with it the taste of bile in the back of his mouth. More footfalls. Five, perhaps six. The cold metal felt like the barrel of a gun. That primal voice that occasionally spoke to him told him to listen to what this man said.

"Where're we goin'?" James asked, letting his accent form around the words.

"You tell us, bud. Folks say they saw you with a dog. A very *particular* dog."

James relaxed and turned. The barrel of a gun now rested inches from in between his eyes. On each side of the barrel were four bullets seated in the revolver's chamber. He could only assume two more were hidden out of sight.

The man took a step back, momentarily startled by James's confrontation.

"Highball, right?" James asked, standing his ground.

"You tell us where you took him." A different man taller than the first suddenly appeared in front of James, his voice an animal growl. "Tell us, and I'll consider letting you live."

James extended his hand, which caused five more guns to be pointed in his direction.

"I, I just wanted to introduce myself, explain . . ." he trailed off. His hands reflexively went palms up in the air, causing the brown paper bag to crash to the ground. Cans of Ken-L Ration rolled out in every direction, the butcher paper wrapped steak bouncing once on the ground before coming to rest on the sidewalk.

"I'm Dr. James Smith. A vet. I found your dog, brought him back to my clinic, and fixed his paw. I just wanted to help."

"Fixed?" Another man called, his gun still pointed squarely at James's chest. He spoke through clenched teeth, an unlit cigar tucked into the left side of his mouth.

"There was glass in his foot. I removed it, stitched him up, and ran out to get some food. That's all, honest."

The man with the cigar brushed past the other two and pressed his nose to James's. The tobacco smelled sweet, and he fought the urge to cough the smell out of his nose. He stayed perfectly still, unsure of what to do. Normally when he was this close to another human's face, kissing was involved.

The man edged back and broke into a raucous laugh and embraced him. James considered the kiss again, but decided against it.

"You're a doc?" He slapped James's back.

"Veterinarian," he corrected.

The man laughed again. "A doctor. Friends." He turned to address the men lowering their guns behind him. "We just found ourselves a doctor."

ONE OF THE SMALLER MEN—A teenager perhaps—stooped to gather the groceries and put them back in the torn bag. His hands gripped the paper, ensuring the contents didn't spill again. His hands were too small for the job, and his wrists flexed under their weight.

James wondered how the boy knew it was his responsibility to do this. Did they decide on their roles each time before they went out? Or did being the smallest, and presumably youngest, automatically relegate him to clean up? Either way, even though the young one struggled to hold it all, James was glad the boy was there to do it. This way he could keep all his focus on the men around him.

The men stepped aside and allowed James to show them the

way to the clinic. They followed him to the back where, happily, Highball was on his feet, equal weight distributed on all four legs.

The dog gave an enthusiastic wag of the tail and danced lightly on his feet when he saw the men. Not that James had much say in the matter, but it did make him feel better knowing the dog belonged with them.

"Is he yours?" James asked the large man with the cigar.

The man reached down and ruffled the fur on the dog's neck before shaking his head. "Naw, my nephew John's. He was in a bit of a…disagreement with some men and Highball got away. Hell of a thing. Had to go to the hospital too to get some stitches. Would have been nice to come here." He stood and walked the perimeter of the room, dragging his finger along the stainless-steel counters.

"I'm a vet," James repeated.

"That's still a doc, right?"

The accusation in the man's voice made James take a step back. "Well, yes, but I'm not authorized to work on humans. My certification . . ."

"Well, Doc, we won't tell if you don't." He winked. "You live here?"

"Yes, upstairs." He should have lied, but the thought only came to him after the words were out of his mouth. His default tended to be the truth, something that he would probably need to work on if he wanted to last much longer in this place.

"Perfect." The man slapped James's back again. "Pete, grab that dog and let's get out of here."

"He'll need to come back in a few days to get those stiches removed. And he'll need daily bandage changes." James rushed to pull out a pad of gauze as the men moved around him.

"Little Al," the man said, snapping his fingers.

The young kid rushed forward and stuffed the material in his pockets. They were about to leave when the man with the cigar turned around, his hand outstretched.

"Name's Frank. Frank Gusenberg. I want to thank you for what you did. I won't forget it. Nor will John or our boss. Here." He reached into his pocket and pressed a wad of money into James's hand before leaving.

James pocketed the money with a nod, shifting his weight slightly with the enormous amount of cash that weighed down the right side of his pants.

The men left him in the room that felt more silent than its usual quiet.

For the first time since he moved to the city fourteen months earlier, James locked the door before heading to bed.

III

THE NEXT MORNING, James was surprised to find three people waiting in the street as he unlocked the door. Two were women with cat carriers under their arms and the other a man holding the leash of a handsome black Labrador retriever.

They wordlessly pushed in and took seats in the lobby. The man gestured to take the woman first. James hurried to put paper in the exam folders before calling them back. He'd let his secretary go the month before. There simply wasn't enough work to justify keeping her. Plus, there wasn't money to pay her.

Each woman was put in one of the two exam rooms, and James went about poking and prodding their cats. Both visits were routine, and the animals looked to be in good health. One of the ladies remarked about how good her cat was behaving while its nails were clipped. James noted they hadn't been trimmed in months. She informed him that the feline hadn't let her cut them in years. She went on again and again about how she couldn't believe how well the visit was going and promised that she'd speak of his virtues throughout the city.

As James walked them out, he struggled to read the handwriting on the pricing guide his former secretary, Marcey, made before she left. The first woman opened the door and was about to let the other lady out ahead of her when James called out to them. "Ma'am, please, let me ready your bill."

They looked, confused, at one another and then back at him. Finally, the taller one with the cat named Ace said, "Mr. Moran said it could just go on his tab."

"Right, my mistake," James said because he didn't know how else to react. They nodded and left. The man with the dog stood and followed James into the back. The paperwork could wait.

His week transpired in much the same way. New patients flooded into the office to the point where he sent a message to Marcey, begging her to come back. Luckily, she hadn't found work yet and was able to start right away.

Most patients walked in and out without stopping at the desk, but a few would pause after their appointments. Those were word-of-mouth clients, not ones sent by the gangster, and were charged on the spot. The others were tallied by Marcey, but it was unclear where, if anywhere, bills should be sent. They piled in her desk drawers until she struggled to close them.

James lived simply and didn't need much, so the lack of money didn't concern him, but Marcey talked about it all the time. He made sure she was paid in a timely manner to keep her from worrying.

He'd sold a few of the possessions he'd collected through the years in order to pay rent when he first arrived in the city. He was relieved that he might not have to worry about getting kicked out for not making payments. It could keep him in the city a bit longer. Part of him wanted to leave, to find a life elsewhere, but he felt a draw to stay, as if some specific purpose inexplicably linked him to this city. He was determined to find out why.

Envelopes showed up weekly that more than covered the debt Moran owed. James put that extra cash away in a safe in the upstairs apartment. He wasn't sure how long the arrangement would last and somehow knew that keeping as much money as he could would serve him well in the future.

Even after giving Marcey a raise and putting some money back in the practice to update faulty wiring in the surgery room, the small safe was bursting at the seams.

James thanked his luck each night for finding Highball.

But he still locked the doors.

IV

THREE WEEKS INTO THE ARRANGEMENT, James's true worth to the gangsters became clear.

The evening was late and bitter cold. The wind howled through the closed windows on the second floor, and he considered getting out of bed and moving to the attic where it was a few degrees warmer. While he knew some relief resided there, he couldn't bring himself to exit what little warmth existed beneath five heavy blankets. He stayed, teeth chattering, until a knock that sounded like a cannon shot wrenched him from his bubble.

Panicked, rough voices accompanied dark outlines through the hand-blown glass on the door. James pulled his robe around himself and opened the door. He braced against the gust of cold air.

Without so much as a word in his direction, three men pushed through carrying a body. It took James a moment to realize he recognized two of them, including the one who was being carried. Frank, the man who'd given him the money for fixing Highball, and Pete, one of the men who was with him. Frank looked about the same, down to the cigar in his mouth. Pete's face, however, was almost as white as the snow outside. James wondered if he was already dead.

James followed them to the largest exam room. They placed Pete, still and silent, upon the table and turned to James.

"Well, what'cha doin' just standin' there, doc? Fix 'em!" Frank barked at James. Whines erupted from the small kennel next door as the three dogs staying for observation and recovery awoke to the strange sounds. James hushed them quietly under his breath and moved toward the table.

"Help me get these clothes off him," James said as he struggled to remove Pete's coat that was half-frozen with blood.

The black and brown-haired men assisted, and soon Pete was naked except for his undergarments which were also stained in blood. Three holes formed dark abysses in the man's torso. One above his right breast and two in his lower left abdomen.

"I'm not sure . . ." James's voice trailed off as he stood over the man.

Frank came so close to him, his lips touched James's right ear. "You *will* fix him."

James nodded.

He took the animal-designed oxygen mask and placed it awkwardly over Pete's nose and mouth, tying it behind his head with several pieces of gauze. He wasn't sure if it would work as well, but soon Pete's chest was rising and falling in more of a rhythm, although the movement also caused more blood to flow from the three holes.

"I need your help to roll him over, I need to see if the bullets have passed."

The men complied and James was relieved to see three holes in Pete's back. One less thing to worry about. He pulled out his surgical tools and set to work, ignoring the cold, and thinking of the gun once pressed into his head, hoping the man would make it through the night alive.

IT WAS A LONG NIGHT, and James's hand felt stiff from the cold and use once the morning light filtered through the small, dirty windows in the exam room. But Pete was alive.

Once the threat of imminent death had passed, the three other men took their curtness off like coats. Frank shook James's hand with both of his, relief softening his features, making him look ten years younger than when he'd walked in.

James learned Pete was Frank's brother, which explained the roughness of their entry. Albert had the black hair, and John had the brown. John also gave a two-handed shake and must have seen confusion on James's face because he rushed to explain the extra show of affection. "You took care of my dog."

"Highball, yes. I was hoping you'd bring him back in here; he needed his stitches out. Not good to leave them in."

John nodded his head. "Oh, I know, doc. I took 'em out the other day. Healin' up real nice."

Worry bubbled in James. "*You* took them out?"

He smiled. "Not me, my girlfriend. She's a nurse. Helps the docs do it all the time. Dog didn't even yelp."

"Good, good to hear he's doing well. He's a nice dog."

"He is," John agreed. In about an hour Marcey would arrive. James doubted she'd think highly of coming across these three men, but he wasn't sure if Pete was ready to move yet. The man was still taking long, deep pulls from the oxygen even though the sleeping gas hadn't been mixing with it for about fifteen minutes.

Behind him, James heard the men talking in low voices. The water splashing off the metal sink did little to keep their conversation from reaching his ears.

"We gotta try again," Albert said, stressing each word.

"And get another one of us shot?" John asked.

"Look, if we are going to get Capone out of here, we gotta *scare* him outta here. Offin' Machine Gun will go a long way to doin' that."

"That's what you said about Patsy and Aleina. But they're dead and buried, and Capone is still in town," Frank said.

"Bugs agrees," Albert said, a childish defensiveness in his voice.

"Of course he does. He's not the one gettin' shot at," Frank said.

A groan behind them put an abrupt stop to the conversation. Pete moaned and rocked from side to side on the table. In moments, all four men surrounded him. James talked in the quiet voice he used for the dogs, but it had no effect on the man. James turned to Frank, hoping he'd see the earnest expression on his face. "I'm gonna have to open soon. My office girl is going to be here any minute. If you are still here . . . " he trailed off. "I don't know how to explain it if you are still here."

Frank nodded. Wordlessly the men picked Pete up and retraced their steps out the front door. James handed John some pills and told him to give them every few hours for the pain.

"You did good work, doc, thanks," John said.

James nodded, hoping "good" turned out to be the appropriate word for what he'd done.

V

THE NEXT WEEK WAS QUIET, with only the cold to keep James company at night. Which, all things considered, was preferable to him. He had a steady book of appointments. Two early litters of puppies. A man came in asking to have a cart horse looked at and was sorely disappointed when he was told only cats and dogs were treated in the clinic.

"What use is a doc that does that?" the man yelled. "A horse makes money, brings livelihood. A *cat* doc." He huffed the ridiculousness under his breath.

James agreed to follow him out, but told him no promises could be made. Luckily a degree wasn't needed to tell what was wrong with the beast. Its feet were grown so long the shoes were held on in awkward angles. James told the man a farrier was what he needed, not a vet. He mumbled something under his breath about money and tugged the poor thing along, lame and hobbling as it pulled a cart laden with crates.

"Could you be any help?" Marcey asked when James got back into the clinic. She had craned her neck to watch the pair out the window.

"Think he was looking for a sucker to pull those shoes for free. Too bad I don't have the tools."

"You would have done it?"

"Sure. Can't see why an animal should suffer because it's burdened with an unsympathetic owner."

She smiled at him. "You're a good man, Dr. Smith."

"I do my best, Marcey."

She stood in front of him a beat longer, playing with some phantom dirt stuck under her nail.

James took the bait. "Can I help you with something, Marcey?"

"I was just wonderin', well, we've got this big ol' window, and I didn't know if you saw some of the stores down the road, but they have all kinds of window displays up for Valentine's Day. Do you think maybe I could put something up? Nothin' too big. Some hearts?"

"That would be fine, Marcey. Take five dollars from the drawer so you can do it up real nice."

Her smile turned radiant.

James found the whole practice fascinating. How cutting out and hanging red hearts was supposed to garner true love was beyond him. The holiday had evolved so much over the years. It used to be chaste notes of affection sent through messenger to a woman whom you had met across the room once and wanted to get to know better. It used to be the beginning of the courting season, but now it seemed like people threw the word love around as if it were no different than a greeting between acquaintances. But if the centuries had taught him anything it was that people were a fickle bunch, full of traditions adopted and abandoned at will.

The day before Valentine's, the clinic looked like the colors red and pink had thrown up on it. If he'd have thought she could have done so much with five dollars, James would have told her to only take two. Lesson learned for next year.

When they closed up the office for the day, Marcey told him she'd be in a bit early the next morning to put the rest of the decorations up. Where they were supposed to go, James didn't ask.

He took out the one dog in the kennel and walked him down the narrow alleyway behind the building to the one small patch of grass in a quarter mile radius. The dog took short, careful steps on the frozen ground, a slight limp when his back left leg had to bear weight.

The poor thing had been kicked by a horse when the dog's careless owner got too close to a cart as they crossed the street. Luckily the break on the back leg was clean. James sewed up the crescent cut and put a splint on. He'd kept the dog more to keep an eye on it than for any medical need. He didn't quite trust the owner who seemed like a careless man, having to come back twice for items he'd left behind. If a man couldn't keep track of his glasses and wallet, how was he supposed to be in charge of an animal's needs, much less an injured one?

As they picked their way back to the clinic, he saw a familiar looming outline near the door. A low growl emitted from the dog, and James reached his hand down to gently smooth the raised hackles on its back.

"Shh, it's all right. Good boy, but it's all right." The dog quieted, but James could still feel its alertness through the dark. "Frank?" James called out.

"Doc," he said, holding the door open.

The dog was put back in its kennel, and the two men walked to the front where Albert, John, and two other men sat. James startled when he saw a fifth man in Marcey's chair.

He was a large man with brown hair combed off to one side. A bit of stubble highlighted the deep cleft in his chin. Coupled with his tailored suit he looked more like a politician than the mob boss James knew he was.

"Mr. Moran," James said, nodding to him.

"Doc, I hear you have done good work for us."

"I appreciate the opportunity, sir," James said, not really sure how to address the man. "How is your brother?" he asked Frank.

"Sore, but already movin' around."

"Good. Keep an eye on those stitches though. Don't want any coming out by him doing too much."

Frank dipped his chin in acknowledgement, but said no more. It was clear they weren't here to talk about Pete.

"Is there something else I can help with?" James asked to break the silence.

Bugs Moran smiled. "Why, doc, so nice of you to ask."

"You got a basement here, right?" Albert asked.

"Yeah, but nothing much down there. Not even heated. I think there are still some boxes from the previous tenant. Anything I put down there froze, so…"

"Cold is not a problem," Mr. Moran said. "It have street access?"

"No, sir, just a staircase from the back of the small exam room.

Even more reason why I don't use it. Got a heavy table right in front of the door. Bear to move."

"Think we'll be able to do it, no problem," Albert said.

"I don't think I'm following," James confessed.

"We've got a shipment coming in tomorrow around ten-thirty in the morning. We need a place to move it, a place that's not being watched, that people won't notice a few guys bringing some crates into it. A place with nice, cool storage."

"Like my basement?"

"Like your basement," Mr. Moran echoed.

"What should I do about my patients?"

"I see no reason why they can't wait one day to see you. Think if you put a sign on the door that you are ill and the office is closed, that will work. We will, of course, compensate you for any lost revenue," Mr. Moran said.

The image of Marcey cutting out little red hearts filled James's mind's eye, and he wondered how heartbroken she'd be to not be able to hang them. Maybe he'd let her do it anyway, send her home then open up later in the day. He'd figure something out.

James nodded.

Albert snapped his fingers, and the two other men followed him down the hall. James heard the scraping of the table being moved, then silence, and the three returned.

"You got lights down there?" Albert asked.

"Yes."

"Leave 'em on and the door unlocked," Frank said. "No need for you to be here. We'll take care of it all, put the table back. In a few nights we'll come back and get it all out, and it'll be like we were never here."

James nodded, although he doubted his consent was really something they needed, or cared to have.

VI

JAMES'S FEIGNED illness did little to garner sympathy from Marcey. She huffed her annoyance as she placed the remaining decorations up and took great care to make a sign to hang in the window announcing the clinic's closure.

In a desperate attempt to regain her approval, he gave her some money out of the drawer and told her to have a nice Valentine's dinner and maybe buy herself a new hat. She rewarded James with a quick smile and a peck on his cheek before rushing out into the cold morning air.

The clock over the door read ten in the morning. James paced the length of the window for what felt like an hour, but when he looked back up, only two minutes had passed. He sighed and decided to go for a walk. He debated taking the dog—who he'd renamed Rufus and decided was not going to go back to his owner—but didn't want to subject the poor thing to his wandering around the city. He'd be all right locked up, safely away from whatever Mr. Moran's men had in store over the next hour.

James wrapped a scarf around his face three times before placing his heaviest coat on and exiting out to the crisp air. The day was a rare glorious one. Cold, sure, but filled with sunshine that caused a film of sweat to gather under heavy layers. He walked the block a few times before something spurred him further north, away from his normal radius of travel.

James wasn't much for exploring while in Chicago, tending to stay in small pockets, venturing out only for necessity. Refilling oxygen tanks, medicines from the medical college, the occasional trip to the Middle-Eastern neighborhoods for tonics and herbs. Two blocks up and he was in unfamiliar territory.

James wished he'd brought Rufus with him just to watch his back. To set an alarm for trouble.

Though, when the trouble was upon him, he detected it just fine.

THE WHINE of the dog caught James's attention first. Then the voices came floating in as if the wind itself had speech. He looked up at the sign announcing the Lincoln Park Garage. It smelled of gasoline and grease. Something pulled him toward it. Told him to enter. Told him to not be seen.

He stood off to the side of the concrete structure crouching between two cars and caught a glimpse of the dog. A jolt of recognition ran through him. *Highball.* He was tethered to the wall by a car, dancing at the end of his leash. Even from a distance, James could tell the injured leg had healed nicely.

Men moved around him, every few passes reaching down to pat him on the head. James realized with a jolt he recognized several of them. Frank, Albert, John, little Al, and even Pete, the latter moving gingerly around the parked cars. Then without warning, Highball stood, ears pricked at to attention. Behind James, through the metal grates on the wall, Mr. Moran walked at a brisk pace, then pulled up short.

James followed his gaze and saw two police officers and two men in trench coats move toward the garage entrance. As if sensing James's presence, Mr. Moran turned and locked eyes with him. He took one hesitant step forward before changing his mind and returning the way he'd come. James lost sight of him just as the police entered the garage.

James crouched, not wanting the cops to see him and think he was associated with the men they were approaching. Especially since he *was* associated with them. Two men James didn't know stepped out and saw the cops first, turning to run before shouts told them to freeze.

James could hear Frank's protests as the officers lined the seven men up. "We ain't done nothin'," he called out. The hard surfaces of the garage carried his voice the hundred yards to where James hid.

The officers growled something he couldn't understand as the men in trench coats checked behind them. Maybe more cops were coming? James looked behind himself to make sure no one was coming in the side entrance he'd used.

The street was empty.

A metallic sliding sound brought his attention back to the eleven men. As if in slow motion, the men in trench coats pulled out long guns with large, circular bellies. The officers held shotguns out. Frank had just raised his revolver when it sounded like the world exploded in front of James.

The flashes and booms brought him back to the various battlefields he'd seen. For a moment he was transported to the fields of France, red with the blood of the fallen. It wasn't until he placed his hand on the smooth, black car next to him that he was brought back to the present and had the wherewithal to cover his ears.

It sounded like a thousand rounds had been fired in the span of a few seconds. The officers and men in trench coats ran out the way they'd come, leaving a bloody pile behind them. And off to the side, still tethered to the wall, Highball screamed and bucked against the horrors in front of him.

VII

A RINGING SOUND reverberated around James's head, making him feel dizzy. He stumbled from the garage and wondered if his hearing would ever return to normal, at least in this incarnation. He was a block from home when he remembered Highball and rushed back to the scene.

James strode to the main entrance of the garage this time and was pleased to have his hearing back to normal, though the shock still filled his insides.

More officers, dozens of them now, filled the space. The smell of blood and bodily fluids now mixed with the oil and gas to form a nauseating stench. James was mere feet from the scene before anyone noticed his appearance.

Two men came up to him, clamping rough hands on his shoulder. Another man tried to calm Highball down, who had taken to laying on the blood-soaked ground, a pitiful cry escaping with each breath.

"Whatcha doin' here? You can't be in here," one of the officers said, shoving James back.

James locked eyes with the unblinking ones of little Al. He looked even younger in death, eyes wide with surprise. An expression as if to say, "Really? This is really how I'm gonna go"?

"The dog," James said after another shove. "I'm a veterinarian. I'm here for the dog."

The man lowered his arms. "Poor thing is ruined, I'm afraid," he said. "Witnessed the whole thing. Looks to be the only survivor."

"I'll take care of him," James said.

"What does that mean?" The other cop asked. "Creature's gotta be destroyed. Was gonna do it myself as soon as we can drag him away from the bodies."

"Let me," James said. He moved forward and put his hand out for the leash. "I'll save you the bullet."

The officers looked at one another, but relented, glad to have this small problem be someone else's.

James knelt down and placed his hand on the dog's head. Highball cowered even further, as if he could bury himself into the concrete. A few soothing words and rubs, and he began to soften enough so he could be picked up. James nodded toward the officers and made the long trek home, his arms straining with the effort of carrying the terrified dog.

THE SUN BURNED high and hot above them, but James didn't mind. For a while he wondered if he'd ever thaw out from the frozen winter. Florida was as glorious as he'd read about, where the closest thing to winter was in the town names. Rufus danced in front of James, begging for the ball to be thrown just one more time. Even though he'd told the dog three tosses ago this was it.

James relented, and Rufus dashed after it.

"You know, you can go, too. Play, chase. I'm not going anywhere," James said, reaching his hand down where he knew Highball would be.

The papers reported the dog destroyed, so James felt safe in the knowledge that no one would come looking for him. It took months before the poor creature stopped crying in his sleep every night. It still happened from time to time, but James's words were able to reach him quicker. James remembered how it was after all the battles he'd seen. He knew the dog would never be the same, but that didn't mean he couldn't be all right.

Rufus brought the ball back and without thinking James picked it up and threw it again. It didn't matter. They didn't have anywhere to be.

When James got Highball back to the clinic he'd packed his bags right away, lining his suitcase with the wads of money from the safe. He tucked a few hundred in an envelope and addressed it to Marcey. Lessen the blow of losing her job, again.

James hailed a taxi and flashed a twenty, and the cabby agreed to take him and both dogs to the train station. Rufus hung his head out the window the whole time, oblivious to the cold burning through his nose. Highball remained silent, his head buried in James's lap.

The dog didn't eat for three days, but a steak finally proved too much to ignore. In small increments, he came back to life. For the first two months James was worried Moran might send someone after them, knowing James witnessed what happened to his men, but he must not have thought James could be any help because no one ever came.

The three moved through their days languidly, bobbing from one moment to the next. James allowed the dogs to dictate their day, when they woke, when they ate, when they slept. It was the one thing James found maddingly unfair about his time here on Earth; dogs lived such short lives. He pledged to make each moment of theirs as perfect as possible. And when they moved on to whatever came after this life, James would move on as well. Find a new city, a new life, but until then—

He picked up the ball and threw it, his heart soaring when Highball launched from James's side, sprinting after Rufus and toward the yellow orb.

AUTHOR'S NOTES – KRISTIN DURFEE

THE SHOOTING at the North Clark Street garage—dubbed the St. Valentine's Day Massacre—remains an unsolved mystery to this day. In January of 1929, a member of Al Capone's gang and his wife were allegedly murdered by Albert Kachellek, Pete Gusenberg, and Frank Gusenberg. They then tried to murder "Machine Gun" McGurn, who put a hit out on the men. Under the pretense of purchasing boot-legged whisky, five members of Bugs Moran's gang (including John May, the owner of Highball) and two associates, were lured to the parking garage. Witnesses say they saw four men enter the garage, two dressed as police officers. Bugs Moran was also supposed to be at the meeting, but was said to have been late and witnessed what he thought were police officers coming to arrest his men, so he took off before being seen.

There is speculation that Al Capone was behind the hit, intending to also take out his competitor Bugs Moran, but no evidence was found directly linking Capone to the crime. While one of the firearms involved was discovered and forensically linked to the case (one of the first high-profile uses of the budding field of firearms forensics), no charges were ever filed.

It is also true that the lone survivor of the shooting was a German Shepard named Highball. There are no records as to what happened to the dog, but due to its stressed state, it was thought the animal was euthanized. I had learned about the massacre through my training as a firearms analyst and the story of Highball always stuck with me. I like the idea that maybe someone took him someplace warm and peaceful to live out his days. Romantic, yes, but with no concrete proof as to what happened to him, it's a thought I'd like to hang on to.

—*KAD*

THE ORCHID MAN

Charles A. Cornell

I

South Vietnam, January 1968

Steam rose from the elephant pond into the thick humid air. Dinh Thanh Hau, ten years old, barefoot and wearing only a loincloth, stood at the pond's muddy edge, an empty straw basket in his hands. His morning chores were done—pigs and chickens fed and goats milked. This afternoon he had to gather river seaweed—fertilizer for the vegetable patch— and then later, help grind coffee beans, another job he hated.

Tia Sang, Sunbeam, the first baby elephant born to the Dinh family's herd, rolled in the shallow pond under the watchful eye of his mother, *Vu Nu*, Dancer.

Do your chores, his mother, Kim had warned Hau. No time for play! The Tet New Year festival would begin soon. Every year at Tet, the Dinh clan picnicked by the Dray Sap waterfalls and swam in its cool lake. Playtime then. Not today. Still, Tia Sang had the boy rooted to the spot with laughter as the baby elephant rolled in the mud and splashed up to his giant mother's feet as if to dare her to join him.

A whipping *thump, thump* beat the air over the rainforest's canopy. White egrets and grey-bodied storks scattered from their roosts. As the helicopter approached the hamlet of Bon Ao Voi, the sound of its thrashing prop frightened Tia Sang. He splashed out of the water and bolted towards the stick-fenced farmyard on the opposite side of the pond. Chained to a post, the baby's giant mother growled, the stumps of her padded feet kicking up red dirt as she turned towards her baby's squeal.

Hau dropped the basket and shouted, "Stop, stop!" He corralled the little elephant with a tall bamboo pole. Baby Tia Sang wheeled around, confused. He ran back across the pond to seek the enveloping comfort of his mother's trunk, her anger marked by flapping ears and a thrashing tail.

The chopper, stuffed with soldiers dangling their feet from its open sides, swooped overhead barely fifty feet above him. It flew so close Hau could see the cigarette packs strapped onto the sides of the soldiers' helmets, and their faces, Vietnamese. Three other helicopters skimmed low over Dak Krong River, churning up the calm waters of the marsh as fishermen in dugout canoes steadied their boats. Two more helicopters followed the first, again buzzing directly over Bon Ao Voi, rustling the thatch of its stilt-raised huts and blowing the bamboo pole out of Hau's hands. The chopper formation flew northeast of the hamlet, towards Buon Kuop on the other side of the Dak Krong, then banked to the west and disappeared above the dense jungles of the hilly Central Highlands. Until today—when helicopters flew over Bon Ao Voi—war was on the other side of the hills, on the banks of other rivers, in the rice paddies and coffee fields of other villages, not Hau's.

His mother, Dinh Than Kim raced across the dusty farmyard, scattering the chickens. Another chopper flew above the hamlet to catch up with the rest. "Run, Hau," his mother said, breathless. "Tell your father to come home."

"What's wrong?"

"Just do it," she scolded. "Hurry!"

Hau ran up the winding dirt road—a wide, hard-packed logging trail, flanked by elephant grass verges that melded into the forest of banyan, teak and sao den, the tree that towered over all the others. This was the road his father, Giang, and uncle, Quy, traveled each day from early in the morning until sunset, on top of the old bull *Vua*, King and the bossy matriarch of the herd, *La Dam*, Queen, beasts of burden whose strength pulled timber through the brush and whose broad backs carried it home.

Hau stopped, out of breath, panting. With the choppers gone, the hills resumed their quiet watch over the river lowlands. Hau continued his trek until he reached a spring that tumbled through the jungle, gurgling over rocks to spill its fresh water over the trail. Suddenly, the sound of a snapping twig and the crackle of dry leaves betrayed the presence of someone behind him. As Hau wheeled around, his mouth was caught in the grasp of a firm hand, his body lifted from the trail by a strong arm around his waist. His assailant dragged the kicking boy into the forest until they reached the shelter of a wide banyan.

"Shh!" the man said. He nestled Hau into a broad crook formed by the banyan's many roots. "Quiet, little one."

Hau bent his neck back to see his captor's face. It was Ru Bo Jin, the young foreign student that had come into his village a year ago from a place far away, a land his father called China. Jin worked the coffee fields in the morning, his untiring arms picking faster and longer than anyone Hau had ever seen. By noon, his promised quota filled, Jin left Bon Ao Voi and would spend the rest of the afternoon deep in the forest. He would often return with the elephants, carrying a basket filled with orchids from his secret garden, an enchanted place whose location only Jin knew. The stranger, now friend to many in the village, slept in the back of Pappy Ayun's hut where he dried the bulbs and ground them into tiny flakes to blend special healing teas. One such tea had cured Pappy Ayun—a M'Nong elder, his mother's father, old and frail—from a fever many said would surely kill him. His mother Kim named Ru Bo Jin, the Medicine Man. But the children of the hamlet called him the Orchid Man because he gave the blooms to the girls for their hair.

"Soldiers," Jin whispered in Hau's ear. "In the forest, up the trail." He released his grip from around Hau's waist and raised a finger to his lips. "Not a word, understand?" Hau nodded and Jin's hand fell from the boy's mouth. "Viet Cong. I see six. But there must be more. We must wait until they pass."

When Hau was little he did not understand why some soldiers worked for the government in Saigon while others hid in the forest. Many villagers tried to be friends to both kinds, hiding food for the ones that lived in the jungle while guiding the government's army into the hills to kill the very same soldiers they had fed the day before. His father had tried to explain. He mentioned a people called the French who had conquered their lands before Hau was born. Some in Vietnam had fought the French with all their might while others helped to keep them in power. Eventually, the French left but the battles continued, between men of the same country, soldiers from the north and soldiers from the south. This battle for control of Vietnam, his father said, was now a war. And that had brought the helicopters, owned by another people called Americans.

A dozen Viet Cong carrying guns and dressed in sweaty cotton rags, pith helmets covered in leaves trapped in nets, walked down the rocky stream and crossed the trail, following the water's path through the jungle. Ten minutes after the last soldier vanished into the brush, Jin rose from their hiding place. "This trail is not safe." He pointed into the forest. "We must go this way."

"But my father," Hau protested. "My mother told me he and Uncle Quy must come home."

Jin knelt and placed two strong hands on Hau's shoulders. "I saw them. This morning. They won't be coming home tonight."

Hau's face soured. Puzzled, he asked, "Why not?"

"They're gone."

"Gone where?"

"High into the hills where the road becomes jungle. These soldiers, the Viet Cong, well…you must be strong, Hau. They have taken your father and your uncle. And your elephants, Vụa and La Dam."

"Taken them where?"

"Far away. It's the elephants they want. And they need men to ride them."

"But why? What will they do with them?"

Ru Bo Jin didn't answer. Jin patted the boy on the cheek, stood up and reached for his hand.

Hau pulled away, and huffed, "I'm not leaving without finding my father."

"Your mother needs you now. You must be strong and tell her what's happened. Follow me. This way. To my secret garden. Do you want to see it? It's on the way home to the village."

Hau looked in the direction of the stream where the soldiers had marched and then back at Jin who had stepped the other way, onto a trail beside the banyan, leading into the bush. Hau dipped his head, "All right."

Jin skirted around the sides of a large clearing of dwarf bamboo and razor grass—an open area where they might be spotted by Viet Cong patrols—then followed a trail barely visible through a stand of broad-leafed banana trees. A half an hour later, the trail led them into a grove of sao den wrapped in strangler figs and dangling with vines. Sunbeams descended through the high canopy like heavenly spotlights, the forest floor dotted with red canna lilies and white camellia bushes. A fragrant scent perfumed the humid air. The path fell suddenly into a shallow hollow of fallen tree trunks layered in moss. They had arrived in Jin's hidden garden, a lush sun-kissed oasis where hundreds of orchids grew everywhere, their delicate multi-colored petals hanging from thin stems like translucent porcelain ornaments.

Jin brushed aside a clump of ferns. Hidden under the foliage was a basket and a canteen of water. He left Hau to quench his thirst and wandered over to a mossy log whose rotting length was covered with orchids. Jin gently touched a bloom with his finger, an orchid with a shiny pink pouch, its creamy yellow petals covered with bold leopard spots. "*Paphiopedilum henryanum*. The Venus slipper," he said. "Powerful medicines are inside each type of orchid. I've studied them throughout your country, sampled their stems and bulbs, catalogued and tested their phytochemicals. Some have properties that kill bacteria and treat cancer, others strengthen the immune system and improve eyesight."

A soft blue spark danced from Jin's fingertip and bounced along the petal's edge. Hau's eyes widened. "Magic?" the boy wondered.

"To the uneducated, science often appears to be a form of magic. But the more I learn about these orchids," Jin continued, "the more I understand the secrets of life on this planet. Soon my work will be done and I will have learned enough that I can leave this forest."

"Leave? Where will you go?"

A distant rumble broke the silence.

"Artillery," Jin said as the first rumble was followed by more of the same, this time louder and more intense. "We must go now. The trail will lead us to the river, by the falls. It will be quicker if we go that way."

They descended through the rainforest until the orange evening light of the setting sun peeked through the trees. The forest ended at the marshy sides of the Dak Krong River, a tributary of the Mekong, the lifeblood of agriculture in Quang Duc province and a means of transportation and commerce. Without it, settlements like Bon Ao Voi and their people could not survive.

Ru Bo Jin and Hau walked along the dikes separating the rice paddies into tidy squares along the river's south bank. The hamlet came into view. When they reached the elephant pond, the whipping *thump, thump* of choppers returned. Like metal flying insects, the helicopters swarmed low over the thatched huts of Bon Ao Voi as they had done at midday, retracing their route back to where they'd come from.

Hau's mother Kim crumpled to the dirt of the farmyard when she saw him walking towards her. In tears, she held him tightly, then wept again as Jin told her about Hau's father and uncle. But she had already suspected their fate, she said. Word had come from villages further north along the river that the Viet Cong were seizing elephants and the men who trained them to haul supplies across the Cambodian border. She had hoped she'd sent Hau in time to warn them. But as the shadows of the day grew longer, she feared he had been captured as well.

"What is the village to do now?" Hau's mother asked. "Will the Viet Cong come for the other elephants?"

Jin had no answers for her.

Night descended on the village, a blackness penetrating body and soul. But the quiet was soon broken. The barking of a dog turned to a yelp, then its voice was extinguished for good. The renewed silence announced the arrival of visitors, phantoms of the jungle bearing AK-47s.

II

COMRADE LE DAO PHONG, the Viet Cong commander, paced the planks of the hut. The villagers had been crowded into the hamlet's *rong*—the stilt longhouse that served as their communal hall—and forced to sit in a row, cross-legged, hands behind their backs, bound with rope. The dim glow of the cook fire lit the room. Outside, Vu Nu bellowed, her guttural growls mixed with the frantic chat of Phong's guerrillas as they tried to steer her into the forest and into their service. She wasn't leaving Tia Sang behind.

"Please," Hau's mother Kim said, looking up at Phong's stern, angled face with its menacing dark pupils rimmed with bloodshot veins. "The elephant will not go. She will kill your men first. And if you kill her, your guns will bring other soldiers here."

Phong slapped Kim, knocking her onto her side. He huffed, turned to a soldier, and said, "We carry the rice ourselves. Tell them to leave the elephant alone." The soldier nodded and left the hut.

"From now on," Phong said, addressing the villagers as he paced, AK-47 in hand, "Bon Ao Voi is under my protection. You will pay tribute in rice and coffee. Some of my soldiers will stay with you to dig beneath your huts by night. By day, they will live among you, as M'Nong. You will dress them as you are dressed. You will feed them as you are fed and go about your usual ways. You will not leave the village out of their sight. If you do, you will be shot. My men will accompany you to the fields to make sure. The liberation of our country continues. You should be honored to be part of it."

Ru Bo Jin sat quietly in the shadows, chin dipped to his chest to hide his face, the fire's light glancing across his shiny black hair. Jin appeared to be in his twenties, smooth unwrinkled skin, broad shoulders, taut strong muscles. Comrade Phong had noticed how much taller he was than the M'Nong men who were much older, leaner and had sinewy bodies toughened by years of hard work in the fields and forest. The young men of the village had been recruited into the ARVN, South Vietnam's army, as soon as they came of age. The M'Nong were a community of independent mountain people who'd co-existed with the Vietnamese for centuries. The young man in the shadows was definitely not M'Nong.

"You," Phong ordered. "Stand up!"

Jin got to his feet, back bent slightly to match the height of the diminutive Comrade Phong.

Phong whacked Jin in the ribs with the butt of his AK-47. "Straighten up!"

Jin complied, his body firm. He expressed no pain from the blow, his eyes fixed on Phong.

Phong shoved the tip of the gun barrel under Jin's chin and pushed upwards. He grabbed the young man's cheeks between the fingers of his free hand and turned Jin's face until it caught the light. "You are not Vietnamese. You are Chinese. Are you a spy? Whose side are you on?"

"Some may call me a spy. I'm on a mission from a place far away from here."

"He's a medicine man," Hau yelled out. "He heals people. He's kind. Don't hurt him!"

Comrade Phong turned towards the boy. "A medicine man? A doctor?"

"He brings us flowers from his secret garden. Magic flowers. They healed Pappy Ayun when he was very sick."

Phong turned back to Jin and poked him again in the ribs. "Explain."

"I'm a student of botany. The rare orchids in these forests have powerful chemicals in their bulbs, compounds I have not seen anywhere else."

"A traditional Chinese medicine man? We have use for someone like you. Medicines are in short supply." Phong turned to one of his guards. "Take him. The boy too."

"No!" screamed Hau's mother as she struggled to her knees. She fell to the Viet Cong commander's feet and pleaded, "No, please!"

Phong kicked her. She fell sideways. He pressed his foot on her neck, pinning her to the floor.

"Don't hurt her!" Hau yelled.

"So, he's your son? Good. Take him!"

The boy was yanked to his feet. Phong glared at his distraught mother. "If you ever want to see your son again, you will make sure your people behave. Perhaps he will come back to liberate you from the oppressive forces of Saigon and their imperialist lackeys, the Americans. That day will come. Until then, obedience and service to the cause is required from everyone. Understand?"

She whimpered as Jin and Hau were led away.

THE VIET CONG patrol of fifteen men, burdened by sacks of rice and grains, moved cautiously up the logging trail under the cover of darkness. The mountain spring marked the point where the soldiers took a detour ankle-deep through its bubbling waters to hide evidence of their passage. As dawn broke, Comrade Phong raised his arm. The group stopped suddenly and crouched. A rustling sound came from the undergrowth to the left. A herd of wild pigs crossed the stream. Phong signaled two men to follow. They drew bayonets and slunk into the jungle. Fresh meat for the first time in quite a while. A change from eating crickets.

The coolness of the night disappeared with the rising sun. They reached a forested plateau, the origin of the stream. Several men peeled off from the main group to shower in a small waterfall. The

Viet Cong encampment was set in a forest clearing with a sharp cliff at its back and a hillside sloping steeply away at its front—the perfect defensive position, commanding the high ground when approached from the river valley, impermeable from attack from behind, and hidden from the air by a triple canopy of overlapping branches. Viet Cong of both genders were busy digging openings and tunnels into the cliff. The camp was big and getting bigger with every shovelful. Too big for just a small platoon of Viet Cong.

A kitchen had been made. Jin noticed an oven with a long metal flue that ran deep into the hill, the flue's pipe pockmarked with holes. A cauldron of soup boiled. The smoke from the charcoal fire dissipated into the dirt ceiling, absorbed to prevent detection.

Phong ordered Jin and Hau towards a rocky outcrop that formed a natural wall. Thick teak posts had been placed in the ground—a row of stakes, each with a heavy chain whose ends were nailed firmly into the wood. The ground around them was freshly disturbed. Banana peels littered the loamy soil. A soldier grabbed the boy and placed a shackle on his foot. A lock was applied.

Phong confronted Ru Bo Jin. "The boy remains unharmed so long as you do as you're told. If you flee, he will be killed."

Jin glanced at Hau. The boy's body shook. His lips trembled. The smell of human excrement around the posts made the boy gag.

"When the Americans come," Phong said, "—and we know they will—we will have a few surprises for them." Phong gathered a fresh troop of soldiers and prodded Jin in the back with his gun. "You come with us."

Phong led his small squad out of camp, back along the trail they'd traveled, back to the stream. Soldiers carried two gray-painted crates strapped to their backs. Beyond the spot where they'd seen the feral pigs, Phong stopped his squad. The stream at this point ran wide and deep. Comrade Phong directed two men with AK-47s to take positions on either bank. The crates were opened. Inside one: yellow metal canisters, each wrapped with a single band of cellophane tape. Phong took a bayonet, picked a canister out of the crate and cut its tape. Flat metal fingers flipped up, forming a crown of strips. The device resembled a pineapple.

Jin's rope bonds were removed. A soldier's rifle barrel pushed him forward. Phong showed Jin how to attach a trip wire to the pineapple bomb and hide it from view in the elephant grass at the side of the stream. Phong and his men sat a safe distance away as Jin wired more bombs into the brush until the first crate had been emptied. Then he was shown how to set grenades underwater, tying their trip wires to bamboo rods. Two hours later, all the booby traps set, Jin's dangerous work was done and the guerrillas returned to camp.

Jin was chained up with Hau. The heavens opened above them. The torrential rains lasted the rest of the day and all through the night, turning the foul-smelling ground around the posts into a pigsty. By morning, rivulets ran through the forest floor, scarring the muddy open areas. When the rain finally ended, the forest became a sauna in the hot sun. Steam rose from the foliage and the forest floor as if the Earth was cooking.

Food arrived in the form of banana, mango, and papaya. Comrade Phong watched them eat. Hau ate ravenously but Jin, despite the previous day's long trek, nibbled slowly at a piece of fruit.

"There's something strange about you," Phong said. "You eat little, but you are not thin. You work hard, but you barely sweat. You know how to follow orders and survive, that I do know. Whoever trained you as a spy trained you well. Have you been sent by Beijing? Or are you a spy for the Americans?"

"If I was a spy for the Americans, why would I be Chinese? Wouldn't they want someone who was Vietnamese?"

"True. But then again, if you are a Chinese spy, why have you not made your presence known to us? They are allies. And we know everything. We have people everywhere. But we do not know you. You speak our language very well. And I've heard you talk M'Nong to the boy as if you were born in his village. How long have you lived in Vietnam?"

"Long enough to find what I came here for. I can take you to the garden of orchids if you don't believe me. Rare orchids like no others found anywhere else. That is why I'm here and nothing more."

"Orchids? Do you think I'm interested in *orchids*?" Fire burned in Phong's eyes. "Killing Americans, that's what I'm interested in. Liberation, that's what I'm fighting for. The liberation of South Vietnam from imperialist pigs. The destruction of the puppet regime in Saigon. *That's* what our struggle is about." He grabbed Jin by the throat. "Orchid Man, friend or foe, your re-education will continue. But I promise, if you are indeed my enemy, I will turn you into an instrument of our victory, whether you wear flowers in your hair or not."

The Viet Cong soldiers toiled through the daylight hours in the jungle's simmering heat. They dug foxholes; created blinds of foliage; hauled bamboo poles under the ground to shore up tunnels. Despite shade from the forest's protective canopy, sweat poured from their young bodies, drenching their flimsy cotton clothes. By early evening, the smell of roasting wild pig wafted through the trees. At dusk, the guerrillas manned posts around the perimeter of the camp and hid along the booby-trapped trails that lead up to it from below. Once in position, they could finally eat a meal of pork and rice, wrapped in banana leaf.

Night fell, a bright moonlit night, stark shadows everywhere.

With Hau curled up asleep beside him, Ru Bo Jin lay awake, tuned to the sounds of the dark forest—the scurrying of monkeys in the trees, the electric buzz of cicadas, the *two-weep, two-weep* of thrushes and warblers. A rustling sound coming from above the rocky outcrop—movement?—caught his attention. Behind the crest of the cliff, due west, lay the Cambodian border. The unnatural rustling grew louder. Comrade Phong rose from his post, a foxhole to Jin's left. Soldiers descended into the camp from the trail above, carrying heavy packs and ammunition boxes, with weapons whose silhouetted shapes Jin recognized: rocket-propelled grenade launchers, mortars, and heavy machine guns. In the next hour, a troop of over six hundred pith-helmeted soldiers—carrying a seemingly endless amount of firepower—marched into the camp under the cover of darkness, filling all of the vacant foxholes and mortar blinds.

Le Dao Phong greeted the troop's leader, a short ten paces from the manacled Ru Bo Jin. The pair whispered for a few minutes as the last of the soldiers took up their positions then slunk quietly toward Jin.

"This is Colonel Quan Van Thi," Phong whispered. "His men are *dac cong,* sapper battalions of the People's Army of Vietnam. Victory, Orchid Man. Victory."

"I'm told you are a Chinese medicine man," Colonel Thi said, his flat, square face ghosted by moonlight.

"Any medicines I might have are back at the village."

"Yes, orchids. I have heard of their properties. Phong tells me they grow nearby in the forest. You will go there tomorrow morning. Harvest more. As many as you can. We will need them."

"You fight with us," Comrade Phong reminded Jin. "No monkey business, remember? Or the boy dies."

III

CHARLIE COMPANY'S PLATOON LEADER, Second Lieutenant Neil Hinman walked around the opposite side of the chopper so his men couldn't see him. Safely hidden, he threw up. He wiped his mouth, picked up his M-16 and returned to his assembled squad of fifteen soldiers from the 101st Airborne.

Hinman, barely three years out of WestPoint, was twenty-four, born and raised in Portland Oregon, tall and gangly with a shock of bright ginger hair, inherited from his Irish mother. His father had been in the army in World War Two. His grandfather in the Great War before that.

He glanced up and down the ragged line, examining every face. Half the squad were brand spanking new, with proper names he couldn't remember unless he read the labels sewn on their shirts. That was just fine. Most of his squad preferred to be called by their nicknames anyway, usually a reference to a bodily feature like *Curly* or *Big Dick*, or by a bad habit like *Smokin' Joe*. The greenhorns in the group had just shipped in from the States, fresh off the heavy lift transports. The other half were just like him, only two years in theater but already weary, sick and tired of the cocky new grunts with their *gung ho* swagger and naïve *time to kill us some gooks* attitudes, some of the newest barely out of high school. Tough enough though, or they wouldn't have made it into the Airborne. His squad was a mix of whites, blacks and Hispanics; drafted to fight in this hellhole of a country from Abilene Texas or Dothan Alabama or the Bronx. It was his job to weld these men into a cohesive fighting force with little time to do it. That reality churned his gut.

"Listen up. Our flyboys have dropped intrusion detection devices in the jungle. They've picked up enemy troop movements. Military intel suspects a large contingent of North Vietnamese regulars have moved down the Ho Chi Minh Trail and crossed into the hill country west of Buon Ma Thuot."

Half the squad smiled, the newbies pumping the air with their fists. The other half either kicked at the dirt beneath their feet, snapped the wad of gum in their mouth, or took a last drag on a cigarette and flicked the butt at Hinman.

"You clowns are going to listen up. Because not listening might cost some of you, your life."

"Stand to attention when the lieutenant is addressing you!" Staff Sergeant Will Washington barked.

The soldiers straightened up.

"The tactical plan is simple," Hinman continued. "Land on the south bank of the Dak Krong River outside the hamlet of Bon Ao Voi, a village that our ARVN friends have bypassed in previous raids. Establish a secure landing zone. Clear the village of enemy combatants. But don't think our job is done after that. No sir. It's just beginning. We'll send patrols into the jungle to draw fire. Yes, you heard me right. *Draw fire*. You want action? Well, we'll get it. Plenty of it. We're about to engage the fuckin' NVA. These guys are the real deal. Don't worry, they're not shy. They'll show themselves. Once the choppers drop us, they'll return to Bu Prang to bring reinforcements if we need them."

"And body bags," a grizzled grunt said.

The Huey's engine coughed. Its propeller whined. The chopper's blades throttled into a full blown hurricane and drowned Lt. Hinman's reply.

Hinman's commanding officer, Major Callum 'Bulldog' Bagnell ran past the platoon to the open side door and yelled back, "So what you bastards waiting for? Let's go!"

Hinman split the squad in two and waved his men to their assigned choppers. Half went with him, the other half with Sgt. Washington. He mouthed the words, "Good luck." Washington saluted back.

Bagnall leaned out of the Huey and twirled a finger in the air—the signal to the chopper pilots to take off. "This is the big one, Hinman," Major Bagnall shouted as Hinman settled into the seat opposite him. "You ready, son?"

"Easy pickings, sir."

"That's the spirit."

Twenty choppers—carrying one hundred men of the 1st Brigade, 101st Airborne, and a further fifty soldiers of the ARVN's 23rd Division—lifted off from Bu Prang Special Forces Base, three miles south of the Cambodian border. This was the third search and destroy mission for Major Bagnell's unit as part of Operation San Angelo. Previous air-mobile strikes had yielded only minimal contact with a few squads of Viet Cong guerrillas.

The helicopter assault group swept through a clear cloudless sky. Two AH-1 Cobra gunships accompanied the strike force. The hills were within artillery range of the firebase at Buon Kuop. If needed, the 101st could also call in air cover from Tuy Hoa Air Base. Hinman kissed the gold cross dangling from his neck. *God bless this firepower*, he thought, as the humid Vietnamese wind raced by the open sides of the chopper.

THE WATER BUFFALO lumbered through the marsh, its hooves sinking into the mud. Dinh Than Kim, broad grass hat shielding her from the bright morning sun, followed behind, filling the holes the beast's feet created with seedlings of rice. A large flight of helicopters approached. The *chop-chop* of their props disturbed the buffalo. It bellowed and reared. She whacked it with a stick to stop it from reversing over her.

A helicopter of ARVN troops landed fifty yards away from Kim, followed by a second, then a third. She winced as turbulent air whipped water, mud, and rice seedlings all around her. ARVN Captain Nguyen Duc Long dipped his head under the chopper's wash and waved his soldiers forward. His men, brandishing M-16s, shouted at the villagers in the rice paddy. One by one the villagers raised their hands in the air and were herded out of the marsh along the dikes.

South Vietnamese troops ran over to the elephant pond, guns aimed into the forest. Vu Nu growled and swayed from side to side. Baby Tia Sang cowered behind his mother. Like aerial buses, more choppers queued in the sky, landed their troops, then lifted off again.

American soldiers swarmed into the hamlet and hauled women and children out of the stilt houses. The infantrymen conducted a careful search, mindful of booby-traps hidden inside the huts. ARVN soldiers arrived from the rice paddy with captives. Pigs and chickens scattered into the corners of the stick-fenced farmyard as the field workers and villagers were herded inside. The soldiers told everyone to sit cross-legged in the muck.

One of the last villagers in, Kim dropped her hands and her eyes wandered over to the longhouse.

The butt of Cpt. Long's pistol smashed into her temple. "Who are you hiding?" Cpt. Long barked in M'Nong. "Where are they? How many? Speak!"

Kim fell into the muck, rolled and moaned. She was too dazed to speak. Blood ran down her face.

"Tell us where the Viet Cong are hiding!" Cpt. Long screamed. He fired a round in the air. He tugged on a shirtless man's loin cloth and searched him for a concealed weapon. "You!" he barked. "You are Viet Cong!" The man shook his head, *no.* He rocked back and forth, his hands clasped as if in prayer.

Cpt. Long pointed into the group of villagers. An ARVN soldier knew what to do. He grabbed Pappy Ayun by the collar of his ragged shirt, lifted him out of the muck and dragged the old man outside the fence.

Lieutenant Neil Hinman and his men marched past the yard to check nearby huts. "What have we got here, Captain Long?" Hinman asked.

"This village is hot. I can smell it. They're hiding Viet Cong."

Staff Sergeant Will Washington called out from a hut entrance, "Nothing in here, lieutenant."

"Maybe not there. But I know how to find them," Cpt. Long said. He walked over to Pappy Ayun, forced to sit in the open yard. Kim feared her face had betrayed him as her father to the South Vietnamese officer.

Long addressed the villagers, glaring back at Kim. "Where are they hiding? We know Viet Cong are here." He placed his pistol to the old man's head and watched Kim's reaction. Her anxious face acknowledged his suspicions. "Speak up," he said, eyes aimed directly at her. "*Now!*"

Kim shuddered and pointed to the longhouse.

Cpt. Long smiled. "Good. Very good." Then he pulled the trigger. Pappy Ayun slumped to the dirt.

Lt. Hinman signaled to his squad. "Look for tunnels over there. Washington, follow me." Hinman and his sergeant crept towards a stilt house close to the logging trail and hid behind its thick pilings. "Cover the left," he instructed. "I'll cover the right." They trained their M-16s into the jungle on either side of the trail.

"Fire in the hole!" a soldier yelled. A muffled explosion sent birds into flight as a grenade blew up inside the tunnel the VC had built under the longhouse.

Jungle ferns waved back and forth, marking the location of guerrillas exiting the other end of the tunnel to escape into the forest. Hinman and Washington opened fire. The Viet Cong returned fire, bullets ripping splinters from the pilings. A sudden thunderstorm of rapid fire rained down on the hamlet from somewhere deep in the brush catching Hinman's squad off guard. Cpt. Long scattered his

ARVN troops. Soldiers were hit. "Men down!" someone cried out. "Medic!"

Hinman called over to Washington, "Did you see the flash? Where's it coming from?"

"Up the trail, left side, one hundred yards. Possibly a 51-cal heavy."

Hinman yelled back at his squad, "Sanchez! Pop smoke up the trail, one hundred yards, left! Curly, get me a Snake on that smoke! Move it!"

A grenade launcher pumped canisters into the air. One by one, they landed in the forest. Red smoke swirled up through the trees. A Cobra helicopter gunship—a 'Snake'—had been circling over the Dak Krong River. It banked hard left towards the crimson smoke-signal, straightened up, and stopped in midair over Bon Ao Voi. The chopper raked the forest with machine gun fire. Shell casings rained down into the farmyard. ARVN soldiers moved the villagers single file out of the fire zone, back towards the rice paddies. Rockets streamed from pods on the chopper's sides. Flames and gray-black smoke bloomed from the foliage.

"That's what I like to see," Major Bagnell said as he slunk behind the piling next to Hinman, teeth clenched. "Good work, Lieutenant."

A rocket-propelled grenade shot upwards from a position behind the elephant pond, tracing an ominous line towards the chopper. A second grenade followed as ARVN soldiers took fire from the brush. The first grenade missed. But the second struck the chopper's rear fuselage below the engine. The fiery explosion left a gaping hole. The chopper's tail rotor stopped. Without the rotor's stabilizing force, the torque of the main helicopter blades spun the Cobra violently in the air. The pilot executed an emergency crash landing into the elephant pond. The chopper collapsed on its side. Mud splashed high in the air as the chopper's blades dug into the water.

Mortar rounds landed in the village. Some hit the stilt houses where soldiers had taken cover. Others burst in open ground sending dirt and shrapnel flying in all directions. Wounded soldiers screamed for help.

"We're sitting ducks, Major!" Hinman said.

Bagnell rolled a toothpick from one side of his mouth to the other. "*Shit!*"

"What do we do? Order an air strike?"

"Not until we find the NVA's main camp. We're not retreating if that's what you're thinking, Lieutenant. No goddamn way!" He pointed to the logging trail. "Lay suppressive fire. Give 'em all you got. In fact, give 'em *hell*. Then get your men up that goddamn trail! We're taking this dogfight to the gooks, understood? So let's find this camp and smoke it!"

"Roger that," Hinman replied. "Washington! Gather your men. We're moving out!"

IV

SUNBEAMS ILLUMINATED THE GLADE. Nature guarded its most precious secrets with a chorus of birdsong and a veil of shade.

Ru Bo Jin harvested orchids into a canvas sack under the vigilant watch of Comrade Le Dao Phong, sitting on guard on a stump, AK-47 balanced in his lap. Phong lit a cigarette, drew a deep breath and exhaled a cloud of foul-scented smoke. The pair had been up since dawn, having left the camp at first light.

The *wump-wump-wump* of helicopter blades drove a troop of frightened monkeys scampering through the high canopy. Phong jumped up, stubbed his cigarette into a clump of moss and clicked the safety off his gun. A second group of helicopters roared overhead. Phong waved the muzzle towards the trail and said, "Orchid Man, we go now."

Jin finished his work. They retraced the route they'd taken to his garden, an hour's trek from camp. Phong brought up the rear. Halfway back, at a spot where Jin's path crossed over the main trail, subtle markings on the trees warned them to detour through the undergrowth to avoid trip-wired explosives and camouflaged spike-laden pits. They reached a large felled teak, its diameter nearly as tall as a man, abandoned because it was too big to haul, even for an elephant. Nestled in a growth of thick bamboo, there had been no way around it. Jin climbed up as he'd done before, but this time at its crest he feigned a slip and tumbled forward.

As Jin's body thumped into the soil, Comrade Phong slung the AK-47 over his shoulder and crawled up. Once on top, Jin's hand grabbed Phong's ankle and yanked him off the log. Phong fell hard. Jin jumped on his startled captor. Comrade Phong, a wiry, battle-toughened and commando-trained fighter, drew a bayonet from the scabbard strapped to his leg. Jin parried the thrust by snatching Phong's wrist. A razor-sharp tip hovered just an inch from Jin's face. Phong clutched Jin's shirt with his free hand and tugged, straining to pull Jin off balance. Phong's arms tensed like steel, his face grimacing.

Neither man had a free hand to reach the gun that had fallen into the brush beside them. Minutes passed by as the two men wrestled in a stalemate. Phong tired, his stiff arms bending under Jin's strength. Jin turned the bayonet towards Phong's chest until its tip pricked through his shirt, right over his heart.

"Let go," Jin said. "I won't kill you."

Phong sputtered, the foaming spit of his supreme effort dribbling down his chin. He sobbed, his eyes full of fear. Whatever strength Phong had left, sapped away. His grip on the knife loosened until the blade's hilt fell limp on his shirt.

Jin tossed the bayonet into the bush, stood up and retrieved the AK-47. "That way," Jin said as he pointed over the log, back towards the orchid garden. "If I see you following me, I'll shoot you."

The *pop-pop-pop* of distant gunfire punched through the peacefulness of the jungle. Jin tossed the sack of orchids at Phong. "You're unarmed. A peasant farmer that harvests orchids. If you meet American soldiers, tell them that. Tell them my story, as if it were your own."

Stunned, Comrade Le Dao Phong did as he was told.

Jin waited until Phong disappeared behind a thicket of bamboo then headed back in the opposite direction towards camp. A few minutes into his journey, the thumps of exploding mortar rounds confirmed Colonel Quan Van Thi's sapper battalions had engaged the enemy. Jin picked up his pace, racing through the brush like an antelope, memory banks knowing where each booby trap had been set, bio-engineered optics in his eyes tuned to see invisible trip wires. He arrived at the camp's perimeter and raised the AK-47 over his head to signal his presence. NVA soldiers in the nearest foxhole let him pass without questioning why Phong wasn't with him. They had other priorities. The army of NVA sappers and VC guerrillas had shouldered their AK-47s, cocked hammers on their machine guns, and pointed every available firearm downhill. The jungle slopes below camp were alive with movement.

A pineapple bomb exploded in a vicious hail of shrapnel. Three legless American soldiers were hurled into the air two hundred yards away. The explosion was the signal for Colonel Thi's forces to open fire with every weapon at their disposal.

Lt. Neil Hinman's men returned fire with an equal ferocity.

Bullets tore into camp, pinging off the rocky outcrop where Hau was chained. Jin fell face first on the forest floor. He crawled on his stomach until he reached the boy and grabbed the lock that bound the shackle to the boy's ankle, covering it with his palm. Blue sparks danced around the weathered iron. Inside, rusty mechanics clicked until the lock's bar jumped free.

"How did you do that?" the boy asked.

Gunfire raged around them, so intense they daren't move. Grenades flew up towards the camp from the tree-line, desperately aimed, falling harmlessly short. One or two finally bit dirt behind the North Vietnamese positions and exploded. Crippled soldiers screamed in pain. In return, Colonel Thi's mortars took their toll on the exposed Americans and South Vietnamese. The relentless exchange continued for hours, neither side yielding ground. The firefight decimated the jungle. Palms were split in two by mortar rounds, their jagged stalks witness to the human carnage around them.

Six hours into the engagement, the intensity of fire directed at the North Vietnamese positions subsided. Colonel Quan Van Thi bounded past Jin, a pair of binoculars around his neck, searching the brush. An order was yelled out.

"The Americans are retreating," Jin said to Hau, the boy curled tightly in a fetal position by his side.

Colonel Thi ran along the lines.

"He's counting casualties, deciding whether to chase the Americans down the hill or not," Jin said. "This may be our chance to escape."

Colonel Thi took out his pistol, waved it like he was shooing birds out of a field, and shouted. Soldiers jumped out of foxholes and over the barricades into the brush, some falling immediately as his retreating enemy returned cover fire.

"Can we go now?" Hau asked. "They're leaving."

Jin didn't answer. His face pointed skyward.

"What's wrong?" the boy said.

Jin moved his head up and down, first staring into the jungle, then up into the air. His face was blank, his eyes not blinking, caught in concentration.

"What are you doing?"

Jin's head cocked to one side, expressionless. "Listening. Radio transmissions. From Bon Ao Voi to pilots." He looked down at Hau, this time with wide eyes as if awakened from a nightmare. "The pilots have answered back. They're getting close. We have to hide…quickly!"

The camp's quarters and tunnels were empty. Even the cooks had taken up arms. Jin lifted Hau off the ground and ran as fast as he could towards the hillside kitchen. A sharp loud *whoosh* accompanied a streaking silver Phantom jet as it screeched above the forest canopy, leaving a sonic boom in its wake. Two gray cigar-shaped canisters tumbled end over end over the camp. Jin ducked into the kitchen tunnel, pushed Hau to the ground and covered the boy's body, tucking his own arms and legs around him so nothing of the boy was exposed.

The pair of napalm bombs exploded, sending an area five thousand square yards wide into the depths of Hell. Burning jellied gasoline raced through the jungle. Flames burst into the kitchen and coated Jin's back. His shirt, pants and hair burned off. Jin jerked and rose to his feet, the flesh of his back sizzling like bacon. A large pot of water sat on the floor. He tipped it over his head, the water running down his seared body.

Hau coughed from the acrid black smoke and stifling hot air. He crawled to the entrance to escape. Jin lurched out of the kitchen in a daze. Hau gasped as the Orchid Man tottered past him. The skin on Jin's back was gone, his spine exposed. Beneath the charred flesh, blue lights flashed. Hau thought he saw the outline of a silver metal box at the base of Jin's neck, throbbing like a glowworm, with thin translucent tubes intertwined among Jin's arteries and veins.

Ru Bo Jin stumbled into the tortured jungle like a puppet with several broken strings. War had blasted ragged paths of destruction among the burning trees. Large craters dotted the hillside. The land was littered with burnt bodies, some still aflame, unrecognizable as anything that once had a name. Further down the hill, outside the blast zone of the napalm bombs, Jin found a cluster of dead American soldiers. His eyes scanned back and forth. He fell to his knees and turned a body over. The man had a bullet wound in his forehead. The ground and foliage were soaked with pooled blood. Jin dipped his hand until it dripped with crimson liquid, then smeared the blood on his chest. Hau stared, aghast, as he witnessed Jin stripping the soldier of his shirt, pants and boots, then dragging the body —naked except for dog tags—into a bomb crater. Jin covered the dead soldier with a layer of palm fronds.

"What are you doing?" Hau asked as Jin bundled the soldier's clothing under his arm. "Why did you scoop up that blood?"

Jin's responded, voice garbled, monotone words interspersed with a clicking sound, "Follow...*click*...my footsteps. And...*click*... you'll be...safe."

Jin, naked, as his clothes had been burned away, navigated through what remained of unexploded booby traps until he located the mountain stream which led to the logging trail. Soon, they reached the forest at the edge of Bon Ao Voi. There, several helicopters loaded troops. The rest were in the air, leaving.

They watched from the brush. A squad of American soldiers

held out Zippo lighters and set the thatch on the huts alight. The village went up in flames. Job done, the soldiers boarded the last remaining chopper. As soon as the Huey lifted off, Jin crossed the hamlet's grounds, towards the elephant pond.

Hau followed. "Where are you going?" the boy sobbed.

No answer.

A large gray mass lay sideways in the pond's mud. A long limp trunk draped over the back of baby Tia Sang. The little elephant pushed against his mother's head with his own, attempting in vain to wake her up. Vu Nu had been shot.

Hau ran past the tottering Jin toward Tia Sang.

Jin grabbed his hand and pulled him back. "No," he said. "Nothing…*click*…you can do."

"Where are you going?" the boy repeated.

"Home…*click*. My…home. Do not…*click*…follow. Too dangerous."

"But what will *I* do? Where will *I* go?"

"Wait here. Someone from the village…*click*…will return. Don't…*click*…follow me," was the stern reply.

V

WITH EVERY STEP since leaving the hamlet, Ru Bo Jin gained strength and agility. The wounds that covered his back had glossed over until a shiny membrane—resembling opaque plastic—hid his spine and protected his burnt flesh. Strangely, the blood Jin had smeared on his chest from the dead soldier had been fully absorbed into his body, diffusing into his skin until tiny spider veins of pink appeared, pulsing gently across his abdomen. His pace had quickened, leaving Hau to scurry behind to keep up. The young boy followed, despite Jin's warning.

Having given up hope that his mother Vu Nu would ever rise from her sleep, and seeing a friendly human face, Tia Sang, the distraught baby elephant, had rushed to Hau's side. As he had done in the past, he followed Hau, a favorite playmate who fed him mangoes.

A mile northwest of Bon Ao Voi, the Dak Krong River forked around an island. The sound of rushing water filled the air. Jin arrived at a shallow crossing of gray cobbled rocks upstream of the first set of waterfalls, Dray Sap, a spot Hau knew well. The annual Tet New Year's festival was nearing. Dray Sap was the place where he and his family would picnic on the banks of the small lake below Dray Sap's beautiful white waters.

Jin crossed the stream and hiked into an old growth forest of banyans and willows. His unyielding pace left Hau and Tia Sang to hurry through the jungle to keep up. Jin followed a well-worn trail deep into the forest, a trail that led north to a bigger set of falls, Dray Nur, where the river fell at several points over a massive granite shelf one hundred feet high.

Above the falls, the Dak Krong tumbled haphazardly throughout the island, falling into narrow canyons of volcanic rock, carving natural showers into the jungle landscape. Cool wading pools formed at their bases and caves peered in the cliff faces behind the roots of overhanging banyans. It was at the base of a small waterfall, down a steep slope of sharp rocks, that one such cave entrance, well hidden, split the canyon. Jin scampered down.

Hau peered over the edge of the cliff. The way down was treacherous, even for an adventurous boy. The rocks were slippery and jagged. One wrong move and it was a sixty foot drop into a shallow boulder-strewn pool. Jin obviously knew the way, grabbing handholds and vines at just the right moment as if he'd done this a thousand times.

Tia Sang nudged Hau playfully, not realizing his strength. The elephant nearly pushed Hau over the edge. Hau cried out, "No! Bad elephant!"

Hearing Hau's shout, Jin paused halfway down the canyon and glanced up. "I told you. You cannot follow me," he said. Jin appeared to be in no pain and his speech had returned to normal.

Hau ignored him and began a tricky descent.

Jin climbed back up towards the boy. Hau lost his grip on the side of the cliff and slipped. He fell into Jin's waiting arms.

"This is why you can't follow me. There is nothing for you here."

"But I'm frightened. And I have nowhere to go. The soldiers may return and kill me. Or I may be captured again and chained up."

Jin hoisted Hau to his shoulder. Without another word, he made his way down the cliff face. At the cave's entrance, he placed the boy under a ledge where the rocks were dry and said, "Night is coming. I will make you a bed of ferns but you must promise not to follow me inside."

"Where are you going?"

"In there." Jin pointed to the cave. "Don't be afraid. Stay here. But in the morning you must leave. I will be gone."

"Gone? Are you going to die?"

There was no answer.

JIN DID what he'd promised. He'd provided a bed for the boy to sleep on outside the cave's entrance. And he'd fetched papayas and bananas for something to eat. Jin had said little except that he'd found food for Tia Sang too and assured Hau the little elephant was safe, content to bed down under the banyan tree whose vines descended down the cliff face. In the hour or so since Jin had scaled the cliff and returned with food, Jin's appearance had changed. His whole body had glossed over as if wet, like the slippery smooth skin of an eel.

Hungry, the boy sat cross-legged on his bed of ferns and ate his meal of fruit. When he was done, he turned around to where Ru Bo Jin had been sitting but Jin was gone.

The sun sat low on the horizon. Night would come soon. Why had Jin left him alone? Where had he gone? Finding the answers compelled Hau to enter the cave.

Light cascaded down from cracks in the ceiling. The further Hau went, the darker it got until the only light came from the cave entrance, now but a point of light behind him. Hau could hear Jin's footsteps in the gloom, a methodical slap on the surface of the wet rocks. The footsteps abruptly stopped. Hau crept behind a stalagmite that thrust upwards from the cave floor and waited. He could see nothing. The only sound came from water dripping from above.

Bursts of pale blue light shimmered from deep inside the cave, a gentle strobe, like waves on the river. Hau heard a hum, a tone that sent vibrations through the rocks. The light washed a blue cast over the inside walls of the cave before dissipating into nothing. It pulsed again, a rapid burst of four or five short strokes, each time briefly illuminating the narrow passageway Jin had disappeared down. Hau heard a rustle, like palm fronds brushing together in a strong wind. Suddenly, the source of the sound emerged from the gloom —hundreds of bats fluttering in a thick cloud of flapping wings. The passage was so narrow several hit Hau in the face on their way out.

The boy covered his head with his hands, fell to the wet floor and tucked into a tight ball, trembling. Several minutes passed as Hau cowered behind the rocks until all of the bats had left the cave. The lights and sounds did not return but the darkness grew deeper. The sun's rays no longer appeared as a point of light from the direction he'd entered. Without light, he could go no further and if he lingered much longer, he would have to stay the night inside the cave. Hau carefully walked back the way he'd come, his hands outstretched in front of him like a blind man.

HAU SLEPT LIKE A BABY, the rushing waterfall his lullaby. In the morning he rose to the sound of trumpeting high overhead. Tia Sang bellowed and paced at the top of the granite cliff. The elephant didn't know how to descend the steep canyon.

Hau heard voices coming from the forest above him. Tia Sang flapped his ears, a sign of distress, then growled. A man with a stick emerged at the cliff's edge and whacked the elephant. Hau could hear other men yelling. They were trying to capture Tia Sang.

Hau scrambled from under the ledge and scampered up the

dangerous cliff face, yelling, "That is Dinh clan's elephant! My elephant! Leave him alone!"

"Hau?" asked one of the men. "Dinh Thanh Hau?"

"Yes," Hau grunted as he hauled himself up the treacherous rocks. "Leave my elephant alone!"

A man descended part way to help. "Your mother has been looking for you," he said. "A captured soldier from the Viet Cong said he saw a boy and man wandering out of the forest near Bon Ao Voi. Your mother was certain it was you. Others thought you were dead. Your elephant has lead us straight to you."

THE ELDERS in the village said the North Vietnamese Army and the Viet Cong had conducted a countrywide offensive over the Tet holiday but had suffered many defeats. Afterwards, more and more American soldiers arrived and their camps grew from small outposts to little cities. Peasant life along the Dak Krong River changed. Hau witnessed a doubling of the steely gray gunboats that patrolled its waters, daily flights of helicopters, and regular artillery barrages that pounded the hills.

Despite the chaos, Hau revisited the canyon near the Dray Nur waterfalls several times, a boy with his elephant, chores done. But there was never any sight of the man who'd protected Hau in the Viet Cong camp, who'd covered him when napalm ravaged the North Vietnamese troops, and whose burnt naked body wandered out of the forest and led him back to safety.

One day, three months after the battle of Bon Ao Voi, Hau and Tia Sang visited Dray Sur again. Hau left the baby elephant to play in the forest at the cliff top while he climbed down the rocks to the wading pool at the bottom of the small waterfall. Hau didn't venture back into the cave. He had a morbid fear of bats ever since he'd tried to follow Jin. Instead, he waited quietly at the entrance; the scattered remnants of a bed of dead ferns a sad reminder of the night when he'd lost a friend. The day grew longer and the little elephant bellowed from above. Time to return home. As dusk approached, the boy and the elephant stood atop the granite shelf beside Dray Nur's raging waterfall. The dull red orb of the setting sun fell into the steam of the Vietnamese jungle.

They tramped down the trail back to their new village. Hau heard footsteps crunching through the brush behind him. He turned, recoiling at the sight of a tall American soldier in army fatigues and black boots, and fell backwards against the baby elephant's side. Tia Sang growled.

"Don't be frightened," the white man with mousy brown hair said. Tiny blue lights flashed inside his pupils. A static charge filled the air, raising the hairs on the boy's head. Tia Sang stopped growling, curled his trunk and bent down on one knee.

"Who are you?"

"The new Jin," the soldier said. "The old Jin is gone."

VI

Forty-five years later, August 2013.

IT HAD BEEN a cold wet summer in Portland, Oregon. Today, a Saturday, continued the trend—gray, overcast, a constant light drizzle.

A rap rattled the aluminum frame of the front porch's screen door. It was followed by the doorbell's chime. Alice Hinman sat knitting in the La-Z-Boy recliner in her bedroom. *Dammit,* she thought, as the pain ran through her diabetic ankles. *I must get a new chair. One with a power lift.*

"I'll get it, Mom," Denise said, running to the front door.

Outside the front porch, a young black soldier with a plastic-covered dress cap, his uniform under a damp raincoat, stood next to Harry Helzberg, president of the local chapter of the Veterans of Foreign Wars. The soldier carried a box wrapped in brown paper.

Denise gasped. "Is that—?"

"The shirt shown in that travel picture we found on Facebook?" Helzberg said. "Yes, it is. The one where your mother thought she recognized the name. One of the guys from the VFW just came back from his reunion tour. He checked it out for you. Well, wouldn't you know it? It was still hanging in that shop in Ho Chi Minh City. How it got there is anybody's guess. It's a blessing nobody else bought it."

Tears rolled down Denise's cheeks. "Mom will be so happy. Please come inside. Dreadful weather. Coffee?"

"Yes, ma'am," the young black soldier replied, smiling.

The house, a bungalow built in the early 60s, was small, barely twelve hundred square feet. Sparsely furnished, the living room sofa had just enough space to fit the beer-bellied Harry Helzberg and the trim Sergeant Jake Watson, US Army, 101st Airborne. Denise arrived with a tray of coffee and a plate of homemade chocolate chip cookies. She placed the tray on the coffee table beside the package then knelt on the hardwood floor.

Alice hobbled into the room with her cane.

"Sit down, Mom," Denise said. A rocking chair sat opposite the sofa.

Alice caught sight of the package and noticed the gleam in her daughter's eyes. "Oh, that isn't? It can't be. Is it?"

"Yes, ma'am," Sgt. Watson said.

Alice's eyes watered. "You open it, Denise. I can't. I just can't."

"Oh mom—"

Alice shook her head.

"Okay," Denise replied. She unwrapped the paper and lifted the lid of the box inside. She burst into tears when she saw the neatly folded, freshly washed army-green shirt. She pulled the shirt out of the box and held it up. Shoulder patches for the 1st Brigade, 101st Airborne, graced one of the sleeves. Above the breast pocket, sewn with black thread, read the name, 'Lt. N. Hinman'.

Denise's hand wandered over the name, a father she never knew. She gave the shirt to her mother who immediately crumpled it to her breast.

"But how?" Alice said. "Has he been alive all these years in Vietnam? What happened to him? Why didn't he come home?"

"My friends took photos of your husband with them," Helzberg continued. "In the hope that someone knew where the shirt had come from. After much searching and a few dollars for information, they tracked down an old gentleman who remembered the American who wore it. The old man said the American was kind and knew a lot about traditional Chinese medicine. But after showing him the photo, the old guy said the man he knew many years ago was not your husband. He didn't have red hair."

"But that man who wore the shirt, might *he* know what happened to Neil?"

"The old man said the stranger was in the city—it was called Saigon back then—for only a very short time in the summer of '68, after your husband was missing in action. The American gave the shirt away and then disappeared. No-one ever saw him again. Maybe he was a deserter. Or just a foreigner disguising himself as an American to make his way out of the country. We may never know who he was or how he got the shirt. But we do know where your husband is, Mrs. Hinman."

Alice gasped and clutched her chest. "You do?"

"Tell 'em, sergeant."

"Yes, sir," Sgt. Watson said. "I'm here to officially inform you that your husband is no longer missing in action."

"What? I don't understand."

"The Defense Department's Missing Personnel Office in DC, with the cooperation of the government of Vietnam, has positively identified remains found at a site in the hills near Buon Ma Thuot as those of your husband, Second Lieutenant Neil Hinman. The State Department is negotiating the return of his remains for reburial in the United States. Unfortunately, ma'am, with all the bureaucracy, that could take a long time."

"He's dead?" Alice sighed. "Yes, I know. Silly of me to think otherwise. I've always known that. But deep in my heart, I wished—" She folded the shirt and placed it on her lap. She paused, then drew a deep breath. "But this news—it means I have to go. Yes. I have to be there. I have to see it. Where he fell."

"Mom, you can't—"

"Oh yes, I can, dear. I damn well *can*. Even if it's the last thing on this Earth I have the strength to do."

. . .

VII

ALICE HINMAN STEPPED out of the jeep onto the dry red soil. She'd bought a broad round hat in the market, a grass one like the locals wore. Still, the intense heat and humidity were like nothing she'd ever experienced in Oregon. Her loose-fitting cotton clothes were soaked with perspiration, stuck to her front and back like cling-wrap. Her daughter Denise paid the driver in US dollars which elicited a hearty smile from the man.

Harry Helzberg took off his bandanna and wiped his face and neck, a lump forming in his throat. This was the first time back 'in country' since 1971. Somehow, despite several opportunities, he'd never plucked up the courage to go with his fellow vets when they went on a tour. He'd been many times to the Vietnam War Memorial in Washington, every year since it had been commissioned. Despite the healing his annual pilgrimages produced, it wasn't quite the same thing as this. Finally, he was here, within a few miles of his artillery unit's firebase at Buon Kuop. Powerful, almost inexplicable emotions welled up from deep within his core. The people of Vietnam had been surprisingly gracious. It made the regrets even more profound.

"Look, Mom," Denise said. "Look how big they are!"

Two Asian bull elephants lumbered towards them. On top of each was a small wooden saddle that could seat two people, or one overweight war veteran. The seats were covered by a wicker arch to provide shade. The elephant driver or mahout sat in front, straddled over the elephant's neck.

Alice grunted as she struggled to climb the stairs that led to the elevated boarding platform. "It's okay, Denise," she said as her daughter fussed. "I've come this far. I'll keep my butt in gear until I can't go on any more."

The pair of elephants took them from the re-created M'Nong village, a new tourist spot, up an old logging road. Their cameras clicked at monkeys in the trees, cheeky little things that loved to steal sandwiches and fruit from tourists, as they had already found out in the grounds of their hotel. After a forty-five minute trek through deep forest, the elephants arrived at another high platform and the trio from Portland dismounted. Beside a sprawling banyan tree, a stick-fenced corral was home to a large bull elephant fluffing dirt onto its haunches with his trunk.

A Vietnamese man in his mid-fifties, dressed in the khaki ranger uniform of the Yok Don National Park, greeted the new arrivals.

"My name is Dinh Thanh Hau," he said. "You can call me Hau." The man bowed. "And this is Tia Sang. His name means sunbeam. He is getting very old. He is no longer used for rides. You say in America, he's retired." The man laughed. "We've been friends for a very long time. But you haven't come to see elephants. Please, follow me. It's not far."

Hau led the group on foot into the forest, down a wide trail flanked by bamboo thickets and shaded from the sun by a canopy of tall teak trees. They arrived at a glade where sunbeams shone through the high forest onto fallen tree trunks layered in moss. Some of the trees were stumps, once blackened and jagged, mellowed by the passage of time and the gentle touch of broad-fingered ferns. Camellias perfumed the humid air. Hundreds of delicate orchids hung from the trees, beautiful petals displaying every possible color of nature's spectrum. Interspersed between the flowering shrubs of the forest floor, small Buddhist statues joined white Christian crosses to silently guard the jungle's peace.

To one side of the glade stood a thatched hut. Outside its entrance sat two old men on hand-hewn stools. They rose as the group approached, steadied themselves on gnarled teak canes, and bowed. One of the men—the eldest, easily into his eighties—had a nasty purple patch running down one side of his flat, square face, the kind of scarring caused by a severe burn.

"This is Colonel Quan Van Thi," Hau said. "And this is Le Dao Phong. They are veterans of the war of liberation. They have been tending this garden for a very long time, since shortly after the war ended. This forest is a holy site. Its grounds hold the bodies of many dead, from both sides; spirits that have found a place of rest and honor. And as you can see—" Hau spread his arm wide as he pointed to the many crosses and statues marking graves. "The orchids in this garden have been waiting with much patience to share their secrets."

Hau guided Alice Hinman through the glade to one specific cross. Soft blue orchids—an almost electric blue in color—grew in a cluster around the base of its white wood stake. Alice fell to her knees, sobbing. She clutched a handful of loamy soil and felt its warmth. A metal chain hung from a nail placed at the intersection of the cross. She wept as she read the name on the dog tags. Alice brought them to her lips and kissed them. "Soon, my love, we will bring you home."

AUTHOR'S NOTES – CHARLES A. CORNELL

ALTHOUGH THE BATTLE at the hamlet of Bon Ao Voi is a work of my imagination, the military scenes in The Orchid Man were written with as much historical fidelity as possible, researched from eyewitness accounts of actions in the Vietnam War such as The Battle at The Knoll and The Battle of Hill 488.

Between January 15 and February 9, 1968, Operation San Angelo was a real air mobile campaign conducted by the 1st Brigade, 101st Airborne from Bu Prang Special Forces Base.

The indigenous M'Nong people still live in the Central Highlands and pursue traditional methods of agriculture and timber felling including the use of elephants as beasts of burden. It is an unfortunate fact, illustrated in The Orchid Man, that during the Vietnam War elephants became military targets, attacked from the air or killed on the ground to prevent their use by the North Vietnamese to carry supplies over the Highlands along the Ho Chi Minh Trail.

Large herds of wild elephants once roamed Dak Lak Province but deforestation, hunting, and the illegal wildlife trade has all but wiped them out. Yok Don National Park was established in 1992 to protect over one thousand square kilometers of lowland forest typical of the setting used in The Orchid Man. In 2009, an elephant sanctuary was established to protect the wild elephant population, their numbers declining from between 1500-2000 by the Vietnam War's end in 1975 to fewer than 100 today. Yok Don National Park is home to more than 858 species of trees, 200 bird species, many reptiles, insects, and 93 types of animal—unfortunately 32 of them on the endangered list.

Place names used in The Orchid Man are true to the period. After the war ended and the two Vietnams came together some place names changed. Quang Duc Province is now Dak Lak Province. The Dak Krong River is also known today as the Srepok. Buon Kuop and Buon Ma Thuot are real locations, as are the Dray Sap and Dray Nur waterfalls.

The Orchid Man also received inspiration from the true story of a real Orchid Man, Mr. Trinh Van Sy who has made it his life's work to grow and preserve over 200 rare wild orchid species in his garden in Vietnam.

The mission of the Defense Department's Missing Personnel Office in DC—officially the Defense POW/MIA Accounting Agency, an awkwardly bureaucratic name—is to provide the fullest possible accounting for missing military service personnel to their families and the nation. At present, more than 82,000 Americans remain missing from WWII, the Korean War, the Vietnam War, the Cold War, and the Gulf Wars/other conflicts.

For more than two decades the U.S. has conducted joint field activities with the governments of Vietnam, Laos, and Cambodia to recover the remains of missing Americans lost in the Vietnam conflict. Throughout these countries, field teams continue to investigate crash and burial sites, as well as interview locals to gain additional knowledge relevant to the fates of missing Americans. Since 1973, the remains of more than 1,000 Americans killed in the Vietnam War have been identified and returned to their families for burial with full military honors. Today, more than 1,600 Americans still remain unaccounted for, a sad legacy of the deadly geopolitical firestorm called the Vietnam War.

Finally, The Orchid Man is an attempt to reflect five different perspectives: the principal military combatants—Americans, Viet Cong, South Vietnamese and North Vietnamese—but also the viewpoint of the innocent villagers caught in the crossfire. There is no attempt to take sides—to say who was right or who was wrong—but simply to reflect the reality of a brutal conflict and remember with sadness and respect all the lives that were lost. I hope you agree that The Orchid Man is a fitting tribute to all of them.

—CAC

DRAGON LURE

John Hope

I

Florida, July 2018

The sweet stench of moldy grass pervaded my senses as I hosed down the mower, shears, and Dad's other lawn-cutting equipment. The morning sun low on the horizon baked the back of my neck as I glared at Dad's half-awake face. Coffee steam rose from his mug and a cigarette dangled from the side of his lip like a dead twig. He lounged against a stack of cinder blocks that he kept next to the garage, for reasons unknown.

I looked over my shoulder. Kathy Daniels and her friend Tammy-something walked down the sidewalk, books cradled in their arms, no doubt on their way to Gavel Middle School.

"Can I go now?" I whined, wiping the sweat from my forehead.

"Cha-ase . . ." he said, in his typical long southern drawl. "Ain't my fault you forgot to hose down the equipment last night."

"I'm gonna be late for school again." I peered at the sidewalk but Kathy and Tammy had already rounded the corner.

Dad belched and sipped at his coffee from one side of his

mouth, still balancing the cigarette in the other side, a feat I'd never seen anyone else master. He sauntered forward in slow, lazy steps. His poor thin face was sunken and blotchy, but his arms and legs were firm from a lifetime of manual labor. His insistence on conducting his inspection of my work wearing only a grass-stained T-shirt and striped boxers embarrassed me to no end. He bent over the mower and trimmers at different angles. His strange obsession with maintaining his equipment never made sense to me.

Water still pouring from the hose, I bit my lip with impatience while the water spilled down the cracked driveway, darkening the surface as it spread.

Dad stepped .uncomfortably close to me. He straightened his back with subtle but noticeable snaps of arthritis. "You'll have to learn to take better care of this equipment once you take over the business."

I sneered. I'd never in a billion years cut grass for a living. This was Dad's business.

Dad sipped at his coffee, narrowing his eyes at me. "The mower's… okay."

I jumped to turn off the hose.

"You still got the blowers."

"The blowers? But Dad–"

"Finish the job." He paced away.

I tensed my grip on the hose, wanting to spray Dad in the back of his balding head. Dropping the hose, I dashed for the trailer hitched to Dad's pickup and pulled out the pair of leaf blowers. Leaning them against the house, I showered each with the hose.

Dad leaned against his truck, as he gazed down the street.

"Dad. Blowers are done."

Dad flicked away his cigarette butt.

"Dad. Dad! Can I go?"

The man breathed, then raised his hand. "Fine."

I dropped the hose, cranked off the water, and rushed into the house for my bag. In a jerk, I reversed direction, darted outside, veered toward the backyard, and hopped over the chain-linked fence to Mrs. Higgins' backyard as a shortcut. I zigzagged around the old lady's maze of overgrown sandspur weeds, a few scraping my bare legs.

Mrs. Higgins, sitting on her back porch in her nightgown, rose and shook her fist in the air. "Get off my property!"

"Hi, Mrs. Higgins!"

"This ain't no shortcut!"

"Have a nice day, Mrs. Higgins!"

I hopped over her fence to her front yard. With this hop, books and notebook paper flew from my backpack across the grass. I squatted and jammed the fallen school supplies back inside. When I stood, the bag tipped and the books tumbled out again. Cursing, I scooped them up and raced down the street with them in my arms.

Just ahead of me down the sidewalk, Jacob and Andrew were beating on a third, smaller kid. I knew the small kid was Bryan before I saw his face. Jacob held Bryan from behind while Andrew tortured the little kid with a noogie to the head.

I raced even faster and once I was in range, smacked Andrew in the face with my books.

The books went flying, and so did Andrew. His butt hit the sidewalk. He looked up, stunned.

I elbowed Jacob and he clenched his back, releasing his hold on the Bryan.

Still on the ground, Andrew said, "Damn, Chase. What was that for?"

I yelled, "Leave Bryan alone!"

Jacob rubbed his back. "He's just a punk kid."

"Take a hike. You're late for school, anyhow."

"Fine," Andrew spat, getting to his feet. "But you better watch your back." He waved Jacob to follow him.

Although he was thirteen like me, with his short, skeletal frame, Bryan could have easily passed for eleven. He was gauntly thin as if he ate nothing but saltines his entire life and he wore small clothes that made him appear even smaller. He patted down his messed-up blonde hair. A faded Rays baseball T-shirt – his favorite team – hung over him like a used hand-me-down he picked up from Goodwill, which was probably close to the truth. He said, "Thanks."

"Yeah. Whatever." I stepped toward my scattered books.

Bryan coughed and wheezed.

I shook my head. "You forgot your inhaler again, didn't you?"

Bryan coughed and nodded.

I patted his back to help him knock out the coughing. "C'mon." We walked toward school.

Bryan focused on the books in my grip. "Can I hold those for you?"

"No. I got them."

"Um… okay." Bryan's weepy eyes reminded me of a puppy denied his favorite treat.

"Fine. Here." I handed the skinny boy my books.

"Umph." His face reddened with strain.

I took back a couple books, leaving Bryan with two lighter ones.

Bryan nodded.

I rolled my eyes and quickened the pace. "C'mon."

THE HALL LEADING to the teacher's parking lot caught my eye. There were only two more periods until dismissal. Ditching art and Ms. Hammerstone's history class wasn't the worst thing in the world. Art was fluff and in history we weren't doing anything but turning in our reports on the Continental Congress, which I had dropped off a day early, a first for me. Opposite the hallway to freedom stood Mr. Evans, the Assistant Principal. He scolded a girl as she twirled the ends of her purple hair.

My heart fluttered as I considered my possible escape. This wouldn't be the first time I ducked out of school before dismissal. The last time, however, Mr. Evans had threatened various *disciplinary actions*, whatever that meant.

I edged toward the parking lot door.

A hand tapped my shoulder.

"Hey, Chase," Bryan said, standing next to me. He smiled, his bunny-like buckteeth prominent.

I waved him away, or least tried to, as I crept closer to the hallway, my backpack scraped a line of sixth grade artwork which dangled on a fishing line attached to the wall.

His smile faded. "What stinks?"

"Andrew stuffed a used toilet brush in my gym locker and it got all over my stuff." I whispered, flapping my shirt.

"Gross," he said, sneering at my toilet water-stained shirt.

"Go away. I'm ditching school."

Bryan's bright greenish blue eyes grew wide. "Again? But… we have detention after school. For being late."

"I know. I know."

Bryan eyed Mr. Evans. "And what about…?" He pointed to the overweight man still talking with the girl.

"I know. I know." I twisted my bottom lip, knowing the little chat would draw to an end shortly. The girl appeared ready to bolt. "Can you run interference?"

"Me? How?"

"I don't know. Make up something." I shoved Bryan further out in the hallway.

Bryan staggered, regaining his balance just as the girl walked off.

Mr. Evans turned toward me.

Bryan raced forward and waved his hands. "Mr. Evans! Mr. Evans!"

The man seemed startled, but composed himself and mounted his hands on his hips. "What is it this time, Bryan?"

"Um… um…"

I froze and held my breath.

Bryan flipped up the bottom of his shirt, exposing his stomach. "My belly button is leaking."

"It's what?"

"It's leaking. Look!" He rotated around the man, forcing him to turn his back to me.

I ran down the hallway. I shot Mr. Evans a quick glance before I sprinted outside and into the parking lot. I raced through the zigzag of parked cars, and to the far end where the ground dipped into a ditch lined with a chain link fence. Tossing my backpack, I scurried up the fence and over, grabbed my bag, and ran.

. . .

II

A HALF MILE LATER, I climbed a tree next to my house, up to the twins' bedroom window. Miles and Mazy, both in second grade, would be home soon. I definitely didn't want them knowing I'd ditched the last couple periods again. Neither understood the necessity of taking such things in your own hands.

Arriving at the branch that extended over part of the roof, I reached out and braced one hand on the window sill. Bending, I pushed up on the window glass with my other palm. It didn't budge at first, and then . . . *urt.* With a little metal-on-metal squeak, the window opened. I eased myself inside, landing upside down on Miles' bed, my heavy backpack thunking against the back of my head.

I panted a second and then heard the clamor of the twins' voices downstairs. Shoot! They were home already.

I righted myself, closed the window, and sprinted for the door.

The twins stomped up the stairs, undoubtedly heading for their bedroom.

I spun and jumped into their closet, closing the door a second before Miles and Mazy bounded into the room.

The twins laughed.

Mazy said, "I heard that joke before."

"Then why're you laughing?"

"Cause it's so stupid."

"You're stupid."

"No, you're stupid."

One of their beds squeaked. Through slits in the closet door, I saw movement with little detail, although I knew they were wrestling.

The rustling stopped. "Hey," Miles said. "You got leaves on my bed."

"I didn't get leaves on your bed."

"Then how'd they get here?" Miles called out, "Mom! Mazy got my bed dirty."

"I did not!"

They stomped out of the room.

Silence.

I pushed the trifold closet door open, tiptoeing toward freedom. Coast clear. I rushed out to my room and ducked inside.

I kept the light off and squeezed my way through the blackness to my computer. With the wiggle of the mouse, the computer woke, casting a harsh glow to the tiny room. It wasn't an actual bedroom, it was just an over-sized walk-in closet. When the twins were born, I helped Dad clear out the stacks of busted school desks he'd acquired but never used when the old school down the street was demolished and the closet became my room. Barely large enough for a bed and the plank I used as a desk, I had to sit on my bed to use the computer. I clicked a couple buttons to hide the monitor's harshness, hoping it wasn't enough to emit a noticeable light from the crack at the base of the door.

I peeled off my tainted shirt. Mostly dry at this point, the thought of toilet water cooties was enough. I flicked it toward the pile in the corner of my room.

Remaining shirtless, I put on my earphones and clicked the Dragon Lure icon on the desktop. An animated dragon crossed the screen, spraying flames in his wake. I logged in as TigerHeart05. My orange and black dragon avatar emerged and I was in the game.

A village of brown, thatched roofs and gray chimneys puffing smoke rested at the base of a grassy valley with a deep blue river snaking alongside. A giant green and orange speckled egg sat mounted upright at the center of town. Villagers darted through uneven cobblestone streets. They worked together to maintain the fires and warm water that surrounded the egg, keeping it the perfect hatching temperature. Hunchbacked elders measured water temperature and supplies while younger ones hauled heavy wood and pails of water.

TigerHeart05 remained perched on a giant tree on a hillside, looking down on the village. He ripped apart a slaughtered sheep gripped in his giant dragon talons and gobbled his lunch. Broken pixelated clouds floated across the sky as a chilling breeze cut across TigerHeart05's dry, reptilian skin.

The egg was the result of hundreds of hours of gameplay. Clues tracked down to locate the hidden caves, fierce battles against computer-generated dragons, and riddles he decoded all lead to this egg and its care.

He was so close to defeating this game. Once hatched, the encased dragon–the legendary Prometheus Dragon–would be under his control and it was just a matter of leading the dragon to its home castle, a mere hundred-mile flight due east.

Ting-ting.

A pop up in-game messaging window pulled me from the game. I clicked the pop up and a chat window appeared, overlaying the village scene. Reading the text, I smiled

`HopeMuster: welcome back`

I typed in my response.

`TigerHeart05: hey, muster... glad to be back`
`HopeMuster: you are looking good today :)`

He hit me with this lame joke every time we met. We'd never actually seen each other and there was no way that he could know.

`TigerHeart05: yeah you too`
`HopeMuster: you are early - school out?`
`TigerHeart05: it is for me`
`HopeMuster: kicked out of school?`
`TigerHeart05: we'll see . . . I ditched school early`
`HopeMuster: ditched?`

I paused, tapping a finger against the sides of the keyboard. I sometimes forgot that my best gaming friend wasn't from America. I had never asked what country Muster was from – revealing such facts about our "real life" was taboo. Besides, nobody really cared except Internet perverts. In any case, English was definitely not Muster's first language.

TigerHeart05: ditched means I left when I wasn't supposed to

HopeMuster: you in trouble with police?

TigerHeart05: not yet ;) so . . . guess who finally has the egg?

HopeMuster: yes. I heard you got it. amazing.

TigerHeart05: you heard? how?

HopeMuster: i mean i noticed how the rest of the game reacted

TigerHeart05: oh, ok. you owe me

HopeMuster: i do?

TigerHeart05: yeah, remember our bet about me getting the egg?

HopeMuster: oh, yes. for a Rays baseball cap

TigerHeart05: and it better be a good one, not some old crap

HopeMuster: ok, a bet's a bet. so how big is the egg?

TigerHeart05: enormous. took me a whole day just to transport it to _

Movement in the village scene captured my attention. "Shoot," I whispered. "Dark-winged Bandits." I clicked away at the mouse, moving my dragon. I clicked back to the messenger.

TigerHeart05: sorry dude. Gotta go

TigerHeart05 unfolded his wings.

Three dragons, all Dark-winged Bandits, swooped from the air toward the village. Villagers screamed and ran in seemingly random directions.

TigerHeart05 dove off his perch, plunging down into the valley to rescue the egg.

The attacking Dark-winged Bandits responded, splitting out of formation and crossing each in mid-flight. The one in the middle spewed flames onto the village. Buildings ignited.

I cringed and clicked through a series of buttons in rapid fire.

TigerHeart05 spun and flung his spiked tail at the middle dragon.

SMACK.

The injured Dark-winged Bandit blinked red, appearing limp.

TigerHeart05 rebounded and smacked again.

The Dark-winged Bandit disappeared.

I smiled, watching my experience points increase. I kept clicking.

TigerHeart05 dove toward the pool surrounding the egg, gulped a mouthful of water, and sprayed it over the burning village buildings, dousing the flames.

Far below, the villagers cheered.

The remaining two Dark-winged Bandits, however, were at the opposite end of the village spewing more flames onto buildings. TigerHeart05 flapped his orange wings, accelerating toward the attackers. He spun, employing the same move that defeated the first Bandit. The remaining two worked together, crisscrossing and sandwiching TigerHeart05 from top and bottom.

TigerHeart05 slowed.

The Bandits swung their spiked tails.

TigerHeart05 blinked red and fell, crashing into a wooden house, splinters flying.

I pounded a fist into my makeshift desk. It made a loud noise and flipped up, nearly catapulting my laptop.

Out in the hallway, the twins spoke in whispers.

Shit.

I waited in silence, hoping they hadn't actually heard me.

Seconds passed.

Ting-ting.

The twins burst out laughing. Stomping feet.

Miles called out, "I got you! I got you!"

Mazy yelled, "No, you missed!"

More stomping feet.

I breathed, returning my focus to the computer. The messenger blinked. I clicked on it.

`HopeMuster: problems?`

`TigerHeart05: a little . . . dark-winged bandits, three of them`

`HopeMuster: use drago acid`

I clicked through my supply list. Nearly empty. Just a couple of heart potions, a bail of a corn seed, and an invisibility cloak.

`HopeMuster: you need to build a stock of drago acid`

`TigerHeart05: no kidding`

`HopeMuster: the mystic caves have a lot if you can find them`

`TigerHeart05: too late now`

The game's animation caught my attention. I minimized the message screen. The village and my egg were at stake.

Villager children stared at TigerHeart05, who lay in the middle of a busted house. Screams from afar. He flapped his wings and rose into the air.

The Dark-winged Bandits had the egg. They lifted it from the ground using a netted rope spanned between the two.

"Dang it!" I said, then covered my mouth and glanced at the door.

The twins' laughter persisted.

I refocused.

Ting-ting.

Another message from Muster.

I ignored him and clicked away at the mouse.

TigerHeart05 pursued the invading dragons. With the egg cradled in the netting, he couldn't attack them like before or they might drop and smash the egg. He dove below them, skimming over the villagers' dwellings. Carefully, he swiped at the netting with his spiked tail. The rope frayed but held.

The Dark-winged Bandits growled, but kept accelerating with every swish of their wings.

TigerHeart05 slashed at the netting again, this time with more force.

The rope snapped in several places.

The Dark-winged Bandits hissed and tried to shift their claws for a better grip, but the net's knots slipped and splayed.

The egg rolled.

TigerHeart05 reached to catch it. The giant egg's weight and forward momentum were too much for his hold.

It slipped.

He watched helplessly as it crashed to the ground, shattering into a million fragments and disappearing into sparkling dots.

I smashed my fist into the wooden plank holding my computer. The board flipped all the way over this time. I dove to the side and caught the computer as I slammed onto the narrow floor between the bed and the wall.

I stared at the laptop teetering on my fingertips, eyes huge from the fright of almost seeing my electronic lifeline crash against the hardwood floor. Rocked with shock, I didn't notice the flood of light against my face until Mom's feet stepped into view.

I looked up.

Arms crossed and face tight, Mom scowled at me.

Ting-ting.

I closed the laptop. Responding to Muster would have to wait.

III

I CRINGED. On my knees, I rubbed Mom's feet as she lounged, feet propped up in the living room's recliner. She sighed and squeezed out a burp, the result of gulping from her bottle of Coke.

"Can I stop?" I asked, tired of her humiliating massage.

She shoved her left foot into my face. "This one needs more." She sipped her drink. "Dig your thumbs in more."

I complied, wishing to be anywhere but here.

"You know," she started. "this is for your own good."

I stopped. "My own good?"

She swung the bottle toward me. "I know you think this is wrong. But you've got to learn. It's hard to see that when you're not looking at the full picture."

"But it's Friday, Mom. And I only skipped a couple classes. And this is a holiday weekend."

"What holiday?"

"Monday is Washington's Birthday."

She rolled her eyes. "That's not a real holiday. You don't even get it off."

"I thought we did. It's a government holiday, isn't it?"

"You ain't no government employee. You're a student. A student who should be in school."

I looked down. "I know," I muttered, digging my thumbs in, knowing full well that Mom was a government employee, working in the D.M.V. for the past twenty years.

"We all need someone looking after us. Gotta stay accountable."

Though, like Dad, she had no more than a high school education, her big words like *stay accountable* always came through loud and clear. Of course I knew skipping school was bad. What she or any other adult didn't see was the desire burning inside me. I needed to play the game because it was the one thing that didn't drive me crazy. She didn't see that. Nobody did.

"Chase… you're on a crash course, boy. So focused on what you want, you're gonna wind up killin' yourself if you ain't careful." She shook a finger at me.

I stopped and glared.

"You hate us now, but this is for your own good."

I tightened my lips and dug my fingers into her rough, smelly feet that felt more like a dried out lizard than human skin.

"Ahhhh…" she sighed, her eyes closing, her body twitching like a purring cat.

I stopped. "Am I done now?"

She breathed, looking down on me. "Now, hit the weeds."

"The weeds?" I whined, falling back onto my butt. "I just did your massage."

"Chase, this ain't your first rodeo. Go hit the weeds."

"Fine."

I stood and stormed off, eager to get away from those feet but dreading my next chore.

SWEAT POURED down the sides of my face, stinging my eyes. On my hands and knees and covered in dirt, I crawled through Mom's front yard flower bed, pulling weeds. I hated this job and Mom knew it. Any sort of lawn work was torture. I couldn't believe Dad did this every day for work, and because he did, we had a well-landscaped yard that I despised.

The game baked in my mind. It had taken me *weeks* to track down and capture that egg. It killed me that something as simple as a few Dark-winged Bandits coming out of nowhere could steal all of that work from me.

"Hey, Chase."

I twisted and squinted, the sun backlighting the kid standing over me – Bryan. "Hey." I thumped forward on my knees, pulling more weeds and tossing them into the plastic bag at my side.

"Detention was awesome. Coach Lester played old Mickey Mouse cartoons on YouTube and we didn't have to write anything."

"Good for you."

Bryan half-stepped back. "Are you mad at me?"

I turned from the weeds. "Why would I be mad at you?"

Bryan dropped his head and made circles in the dirt with the toe of his shoe. "I don't know." His drooped head and freckled cheeks made him look even younger than he already appeared.

I returned to the weeds. "My parents caught me at home. But..." I whirled my head back and forth. "...but they don't know about me being tardy. So don't tell them."

He dropped to his knees next to me. "Didn't you say it was your dad's fault that you were late?"

"Yeah."

"So why would you get in trouble for being late?"

I shook my head. "They're idiots. That's why." I shifted my weight. "Dude. You're in my way."

"Sorry." He stood. "Can I help?"

I shook my head. "If Dad caught you helping me, he'd accuse me of being lazy." I wiped the sweat from my forehead. "The only way you can help is to make the sun go away."

Bryan sprang into a stance, hands up and pointing skyward as if ready to attack. "Back, sun! Back! Or suffer my wrath." He spun and kicked to the sky. "Ya-ya!" His backpack flung around and smacked him in his face. He collapsed, rubbing his nose. "Ouch."

I cracked a smile. "You're such a spaz."

Bryan's right ear was small and twisted and his left didn't work well. He was born nearly deaf. When he was five doctors reconstructed his left ear using skin from the back of his leg. I suspected most of the first years of his life he spent in his head. The result was this weird kid in front of me. Aside from him always tagging around me, I secretly liked his weirdness. When I'm gaming, I slip on my headphones and peel away from everyone else. I could always relate to people who were a little different, who weren't just bad copies of other idiots at school.

He squatted next to me. He reeked with his own strange smell, like a pile of old laundry. I imagined he washed his clothes infrequently.

A thought hit me.

"Bryan?"

"Yeah?" He straightened and smiled.

"What are you doing at nine tonight?"

"Um..." He tilted his eyebrows as if I'd suddenly quizzed him on the Battle of Gettysburg. "At nine?"

"My parents are going out drinking with their friends tonight. The twins should be asleep by then."

"Uh, well. I'm not allowed out after dark."

"No. I mean, me coming over to your place."

His eyes grew huge. "Uh... you can't."

"C'mon. You got internet, right?"

"Well, yeah."

"See... I just lost this huge thing in this game I've been playing and I gotta get another one, and fast. Before the chamber closes."

"The chamber?" His eyes narrowed with a thoughtful stare.

"It's complicated." I placed my dirty hand on his boney shoulder. "Please. It'd mean a lot."

He stiffened and stared at my hand. "Um. I guess."

"Great." I stood, brushing off the dirt from my knees. "Your house is the light blue one at the end of Evans, right?"

"Well. Sort of."

"Sort of?"

"I'll meet you there at nine. Okay?"

I smiled. "Great. See you at nine." I stepped forward and attacked the next set of weeds with more vigor.

Bryan lingered, but sort of wandered away.

JUST AS PLANNED, after putting the twins to bed with a warning of death if they got up, I snuck off. I cut through Mrs. Higgins' yard and ran down to the end of Evans Street to what I thought was Bryan's house.

He paced out front, his face tense and faking a smile in the dim overhead street light.

I patted his shoulder. "Ready?" I stepped toward the house.

He resisted. "No, wait."

"What?"

He hesitated with a pained look, then waved me to the side. "C'mere."

I followed him to the chain link fence that lined the edge of the front yard. Rounding it, we walked into a gap between this fence and another one that marked the edge of the next door neighbor's house. For as many times as I'd passed by these houses, I'd never noticed the two parallel fences – typically a single fence did the job of separating properties.

We walked between the length of the pair of fences, light from both houses' living room windows lighting our way. Past their backyards, the chain link fences ended at a doublewide trailer surrounded by dirt and crabgrass.

I stopped.

Bryan walked a few steps before realizing I wasn't with him. He gave me a weak backward glance.

I asked, "You live here?"

"We can go to your place."

"Can't. My mom took away my laptop and I don't know the password to theirs."

"Um . . . okay."

He led me inside, but tapped his lips with his finger.

I nodded and tiptoed close behind.

The entrance led directly into a narrow kitchen reeking of wet pasta and sauce. Tiny LEDs on the face of a rumbling refrigerator provided the only light. Commercial jingles from a TV in the approaching living room gave me chills, like I was about to rob a bank rather than entering my friend's home.

The living room was almost as dark as the kitchen, aside from the harsh flicker of the TV. In front of it, an old lady rocked in a wooden rocking chair, her body as stiff as a corpse beyond the subtle kick of her feet against the plastic, grayish carpeting.

Bryan continued to creep, keeping his eyes on the old woman. I did the same. He stepped to a closed door. Carefully, he placed both hands and his ear to the door, listening. He clicked it open and stepped in. I followed until he stopped me with a hand to my chest. He tapped his finger to his lips, looked to the old woman, and then signaled that I remain outside.

I nodded.

He disappeared into the black room.

The floor squeaked with his footsteps and I eyed the woman.

She stopped her rocking.

I held my breath.

Then she resumed.

Bryan returned with an opened laptop in hand. He nodded his head to the side and I moved, allowing him to pass. He closed the door behind him, and then crept down to the next door. Opening it, he nodded at me to follow him in.

I closed the door behind me. The room was pitch-black.

With a click, a shade-less lamp glared, lighting the small room, which was only twice the size of my closet.

Bryan set the laptop on a card table in the corner of the room, clicked the computer's power button, and sat in a lawn chair next to the table.

I sat on the corner of the bed, next to his seat. I surveyed the room. Posters of knights and castles lined the walls and a pile of dirty laundry lay heaped near my feet. Everything reeked of Bryan.

He smiled weakly.

"Nice room," I whispered.

He shrugged, scratching his nose.

The computer booted up to the desktop. With a few swipes of the mousepad and a couple clicks, Bryan opened a window covered in several dozen Dragon Lure dragon icons, all of different colors.

"Holy cow," I said, a little louder than I intended. I spoke softer, "How many profiles have you started?"

He shrugged.

I grabbed the sides of the computer and angled it toward me. I hovered the mouse's pointer over one icon at a time, each popping up the profile name associated with the corresponding icon.

BlueKnight. BiscuitAndEggs. DragonFly. TigerHeart05.

Wait. Did that say TigerHeart05? The icon with this name was the same orange and black as the one profile that I had on my computer.

"How did you . . ." I stopped.

Bryan's weepy, angled eyebrows looked as if he was prepping himself to be pummeled.

I double-clicked the TigerHeart05 icon. The orange and black dragon crossed the screen. Seconds later, the screen lit with the familiar village where I'd left off earlier, the villagers busily cleaning up the area at the center of town where the egg used to be perched.

I nudged Bryan. "This is my game. My profile."

"Yeah."

"Why do you have it?" I angled myself more toward him, as if readying myself for a fight. "How'd you get into it?"

He opened his mouth to speak, but a loud crash and a rattle of the walls ripped our attention away.

We turned toward the bedroom door just as it flew open and three men in suits burst into the room.

I leapt from the bed, but a heavy body slammed me face-first to the floor.

A sandpapery voice spoke. "Settle down, Chase."

My arms were twisted behind my back and then handcuffs clamped against my wrists.

IV

I SHIVERED IN A STARK, brightly-lit room that felt as hollow as Mr. Evans' office. The room wasn't cold, but my fear forced a constant rub between my clammy shoulder and Bryan's. Our hands still handcuffed behind our backs, we sat in side-by-side aluminum chairs with a small wooden table in front of us. The giant men who dragged us into this room and slammed us into these chairs stood outside a translucent glass door. Their muffled chatter reminded me of the low-toned *wah-wah-wah* of Charlie Brown's parents and the teachers lecturing him.

I turned to Bryan. His trademark weepy eyes appeared ready to cry.

"What'd *you* do?" I asked in a near-whisper, but harsh enough to let him know that I blamed him for this.

"Huh?"

"They busted into your house. You selling drugs or something?"

"No."

"Is your grandma?"

"No."

Fuzzy outlines of the men shifted with the low mumbling of their voices. I fidgeted, the handcuffs pinching my wrists behind my back. I wished for home, regretting yet another decision of mine. I wondered if the twins were still in bed. I yearned to be in mine. Though I tried to hide it, I shivered. I secretly kept Daniel, my well-worn stuffed animal tiger, tucked underneath my bed for nights I felt like this, especially following a bad dream or when I was sent to my room as punishment. I wiggled my fingered and wished I was holding him close to me now.

"I was trying to help," Bryan pleaded.

"Huh?"

"I was just trying to help."

"Help what?"

"Your game. Dragon Lure. I hacked your account just to help you out."

I nodded toward the door. "You call this help? For all I know, your hacking is why we're in this place." I shifted again. "My dad's going to kill me." My nose itched. I attempted to rub it against my shoulder. "How was hacking my account supposed to help?"

"The egg. You were almost there so many times, but other dragons kept relocating it just when you were getting close. Remember those notes that started popping up in your home cave?"

I frowned. "Notes? You mean the ones that I got from… wait. You put them there? I thought it was…"

"The messengers?" He shook his head. "They were just a distraction."

I stared at him. "All this time, I thought I'd solved the puzzles myself. But it was you."

"Well, you had to fight off the bad dragons. I suck at that. I just… helped."

I glared at him, unsure how to respond. I had never considered him as someone who knew how to game.

The doorknob clicked and the door opened. In walked a pair of white-collared men, one with a huge potbelly and the other with thick geeky-looking glasses. Both carried paper cups in one hand and a notepad in the other. A steamy scent of old coffee wafted in the air. They strode in with frightening confidence. Mr. Glasses closed the door behind them and they sat in metal chairs across from us.

"Gentlemen," Potbelly said with a weird smirk, the kind of look adults loved to give seconds before lecture time. "You two've been busy."

"Bryan hacked my account," I blurted, though I immediately regretted it. Bryan would have never tattled on me. He often lied for me, like that weird "My belly button is leaking," thing he said to Mr. Evans. I sucked in and wished I could suck the words back into my mouth.

"Excuse me?" Glasses asked.

Despite my regret, I kept on ratting him out. "He didn't ask or anything. I never knew about it until just now."

"Right," Potbelly said, his facial hair twitching.

"Honest," I pleaded.

Bryan's head sunk lower as he took the accusation without question.

With my eyes, I tried to tell him I was sorry.

Potbelly sipped his coffee and then rested it at the corner of the table. "It's obvious you two worked together."

"It's just a game," I said.

"Oh," Potbelly leaned in. "Your activities were no game."

Glasses nodded. "Stealing from the government should never be taken lightly."

"Wha…?" My mouth dropped. "We… I didn't steal anything."

"And don't think your ages will shield you from the consequences of your actions. Penetrating top secret government databases is punishable at the highest level. Do you realize how many lives you put at stake due to your–"

A clamor of voices and the slam of something heavy jolted all of us. The men twisted toward the door behind them.

Potbelly muttered. "What the…?"

A pair of gunshots.

The men dove to the floor.

More gunshots.

I bent to the side. Bryan and I thunked heads and tumbled to the floor, our chairs tumbling out from underneath us. I held my breath, frightened so much I peed a little.

More gunshots and the translucent glass covering the door shattered, raining glass over the floor.

Potbelly and Glasses yelled something.

Bryan, lying on top of me, his face so tight tears squeezed out the corners of his eyes. I, too, wanted to cry.

The door flew open.

Gunshots.

Grunts.

The table flipped.

Bryan was lifted off me.

A woman in black stood next to a broad shouldered man, also in black. The man held Bryan up with one hand as if he were a bag of groceries. Both adults held guns.

The woman, brawny enough to be a gym teacher, smiled at me. "Chase. I am so glad to at last meet you in person." Her short, black hair rocked as she spoke in a heavy accent, like Russian or something like that. She reminded me of our neighbors, the Janiszewskis, from Belorussia.

"Uh… in… person…?" I stammered, so scared I felt ready to pee myself.

She smirked, exposing her narrow teeth. She squatted in front of me and sat me upright. "I am who you call… Muster."

I gasped, a chill sprinting up my spine.

V

FINALLY FREE OF HANDCUFFS, I rubbed my sore wrists as I tipped into Bryan, seated next to me in the backseat of the car. The fresh leather-scented vehicle provided little comfort as we sped down darkened alleys, occasionally screeching its tires in tight turns. Sweat trickled down my back and I found it hard to swallow. Bryan swung his legs back and forth, occasionally tapping his thighs together in nervous jerks. No police trailed us yet, at least as far as I could tell, but the way Muster's partner was driving it was just a matter of time.

Muster sat diagonal to me in the front passenger seat. She rattled off commands to the driver in a foreign language. He responded with one hairpin turn and another.

My stomach grumbled. I often got hungry when I was scared, like now.

Bryan nudged me.

I gave a wordless, "What?"

He whispered, "She's HopeMuster?" he asked as if he still couldn't believe it.

I nodded. "How do you know her?"

"She messaged me in the game."

"You mean she messaged me while you were playing in my profile?"

He shook his head.

I said, "So she was really messaging me."

"No. She always said, *Hello Bryan* when I played."

"She—"

"Oh, yes, Chase," Muster said from the front seat, butting into our whispering. "I knew quite well who was playing." HopeMuster twisted back to glance at me. "I could not let on I knew you."

"Why not?"

"You're too… how you say… skittish."

Me? Skittish? I frowned at Bryan. "So you all were in on this… whatever this is?"

Bryan shook his head.

Muster said, "No. Bryan knew nothing, aside from a clue or two from me. But even we didn't know how to crack the puzzle. It took both of you."

Frustrated with her confusing comments, I grabbed the back of the front seat and pulled myself forward. "What's going on? I mean, what is all this? Why were we kidnapped? Twice! And what's all this have to do with the game? And where are we going? And when are we eating? I'm starved!"

Muster dug into a brown paper bag between the two and pulled out a pair of wrapped Twinkies. She tossed them to the backseat. "Eat well."

Bryan caught one. "Cool. Twinkies!"

I waited, watching Bryan devoured his snack. My heart rate slowed, realizing we weren't in immediate danger, as least so it seemed. "So?" I at last demanded.

Muster looked to me, eyebrows raised.

I said, "You gonna answer my other questions or what?"

She smiled. "This is what I like about you. You're… how you say… impetuous."

I hadn't a clue what impetuous meant, but the way she said it reminded me of the various patronizing comments teachers and adults made to me and my friends to our faces anytime they thought they understood being a teenager better than we did.

"Fine," I spat. Leaning forward, I wrapped my hands around the driver's head and covered his eyes. "How about now?"

Tires squealed as the man slammed the brakes and fought to peel my fingers from his face.

Muster grabbed my arm, but I slipped from her grip and slapped my hand back across the driver's eyes.

"Chase! Stop!" Bryan screamed.

I hesitated, then let go, for Bryan's sake.

The car jolted back and forth as the man barely avoided a mailbox on the sidewalk. He straightened and resumed his course down the desolate city streets. He nervously scanned his surroundings, likely looking for cops or others who may have witnessed the erratic driving.

"You're crazy," Bryan said to me. "We coulda died." He had a scowl I'd never seen from him before, his eyebrows taut and eyes glared, bits of Twinkie dotted the side of his mouth.

Muster appeared equally disturbed. She panted, staring at me. "Okay. I will explain. But please—" she pointed to the driver. "—do not repeat."

"Fine."

"First. My name is not Muster."

"No kidding," I said with as much sarcasm as I could cake on.

"It is alias. HopeMuster is game profile. It is an anagram."

Bryan asked, "Anagram? Is that when you rearrange the letters?"

"Yes," she said. "HopeMuster rearranged is Prometheus."

I said, "As In . . . *THE* Prometheus? As in–"

"The Prometheus Dragon." She nodded.

"You're *THE* Prometheus?"

"No. I . . . actually all of us . . . are just acting on his behalf."

Bryan grabbed the back of the seat, leaning forward. "You mean Prometheus isn't just a character in the game?"

She shook her head. "He is a visitor. Though he has been amongst us for some time. For generations."

"Generations?" I repeated, glancing at Bryan who has the same confused look as I felt. "How old is Prometheus?"

"We do not know. But such details are not important to our mission."

"What . . . mission?" Bryan asked, sinking back in his seat. His sudden fright in his voice worried me.

Muster explained, "I chose HopeMuster because this is our task for mankind. To muster hope for the American empire. We pull strings of this society to stave off its eminent collapse."

I sat speechless, waiting for her to explain herself.

"If you study the progress of ruling empires over the centuries, there are common patterns to which they adhere. Now, this is America's time. But time is fleeting, and soon the natural ebb will pull back and other nations will rule. Until then, it is our task to support the current giant. It is like a frog leaping from lily pad to lily pad. He jumps to the largest lily and keeps it steady so he doesn't slip into the pond. When the lily starts to sink, he jumps to the next."

All I could think of was: is she for real? My focus shifted to Bryan. With my eyes, I asked, are you buying any of this? His wide eyes and dangling mouth showed that he was.

I said, "Are you trying to tell us that you're, like, in control of all of America?"

She smirked. "No. We are simply playing our part." She leaned closer. "As are you."

I leaned back. "No. We're just playing a game."

She swung a hand. "We are all playing a game. Bankers. Teachers. Engineers. Taxi Drivers. Grass cutters." She eyed me, as if awaiting my reaction.

I tried not to react, but I swallowed anyhow.

"We are all a part of this web of society. It is all one game."

"But . . ." I searched my brain for the words. "But what does the game . . . Dragon Lure . . . have to do with us, and you, and why we're in the backseat of this stupid car?"

"The game is where you come in. Of what we understand about Prometheus, his primary objective is one thing: information. The game provides this. Or at least, it enables us to acquire information."

I lifted an eyebrow. "What information?"

"Secrets. Government secrets."

"Like spies and stuff?"

"Yes."

I said, "You mean Prometheus is just some sort of government spy?"

"No. We are the spies. Prometheus is the keeper of the information. He gathers information from many peoples, not just us."

"So, he's collecting information to . . ." I tried to recall how Muster phrased it. " . . . to pull the strings? To control America?"

"No. That's our objective." She grinned. "We provide Prometheus with the information he desires. In the process, we use the information for our own objectives."

"Which is saving America," I filled in, not totally believing Muster's honorable intent.

"Exactly."

Then I remembered her analogy. "Until you jump to the next lily pad."

She nodded.

I wanted to probe her more about why they are so concerned about saving a country that, based on her accent, she's likely not from, but Bryan spoke up.

"Um . . ." Bryan's voice squeaked. ". . . how does the game work? I mean, how . . ." he trailed off.

"How does the game gather information?" Muster finished.

He nodded.

"America has formed a society of machine networks. People connect by electronic means. This is where the secrets are hidden. I needed a way to tap into these networks."

"To spy?" Bryan asked.

"Yes," she said. "But this activity is not encouraged in this society. I needed spies working for me, gathering information, without them realizing that they were spies. This is where the game comes in. The game is designed with a clever interface into the Department of Defense's most secure computer networks. From your point of view, you are playing a game. Dragons. Caves. Villages. And . . . the egg. These are symbols. Each represents servers, firewalls, switches, routers. All of the components of computer network security."

"So . . ." I started, trying to piece this puzzle together. "When Bryan and I were figuring out the game and unlocking different parts . . ."

She finished, "You were . . . how you say . . . hacking their system."

I looked to Bryan.

He gasped. "Holy boogers."

I couldn't have said it better.

"So," I said. "What now? You just bringing us back home?"

"I am afraid not. You will need to retrieve the Prometheus egg." She twisted back to Bryan, then to me. "Both of you."

I said, "What about my parents? They'll be going ballistic soon, once they get home all drunk and mad."

"The C.I.A. has already taken care of that when they kidnapped you."

Bryan asked, "What do you mean by that?"

"As far as everyone knows, you two have run away from home. You have even left goodbye notes behind, hand-written, in the likeness of your hand."

"I—" I took a few seconds longer than I normally would to try and understand what was happening. "If the government did this, how do you know all of this?"

She smiled. "This is how they always do it."

"Always?" I asked. "You mean we're not the first ones y'all have kidnapped?"

She looked to the driver, then to us. "You two are good. Very good. But you are not the first the C.I.A has taken. Nor are you the first that we have taken from the C.I.A."

"Well how come the game's still working if the Department of Defense and the C.I.A. already know what you're doing? Shouldn't they have stopped it by now?"

"They can't. Internet security and hacking are matters of sparring minds. They build a lock, we learn how to pick it. They build a better lock, we learn how to pick that. We have engineers continually updating the game. And we have fresh minds—you—to continually crack the codes."

All of this sounded fishy. "Are you telling me the government's most top secret stuff is just out there, waiting for some hackers to get it? Seems like they wouldn't allow that to be accessible from the internet."

"You are smart one." The corner of her mouth rose. "But fortunately, the laziness of government workers are their undoing. In recent years, they have insisted on working from home. This has required internet access to their databases."

I filled in, "So making it easy for them has made it easy for you."

"Exactly."

I thought about Mom and her government job working at the D.M.V. For as long as I remembered, Dad complained about Mom's laziness. I always thought this was just the normal husband and wife spat that every parent in my neighborhood had. I wondered if all government workers were truly as lazy as Dad claimed. Or, if there were just enough for people like Muster to take advantage of them.

The car grew quiet as the weight of our situation fell on us like a dark cloud. The revving engine and squealing tires provided the only sounds beyond the pounding of my heartbeat in my ears.

At last, Bryan spoke. "Are we never going back home?"

There was long pause before Muster answered. "We will see."

VI

BRYAN and I sat side-by-side in metal folding chairs in what felt like a bomb shelter, low ceilings and harsh lights. We'd entered a warehouse-looking building and descended a couple flights of stairs getting here. The computer before us was an impressive multi-core processor computer with two widescreen monitors each about the size of a big TV. They handed me the trackball and I logged into the game under my profile. Bryan sat with his arms twisted in his lap. He shivered.

Adults hovered behind me; Muster, the driver, and a man, this one with a big, shaggy beard and deep-set eyes reminded me of someone who kills people for fun. Their staring felt like people watching me pee. A fourth adult sat at a separate computer to our left. His had three monitors and he clicked through a number of windows, occasionally muttering, "Yup . . . looks good." I hadn't a clue what he was monitoring but I suspected it had something to do with the game.

A hand touched my shoulder.

I jerked and saw Muster's cool, dark face next to me.

"It is the egg we seek," she said.

"I figured." I stared at my orange dragon, perched on his tree that overlooked the village that I had left the last time I played.

"Why do you wait?"

"Um—everyone's staring." I turned to the man at the three monitors. "Who's that guy?"

"He maintains the game and will stop Department of Defense network penetration specialists from closing off our access."

"Our access?"

"From their systems. You must understand. This is a game. At least it is to anyone watching. We must maintain our illusions."

I tapped my fingers against the desk in front of me. Bryan nibbled on his fingernails.

Muster lightly gripped my shoulders, centering me on my console. "Perhaps you should retrace your steps. Return to the cave where you ultimately found the last egg."

"No," Bryan said with a shake to his voice.

"No?" Shaggy Beard Man said, his voice rough. "How come?"

Bryan rubbed his nose, wheezing, signs of his nervousness. "Um, well. The . . . the cave where I—I mean Chase—where he found the egg. Well, that cave was destroyed."

"Right," I chimed in. "It collapsed 'cuz of that self-destruct thing that went off when I dislodged the egg."

"So what do you suggest?" Shaggy Beard Man demanded.

"Well . . . " I started.

Fortunately, Bryan spoke up. "Dark-winged Bandits. They have . . . have to travel the coast. Because of their wings."

"Their wings?" the Muster asked.

I smiled, realizing what Bryan was getting at. "Yeah. Their wings need to remain moist or they'll dry out and they can't fly. It's especially humid along the shoreline. They're forced to follow it for long flights." I tightened my eyebrows and focused up at Muster. "This is your game. How come you don't know this?"

"My specialty is maintaining a stable government. Game details . . . elude me. So, the coast?"

"Yeah," Bryan said, at last beginning to sound less scared and more his typical enthusiastic self. "Either north or south. I'd guess south."

"Why?" I asked.

"They have no use for the egg. They probably headed to Zodd to barter it."

I clicked away at the trackball.

TigerHeart05 swooped into the air and ascended skyward.

I smiled, tickled that I was back into the game. Bryan and I continued our back-and-forth, verbally hammering out moves.

After arriving at the village of Zodd, a town populated with a wide array of creatures both larger and smaller than TigerHeart05, he snuck through the alleys, searching for traces of Dark-winged Bandits, asking the occasional visitor for information.

Textboxes scrolled through dialog.

With every potential lead, Bryan and I volleyed probable next steps and ideas. At one point, I found myself smiling at him. Though I always considered him my friend, he was never really an equal. His undersized, frail stature and tendency to get beat up made him seem more like a younger sibling.

The adults paced the floor behind us. Lost in the game and our pursuit, I kept forgetting they existed. But the occasional squeak of their shoes and mutterings under their breaths reminded me we were still their captives.

"Um . . . Muster." I twisted back.

"Yes?" She stepped toward me, her face and body stiff and anxious.

"What's actually inside this egg?"

She eyed Shaggy Beard Man, hesitating as if she didn't want to tell us. Then she said, "They are launch codes."

"Launch . . . codes?" I spun from the game, emphasizing each word at a time. "You're kidding. Like missiles?"

She nodded. "They are armed due to follies in recent international relations."

"International what?" I asked, once again unsure what she was talking about.

"Missteps with North Korea, Mexico, and Afghanistan, to name a few."

More and more, this sounded like an old 1950s nuclear holocaust movie, where the bad guy was just seconds from pressing the button to kick-start World War III and annihilate every human being on earth. I watched those old movies with my dad back when I was little and we got along. They scared the heck out of me when I was five. I had nightmares of creepy military men pressing a giant red button and blowing up half the planet. I once woke my mom in the middle of night, which led to a fight with my dad and restricted me to watching nothing more violent than Pokémon for the next few years of my life.

I tensed. "Why would you want launch codes?"

Muster crossed her arms. "So we may change them."

"Change them?"

"As I have said. We must save this empire from itself. Otherwise, they are doomed to . . . how you say . . . suicide."

"Suicide?" Bryan asked.

Shaggy Beard Man said, "America's on a crash course. This is for its own good."

His words echoed in my head, bouncing around as if I'd heard it once before. I said, "Puppets."

"Uh?" Shaggy Beard Man said.

I recalled helping out my church's puppet shows that taught the little kids various Bible stories. We worked with hand puppets but had props like miniature doors that we'd open and close using rods and wire, all hidden behind curtains and sheets to give the illusion of reality to the kids. I said, "It's like a giant puppet show. Everyone's watching this stuff closely, yet you're all controlling things behind the scenes."

Muster smirked. "This is why you are good at game. You are perceptive."

The computer buzzed.

I spun back to it. It flickered and froze. I moved the trackball.

Bryan said what I thought. "What's wrong with the game?"

The man at the three-monitor computer to our left said, "We have a penetrator." The veins on his forehead grew visible and his voice sounded edgy. He feverishly clicked through a number of windows and tapped at the keyboard. "Ayermo! They got in through ten ports at the same time."

Muster asked, "Can't you block them?"

"I'm trying. I'm trying." More typing. "There." He looked to Bryan and me. "How is it?"

I moved the trackball. TigerHeart05 responded without issue. "Fine."

Muster said to me, "Please. Progress quickly. We don't have much time."

Bryan and I shot looks to each other, then continued our game-play, unraveling the puzzle one clue at a time.

VII

HOURS PASSED. I grew tired despite the endless supply of Twinkies and Coke that Muster produced. I consumed little of each, my stomach feeling twisted and achy. Bryan didn't have the same problem. He gobbled down the sugary junk as fast as they gave it to him. He wiggled and bounced in his chair and occasionally burped and farted. Every once in a while, the screen flickered and the man at the adjacent computer responded with several clicks of his mouse and rapid-fire typing.

TigerHeart05's search led through a cave that went deeper than he had ever traversed before, zigzagging twists and turns until the underground maze opened into a subterranean river and waterfall.

"The egg!" Bryan shouted, loud enough to echo through the room.

Shoes squeaked with everyone crowding behind us.

I searched the screen. "Where?"

"The water. Look!"

TigerHeart05 lowered the torch in his grip, illuminating the dark, flowing river. The barely discernable outline of a giant egg took shape below the bubbling waves near the base of the waterfall.

Bryan nudged me. "Quick. Dive in."

I resisted.

TigerHeart05 searched the water's surface. Aside from the rippling water, dots occasionally sparkled just below the surface. TigerHeart05 waved the torch from side to side, easing his dragon face closer to the surface. A splash. TigerHeart05 jumped back.

Muster spoke from behind me. "What was that?"

"Eels," I said.

Bryan added, "Calorian Eels. We should have guessed as much."

The adults stared, again waiting for Bryan and me to solve yet another problem.

Then, an idea struck me. "Heat."

"Uh?" Bryan said.

"Don't they see and attack by heat?"

Bryan smiled. "Oh, yeah. They attack their prey's body heat."

I moved the trackball, rotating my dragon-self and the torch he held. "The mud."

"But…" Bryan spun in his seat. "…won't that wash off in the water?"

"I'll just be in long enough to pull out the egg."

Shaggy Beard Man said, "I hope you two know what you're talking about."

I gave him a crooked smile. "Me, too."

TigerHeart05 staked the torch into the ground next to his foot. He jumped into an area of mud that lined the river. Rolling, he caked his orange and black scales in deep brown mud. TigerHeart05 righted himself, poised and ready to leap.

I hesitated before my next move. "Ready?"

Bryan nodded.

TigerHeart05 dove into the water. Eels darted back and forth through the bubbles dancing over TigerHeart05's now mud-coated surface, but none attacked with their venom-filled teeth.

TigerHeart05 reached the egg. Wrapping his claws around the slick shell, he pulled. The egg jolted, but wouldn't lift.

"Look!" Bryan said, pointing.

TigerHeart05 spun.

A curved clamp wrapped the egg's perimeter. At the center was a black and white LED display with dashes. Buttons lined the top of the display.

"A combination," Bryan said, reading my mind.

"Yeah . . . but what?" I turned. "Nobody said anything about a combination lock."

"What numbers are important?"

"Important?"

"Yeah." Bryan twisted back to the adults surrounding us, whose faces were bright with urgency. "You said it was the Department of Defense we were stealing from. They would have locked this using a number that other agents would know, right?"

The man at the three-monitors next to us shook his head. "They have enormous lists of random numbers that they use to code–"

"But why would they just stick the egg here where anyone could get it?" Bryan said. "It's not guarded other than by the eels. And they're probably running automatically."

Muster spoke up, "What are you saying?"

"They wouldn't be fully staffed this weekend. I think they stuck it here to pass it off to someone else."

Muster spoke up, "Why would they do that?"

Bryan smirked at me.

I smiled back, as if I finally read his mind. "The Department of Defense. They're government."

"So?" Muster said.

I said, "This is a holiday weekend. Washington's birthday. They're always low staffed on holidays."

A flash caught my eye.

I spun to the monitor.

TigerHeart05's life points had decreased. The eels surrounding TigerHeart05 jerked and occasionally nipped. The mud had almost completely floated off TigerHeart05's scales.

I rolled the trackball, reaching my dragon's claws toward the LED display.

"Quick," I said. "Gimme some numbers."

"Uh . . ." Bryan said, "Try Washington's birthday."

"That's . . . uh . . . February something? What day? What year?"

Shaggy Beard Man pulled out his iPhone and tapped away. "February twenty-second, 1732."

TigerHeart05 tapped the buttons until the display read, "02221732". The display blinked red.

"That didn't work," I said. "Quick. Another one."

A pair of eels nipped. The screen flashed. TigerHeart05's life points decreased.

Bryan said, "Monday is also called President's Day, not just Washington's Birthday, right?"

"Yeah," I said. "To celebrate Lincoln's birthday, right? When's his birthday?"

Shaggy Beard Man looked it up. "February twelfth, 1809."

TigerHeart05 tapped the buttons.

The display blinked red.

"No," I said. "Quick. Another one."

Eels bit. TigerHeart05's life decreased, the numbers changing to orange, an indication of nearing death.

"Hurry!" I said.

My eyes shot around, as if searching for help. The surrounding frightening faces appeared blank. Muster. Shaggy Beard Man. The man at the monitor. Bryan.

My mind scrambled. I mumbled, "The Department of Defense. The Department of Defense." I recalled the report I had to do on the Continental Congress in history. They formed the Department of Defense a year before the signing of the Declaration of Independence, which I thought was strange – essentially an army before the nation was a nation. Today, their formation coincided with Flag Day on June fourteenth. I said aloud, "June fourteenth, 1775."

"What is that?" Muster asked.

I said, "June fourteenth, 1775. The formation of the Department of Defense."

TigerHeart05 tapped the buttons.

Eels nipped.

The screen flashed.

Life points decreased.

The display blinked once, then turned green.

The surrounding clamp released.

TigerHeart05 grabbed the egg with his claws and swam to the surface. Wings free of the water, the dragon flapped with all his might and soared into the air.

VIII

EARLY DAWN CREPT in on the stale smell of dew. The car stopped in front of the pair of houses that stood in front of Bryan's doublewide trailer. The sky was covered in a deep purple. My eyes and body felt the weight of having stayed awake all night. I yearned for the warmth of my bed tucked within my closest-like bedroom.

Muster twisted back to Bryan and me. "Your assistance has been invaluable."

Bryan at last had a look of relief on his face, the soft comforted look that he had anytime it was just him and me walking down the street together. I said, "I guess it's game over." I paused. "For us, at least."

Muster nodded. "Yes. You will not be able to access the game further. We will need to go through a different user account. And use different spies."

"Can't . . . " Bryan bounced in his seat as he spoke. "Can't we just log into a different account? I started a bunch."

Muster shook her head. "For the sake of both of you, no more Dragon Lure. The burden of our mission lies with us. Returning you now, you are blameless. Your government will question you, but you were not at fault. Remember, we kidnapped you. And now, your involvement has come to an end."

"Okay." I nodded, mostly understanding their logic. "So to them, we were just playing a game."

"Correct. No more . . . spies."

"And we will be questioned?"

"Most definitely. You will be interrogated."

Bryan asked, "What are we supposed to say? Like, if they ask about you all?"

Muster smiled warmly. "Tell them the truth. We kidnapped you and forced you to play. It is okay. We have ways of keeping ourselves underground."

I swallowed. As fun as it was to re-capture the egg and effectively win the game, still lingering in the back of my mind was the fear that Bryan and I might have helped some terrorist who may be using the launch codes to destroy America rather than save it.

Muster said with the sweep of her hand. "Please. We must be leaving." She looked to the driver, Shaggy Beard Man.

I opened the door.

"Wait," she said. Opening the glove compartment, she pulled out a Rays baseball cap and held it back toward me. "Here. A bet's a bet."

I took the hat. It felt stiff and new. "Thanks."

Bryan and I stepped out, taking a closer look at my prize. "Wow. Cool."

I said, "Bye, Muster."

"Good-bye my friend."

I closed the door.

The car sped off down the empty, quiet street.

We remained there for several seconds, neither of us saying anything. The fresh scent of grass touched my senses and I heard the distant rumble of a lawnmower. I couldn't tell for sure, but I guessed it was Dad prepping the mowers for the morning's work. Mornings like this, I'd occasionally glance down neighborhood streets, at the beautifully groomed lawns and little flower gardens, and quietly marvel over the amount of painstaking effort involved in making everything appear so nice and pretty. Punk kids like Jacob and Andrew would never in a billion years realize the work going on behind the scenes to make up what they call home – the secret puppetry keeping their lives in balance.

Bryan at last spoke, "I can't believe that just happened."

I patted my friend's shoulders. "It's not over yet. We still gotta explain to everyone that we didn't run away from home. Remember what Muster said. They wrote notes in our handwriting."

"Yeah." His smile faded, worry taking its place.

"Bryan?"

"Yeah?"

I played with my bottom lip, trying to find the words. "I'm . . . I'm sorry."

"For what?"

"I ratted you out the second we were caught. Remember? I told those guys that you hacked into my account."

He stared.

"You wouldn't have done that to me."

"It's okay."

"No, it isn't." I rubbed my nose. "You're my best friend. Friends should stick together."

His eyes brightened. "Best friends?"

I realized I had never called him my best friend before. In fact, I don't believe I ever given anyone that label. "Yeah." I placed a hand on his shoulder. "Even if you're . . . weird and stuff."

He gave me an embarrassed smirk.

"Weird is good." I looked down the road. "And don't worry about all that Dragon Lure stuff." I mounted my new cap onto Bryan's head. "We'll be fine."

He touched the brim. He didn't outright say thanks, but his eyes said enough.

"See you later, Bryan."

"Bye, Chase."

We left each other. For the first time since I'd known Bryan, I felt the pull like I didn't want to part. Still, home was waiting.

I jogged back home, cutting through Mrs. Higgins' yard. The second I hopped over her fence and into her weedy backyard, my foot caught an overgrown vine and my chest slammed to the ground. I coughed, sat up, and froze at the sight of a pair of wrinkly legs. I slowly rose, standing face-to-face with Mrs. Higgins in her nightgown. The morning sun highlighted her blotchy skin sagged from her face and arms.

I tried to smile, though my tiredness made it hard. "Good morning, Mrs. Higgins."

Her wrinkly face twisted, and frail arms crossed. She looked ready to slug me, not that it worried me. A stiff wind could have toppled this old lady. "Cuttin' through m'yard again, eh?"

"But it's such a beautiful yard, Mrs. Higgins. It's a shame more people can't—"

"I guess I'll let it go, this time." She shifted. "After all, you did get m'egg."

"I . . ." My mind scrambled, partly wondering if I heard her right. "Your . . . egg?"

She reached and brushed off grass from the side of my face. "Don't you worry none. They told you the truth. Muster and her bunch are honorable."

I pursed my lips, trying to form the words stuck at the edge of my lips. "You . . . you're . . ."

"Just a little old lady," she finished, winking. "That's all you need to tell everyone."

"Um. Okay." I looked side to side, my mind scrabbling. "But, uh, what about you? Why are you collecting information? What—"

"Don't worry your little head over it. We're all playing our part. You play yours."

Her answer didn't quite satisfy my confusion. Nothing I'd learned tonight did.

She patted my shoulder. "Head home. Your mom's worried sick." She stepped aside.

I eased forward. "Th . . . thanks, Mrs. Higgins." I found my legs and trotted home.

AUTHOR'S NOTES – JOHN HOPE

AMONGST MY VARIOUS WRITING ADVENTURES, I've spent the past twenty years slaving away as a software engineer, designing integrated systems, artificial intelligence self-monitoring tools, and complex data analyzers that challenge current technologies. Boring, eh? Fortunately, such background occasionally provides an interesting perspective into computer hacking and software security, from which stories like Dragon Lure are born. I wrote the story specifically for my thirteen-year-old son, who plays online games like the fictionalized Dragon Lure as if his life depended on it. In fact, I consulted with him about Dragon Lure game details – how should it work and what should the players want to accomplish? This mixture of software realities, game play, and bit of international intrigue came together nicely in this story. Since Dragon Lure's publication, I've been repeatedly requested to expand this into a full-length novel. I just may do this.

—JH

ABOUT THE AUTHORS

JADE KERRION
KEN PELHAM
BRIA BURTON
ELLE ANDREWS PATT
T.L. WOOLSLEY
KRISTIN DURFEE
CHARLES A. CORNELL
JOHN HOPE

JADE KERRION

"...This is the kind of series you'd expect to see with a movie deal"
—Full Time Reader, *Amazon Reviewer*

USA Today bestselling author Jade Kerrion defied (or leveraged, depending on your point of view) her undergraduate degrees in Biology and Philosophy, as well as her MBA, to embark on her second (and concurrent) career as an award-winning science fiction, fantasy, and contemporary romance author.

Her debut novel, ***Perfection Unleashed***, published in 2012, won six literary awards and launched her best-selling futuristic thriller series, ***Double Helix***, which blends cutting-edge genetic engineering and high-octane action with an unforgettable romance between an alpha empath and an assassin.

Earth-Sim and ***Eternal Night*** won first place Royal Palm Literary Awards in the Young Adult and Fantasy categories respectively. ***Life Shocks Romances***, Jade's sweet and sexy contemporary romance series, features unlikely romances you will root for and happy endings you can believe in. They prove that, at the very least, she knows how to alphabetize books.

If she sounds busy, it's because she is. Jade writes at 3:00 am when her husband and three sons are asleep, and aspires to make her readers as sleep-deprived as she is.

www.jadekerrion.com

KEN PELHAM

Ken Pelham lives and writes in Maitland, Florida. His thriller, ***Brigands Key***, won first place in the Florida Writers Association's Royal Palm Literary Awards and was published in hardcover in 2012 by Cengage/Five Star Mystery. The ebook edition was released in 2013.

> *Brigands Key is "... a perfect storm of menace ... breathtaking!"*
> *—The Florida Weekly*

His *BK* prequel, ***Place of Fear***, also a first place winner of the Royal Palm Literary Award, hit the electronic shelves as an ebook in 2013, and the wood shelves in softcover in 2014.

Ken co-founded the Alvarium Experiment with Charles A. Cornell. The Alvarium has crafted three previous award-winning anthologies of speculative fiction, ***The Prometheus Saga***, ***Return to Earth***, and ***The Masters Reimagined***.

Also available on Amazon.com:

Tales of Old Brigands Key, three stories about the sordid, unseemly past of Brigands Key. Contains "The Light Keeper," a finalist in the 2014 Royal Palm Literary Awards, and "The Wreck of the Edinburgh Kate," 2nd-place winner of the Royal Palm for Published Short Story.

Treacherous Bastards: Stories of Suspense, Deceit, and Skullduggery, three stories in the Hitchcock tradition, including one about little Brigands Key.

Out of Sight, Out of Mind: A Writer's Guide to Mastering Viewpoint, a concise guide to viewpoint in the narrative voice. Winner, 2015 Published Book of the Year, Royal Palm Literary Awards.

Great Danger: A Writer's Guide to Building Suspense, the tricks and techniques of suspense in fiction.

In Shadows Written: An Anthology of Modern Horror. Multiple authors, edited by Ken, an anthology of stories guaranteed to cause insomnia.

Shadows and Teeth, Vol. 2, Darkwater Syndicate. Multiple authors, contains "The Queen Beneath the Earth," a horror story set in modern Ireland.

Visit Ken at **www.kenpelham.com** for updates on his work, and musings on suspense fiction.

BRIA BURTON

Award-winning author Bria Burton lives in St. Petersburg with her wonderful husband, her darling son, and two wild pets. Her fiction has appeared in over twenty anthologies and magazines. Her novelette, *The Running Girls*, was a 2017 Royal Palm Literary Award Finalist. Her novella, *Little Angel Helper*, won a 2016 RPLA.

"**Little Angel Helper** is a well-told, uplifting novella that readers looking for a truly inspirational, heartwarming story are sure to love."

—Judge, 25th Annual Writer's Digest Self-Published Book Awards

While Bria writes, her dog and cat do their best to distract her, which is why they star in her family-friendly short story collection, ***Lance & Ringo Tails***. She writes under pen name Shayla Cole for her epic fantasy trilogy, ***Livinity*** (awarded a First Place RPLA in unpublished fantasy). At St. Pete Running Company, she's a blogger and customer service manager. A member of the Florida Writers Association, she has led the St. Pete chapter and served on the statewide FWA Board.

It's an honor for her to contribute to another project by the

Alvarium Experiment. In *The Prometheus Saga*, "**On Both Sides**" serves as a companion piece to "Her Midnight Ride." Visit her website where there are links to all her books and stories:

www.briaburton.com

ELLE ANDREWS PATT

Elle Andrews Patt was invited to join the Alvarium Experiment during its 2014 inception. Her work has appeared in online magazines such as Dark Fuse, Saw Palm and The Rag and several anthologies. Her work has won multiple awards from the Florida Writers Association and the Writers of the Future contest. Elle's novel-length fiction is represented by the Donald Maass Literary Agency.

Visit Elle at **www.elleandrewspatt.com** to read award-winning "**Becky's Story**" for free and for links to her other work and publishing news.

Amazon Author Page: Elle Andrews Patt
Follow Elle: FB: @elleandrewspatt
Twitter: @LAndrewsPatt
Instagram: elleandrewspatt
Goodreads: Elle Andrews Patt

***The Prometheus Saga*: Manteo**
1587. Roanoke becomes ground zero in the cultural clash

between English colonists and Native Americans. The alien probe, Prometheus, watches as native Manteo's love and loyalty is shredded between them.

***Return to Earth*: Someday Loyal**

Alien invaders are lobbing fireballs at Peoria, but Grandmama is holding tea. When the military arrives, unassuming Alice discovers her Grandmama and neighbor Mrs. Suniol have a shared past she never could have imagined.

***The Masters Reimagined*: Regarding Mr. Bulkington**

As the Pequod plunges into the hunt for Moby Dick, Ishmael discovers the power behind Captain Ahab's mastery of the sea lies within the mysterious skills possessed by Mr. Bulkington. Are some secrets worth keeping to the grave?

T. L. WOOLSLEY

T. L. Woolsley is the pen name of writer Kim Campbell, who lives and works in the Fort Lauderdale area. She has been interested in science fiction since junior high, when she discovered that those fascinating creatures, boys, read SF, too. Then it was re-runs of "Star Trek" after school and "Dr. Who" (the fourth Doctor) on Friday nights.

Freelance nonfiction writing honed much of her writing skills while college, a career in public relations, and life experience rounded out the skills she brings to the page.

She is managing editor at a book publishing firm in Fort Lauderdale. At night and on weekends she writes short stories and works on ***Whisper Sister***, a novel about a woman running a speakeasy in 1929 New Orleans.

Visit T. L. at **www.tlwoolsley.com** for updates on her work, and ramblings on writing, life, and the writing life.

KRISTIN DURFEE

Kristin Durfee lives and writes in Apopka, Florida. Her first book, ***Four Corners***, is a Young Adult fantasy novel published by Black Opal Books.

Four Corners *is "a fun, magical adventure that is beautifully written… This story has a nice balance of adventure, action, and relatable friendship that is just perfect."*

—Janella Fila for Reader's Favorite, 5-Star Review

*"I devoured [**Four Corners**]! I could not put it down. I give Four Corners 4 out of 4 stars. While it is geared towards young adults, any adult looking for a fun and fast read would enjoy this book."*

—Official Review from Onlinebookclub.org

Two Worlds, the second book in the Four Corners Trilogy, was published by Black Opal Books in the fall of 2016.

One Earth, the final book in the Four Corners Trilogy, was published by Black Opal Books July 2018.

She has proudly contributed stories to several anthologies, including the Alvarium Experiment: Return to Earth anthology entitled ***Project Bright Star,*** The Masters Reimagined anthology entitled ***The Lottery***, as well as the Thrill of the Hunt anthologies and the upcoming Demonic Household anthology. All projects are available through book and e-versions through Amazon.

CHARLES A. CORNELL

When Charles isn't trying to survive the chaos of everyday life, he's dreaming up all kinds of crazy speculative fiction ranging from the mysterious to the macabre; blending science fiction, fantasy, alternative history and horror. He is a regular contributor to podcasts, seminars and conferences, and conducts webinars and workshops on his specialty, retro-punk fiction (Steampunk, Dieselpunk).

Charles A Cornell was born in England, raised in Canada and now lives in Florida.

His first published novel, ***Tiger Paw***, won the 2012 Royal Palm Literary Award for Best Thriller from the Florida Writers Association.

His dieselpunk work, ***DragonFly*** is a retro-futuristic collision of science fiction and fantasy with a generous dash of alternative history. ***DragonFly*** was a 2014 Royal Palm Literary Award Finalist in Science Fiction, has received numerous Amazon Five-Star reviews, two prestigious Reader's Favorite Five Star Reviews, and won the 2018 Reader's Favorite Silver Medal in the Young Adult - Action category.

Charles's short stories and novellas have appeared in the anthologies, ***The Prometheus Saga***, ***Return To Earth*** and ***In***

Shadows Written. His ***Prometheus Saga*** science fiction story ***Crystal Night*** won the FWA Royal Palm Literary Award for Best Novella in 2016.

Please visit him at **CharlesACornell.com** for news on his latest projects and for musings on dieselpunk and retrofuturism. Also check out his worlds of Steampunk at SteampunkNovels.com and ***DragonFly*** at DragonFly-Novels.com featuring galleries of retrofuturistic aircraft and other illustrations from ***DragonFly***.

www.CharlesACornell.com
www.SteampunkNovels.com
www.DragonFly-Novels.com
www.Cornell-SciFi.com
www.BigCorpSurvivor.com

JOHN HOPE

John Hope is an award-winning short story, children's book, middle grade fiction and nonfiction history writer. His work appears in science fiction/fantasy anthologies and multiple collections of the best of the Florida Writers Association. Mr. Hope, a native Floridian, loves to travel with his wife, Jaime, and their two kids. He enjoys running, reading, and writing, and has a weakness for good barbeque and sweet tea.

Read more at ***www.johnhopewriting.com***, including the following award-winning books:

Silencing Sharks

Deaf and bullied, thirteen-year-old Peter discovers he alone can talk to sharks. And he must put this unique skill to use to rescue them from poachers, while surviving neighborhood bullies and saving his blackmailed dad from getting fired.

Secret Adventures of Foxfire: Busting Walls

Deep within Sebastian's vivid imagination, international spy Foxfire is tasked with her most difficult mission yet while Sebastian and his middle school friends construct a secret tree fort. Foxfire's secret adventures sooner or later intertwine with Sebastian's struggles.

No Good

Set in the late 1940s Sanford, Florida, twelve-year-old Johnny "No Good" and his newly adopted brother find themselves in the middle of a manhunt for a small town murderer when No Good learns the other is connected to the prime suspect.

Pankyland

A pair of neighboring, rival families visit the Florida theme park Pankyland. When eleven-year-old Panky inadvertently loses his younger brother, Craig, he is forced to team up with his nemesis and neighbor Benji to find the little boy before his parents find out. **Sequels: Pankyland 2: The Movie, Pankyland 3: Be Little World**

Colby in the Crosshairs

After Colby's estranged father returns to his white trash home, the nine-year-old struggles to survive a promiscuous neighborhood mother, money sharks, and an uncontrollable autistic older brother while discovering the true cost of living and brotherhood

MORE FROM THE ALVARIUM EXPERIMENT

The Prometheus Saga was the premier project of the Alvarium Experiment, a consortium of accomplished and award-winning authors.

The *Saga* spans the range of the existence of *Homo sapiens*. The stories do not need to be read in any particular order; each story is an entry point into the overall story.

The Prometheus Saga 1 stories & authors are:

"**The Pisces Affair**" by Daco Auffenorde. CIA operative Jordan Jakes meets Prometheus when the Secretary of State becomes the target of a terrorist attack at a head-of-state dinner in Dubai. Visit Daco at **www.authordaco.com.**

"**On Both Sides**" by Bria Burton. When a mysterious woman vanishes during the American Revolution, young Robby Freeman searches for answers from a cryptic sharpshooter who deserted Washington's Continental Army. Visit Bria at **www.briaburton.com.**

"**Ever After**" by M.J. Carlson. Two mysterious women convey the same Cinderella story to Giambattista Basile in 1594 and Jacob and Wilhelm Grimm in 1811. How different cultures retell this story reveals humanity's soul to those who listen. Visit M.J. at **www.mjcarlson.com.**

"The Blurred Man" by Bard Constantine. FBI agent Dylan Plumm's investigation of a mill explosion puts her on the trail of the Blurred Man, a mysterious individual who may have been on Earth for centuries. Visit Bard at bardofdarkness.wix.com/bardconstantine.

"**Crystal Night**" by Charles A. Cornell. Berlin, 1938. On the eve of one of history's darkest moments, a Swedish bartender working in Nazi Germany accidentally uncovers a woman's hidden past. Can he avoid becoming an accomplice as the Holocaust accelerates? Visit Charles at **www.charlesacornell.com.**

"Marathon" by Doug Dandridge. Prometheus, posing as a citizen of Athens, participates in the battle of Marathon alongside the playwright Aeschylus. Visit Doug at www.dougdandridge.net.

"**The Strange Case of Lord Byron's Lover**" by Parker Francis. Writing in her journal, Mary Shelley recounts a series of perplexing events during her visit with Lord Byron—a visit that resulted in the creation of her famous Frankenstein novel, but also uncovered a remarkable mystery. Visit Parker at **www.parkerfrancis.com.**

"**Strangers on a Plane**" by Kay Kendall. In 1969 during a flight across North America, a young mother traveling with her infant meets an elderly woman who displays unusual powers. But when a catastrophe threatens, are those powers strong enough to avert disaster? This short story folds into Kay's mystery series featuring the young woman, amateur sleuth Austin Starr. Visit Kay at **www.kaykendallauthor.com.**

"**East of the Sun**" by Jade Kerrion. Through a mysterious map depicting far-flung lands, a Chinese sailor in 1424 and a Portuguese cartographer in 1519 share a vision of an Earth far greater than the reality they know. Visit Jade at **www.jadekerrion.com.**

"Manteo" by Elle Andrews Patt. In 1587, Croatan native Manteo returns from London to Roanoke Island, Virginia. Can he reconcile his strong loyalty to the untamed land and people of his home with his desire for the benefits the colonizing English bring with them before one of them destroys the other? Visit Elle at **www.elleandrewspatt.com**.

"**First World War**" by Ken Pelham. 40,000 BC: As the last remaining species of hominid, *Homo sapiens* and *Homo neanderthalensis*, fight a desperate battle for ownership of the future, the outcasts of both sides find themselves caught in middle. Visit Ken at **www.kenpelham.com**.

"**Lilith**" by Antonio Simon, Jr. In this retelling of the Adam & Eve story, a hermit's life is turned upside-down by the arrival of a mysterious woman in his camp. As the story of their portentous meeting carries forward through the millennia, only time will tell if Lilith is a heroine, a victim, or a monster. Visit Antonio at **www.DarkwaterSyndicate.com**.

"**Fifteen Dollars' Guilt**" by Antonio Simon, Jr. 1881: After a close brush with death in a steamship disaster, Prometheus encounters another survivor who gripes about how aimless his life has become. Prometheus helps him find his calling, inadvertently setting in motion the assassination of President Garfield. Visit Antonio at **www.DarkwaterSyndicate.com.**

www.ingramcontent.com/pod-product-compliance
Lightning Source LLC
LaVergne TN
LVHW091119080826
845145LV00008B/1981
9781960974051